COREY ANN HAYDU

SIMON PULSE

New York   London   Toronto   Sydney   New Delhi

SIMON PULSE

An imprint of Simon & Schuster Children's Publishing Division

1230 Avenue of the Americas, New York, New York 10020

First Simon Pulse hardcover edition July 2020

For information about special discounts for bulk purchases, please contact Simon & Schuster Special Sales at 1-866-506-1949 or business@simonandschuster.com.

The Simon & Schuster Speakers Bureau can bring authors to your live event. For more information or to book an event contact the Simon & Schuster Speakers Bureau at 1-866-248-3049 or visit our website at www.simonspeakers.com.

Jacket designed by Heather Palisi

Interior designed by Mike Rosamilia

The text of this book was set in Adobe Caslon Pro.

Manufactured in the United States of America

2 4 6 8 10 9 7 5 3 1

Library of Congress Cataloging-in-Publication Data

Names: Haydu, Corey Ann, author.

Title: Ever cursed / by Corey Ann Haydu.

Description: First Simon Pulse hardcover edition. | New York : Simon Pulse, 2020. |

Summary: To save her sisters from a spell that has forced them to be Without, Princess Jane of Ever must work with Reagan, the very witch who set the curse on her family.

Identifiers: LCCN 2019039629 (print) | LCCN 2019039630 (eBook) |

ISBN 9781534437036 (hardcover) | ISBN 9781534437050 (eBook)

Subjects: CYAC: Fairy tales. | Princesses—Fiction. | Magic—Fiction. | Blessing and cursing—Fiction.

Classification: LCC PZ8.H323 Ev 2020 (print) |

LCC PZ8.H323 (eBook) | DDC [Fic]—dc23

LC record available at https://lccn.loc.gov/2019039629

LC eBook record available at https://lccn.loc.gov/2019039630

To Anna Bridgforth, and to all life-changing friends who save you, who know you, who love you, who push you

Dear Reader,

Ever Cursed includes content involving sexual assault.

It may also be triggering if you are struggling with, being treated for, or are in recovery for an eating disorder or disordered eating.

As always, read with care, being mindful of what content is safe and comfortable for you.

With love,
Corey

1.

JANE

Outside the walls of the castle, standing before the moat, looking out at the stream that separates us from our subjects, there is a woman in a box. She is tall and blond. She has an ivory dress and pale skin and a shock of a red mouth. She doesn't move. Not even when the townspeople wave and clamor for her attention. Not even now, when I am looking into her unblinking eyes. She doesn't move. She can't.

The woman is my mother.

I tell myself these facts every day, a story I repeat in my head. A true story that can feel untrue, which is why I find myself saying it over and over. *My mother, the queen, is frozen in a box. We have to break the spell.*

"What'd you say?" Olive says, pulling on one side of my dress, then the other, as if there is a perfect way to wear it, but my body isn't cooperating. I must have said the words out loud. Years of hunger have broken down my defenses, and thoughts slip out too often now, forgetting to ask my permission first.

"We're going to break the spell today," I say, testing out

the words for my attendant. They sound true enough. They sound possible, at least.

Olive pauses. Her hands are on my back, pulling and stitching fabric that was meant for someone softer, someone fuller, someone fed. It's her job to make my dresses fit me, and that means her fingers are always calloused from the needle, her eyes always squinting from the delicacy of the work, the impossibility of making my body look anything but Spellbound. "I hope that's true," she says at last.

There's a clatter from the dining room, one floor below us. I used to like this part of the castle. It always smells like whatever is cooking. And whatever is cooking is always delicious. Now it's a pointed kind of torture, to smell everything I haven't been able to eat for five years.

Dad's offered to move me into a different room a hundred times, but it feels like admitting defeat, so I stay. "Queens don't complain," I've reminded him more than once. A lesson my mother taught me, when she was out here and not in that box.

"They're having scones," I say now, smelling the air. "Cherry."

"Chocolate cherry," Olive says before shaking her head and correcting herself. "I'm sorry. I don't know why I said that. You don't need to know that."

"Chocolate-cherry scones," I say. "Don't know that I've ever had them."

"For Eden's birthday, whatever she requests is what gets made," Olive says, repeating the rules to me as if they aren't my own, as if I don't live with them every day. Across the generations

2

many things have happened on Thirteenth Birthdays. Engagements. Weddings. Treaties between nations. And of course, eighty years ago, a kidnapped princess, the start of the biggest War. The War We Won.

I'm begging tonight to matter the way so many other Thirteenth Birthdays have.

Downstairs, my sisters are laughing at something. I can practically hear their tongues in their mouths, their hands wiping their lips, their throats swallowing. It's not just food I miss. It's everything that comes with food. The way my father used to spread the butter on my bread for me, always caking on extra. The jokes at the table. The loveliness of a heavy silver fork in my hand. Even the way meals mark the passing of time, giving a long day balance and breaks.

Now a day is just an endless stretch of hunger that goes from dawn until dusk without a single breath of relief.

Even today.

"I think you'll be able to break the spell," Olive says, working on fitting the sleeves of my gown around my wrists. This dress fit fine a month ago, but it's now swallowing me whole. The Slow Spell is Quickening. Time is running out.

Ever since the spell was cast, I've been counting down to Eden's Thirteenth Birthday, when the witch promised she'd return to tell us how to break the spell before it turns True.

I wonder if the people of Ever have been thinking about it too. They cried the day the spell was cast. They watched from the other side of the moat when the witch appeared on the Grand Yard, arms raised, a cape flying out behind her. She was a young witch. My age. Her voice was thin as it recited a magical chant. She called out our fates one by one, telling us what malady would befall us on our Thirteenth Birthdays. "When you each reach my age," she said, "that's when the spell will bind you. On your Thirteenth Birthday. When it binds the last of you, in five years' time on Princess Eden's birthday, I'll return. I'll give you one chance to break the spell."

I waited for Dad to react, to boom out a hundred questions. Most importantly, *Why are you doing this?* and *Don't you know what our agreement is?* and maybe also *Do the older witches know you're here; are you confused; can someone fetch this young, unhinged witch and return her to her Home on the Hill?*

Instead, he was quiet. We were all in shock. Witches were our partners in keeping Ever safe. We protected them. They protected us. Perfect symbiosis. Everything about this witch, from her age to her words to the spell itself, was wrong. More than wrong. Impossible.

I was shaking from the impossibility of it.

Mom was quiet too. Queens are quiet, and she was always, always a queen first.

I stayed quiet for as long as I could, because I wanted to be queen. But as long as I could turned out to be twenty-two seconds.

"Why would you do this?" I said. My voice was small at first, then louder, because she didn't answer, and her face only got harder, more sure. "This is— What are you doing? We're princesses, and you're . . . We don't do this to each other! Why would you do this?"

4

Mom had told me a hundred times that silence is more meaningful than words. I was failing at following Mom's rules, but I didn't know how to be quiet in the face of this witch.

The witch kept her mouth closed. She wouldn't look at me. She looked everywhere else, though. She looked at the castle—its stone, its turrets, its incredible size.

I tried to say only the most important thing in the enormous valley of my parents' silence. "Please," I said. "No."

"I have to," she said. She looked a little sad saying it. Or maybe I'm just remembering it that way.

I was the oldest, three days from my Thirteenth Birthday. The rest of my sisters would have more time to prepare for the spell. Nora would have over a year. Alice another year beyond that. Grace would have nearly four years to think it all through. And Eden would have the whole five years. I had three days. My heart beat out the number. *Three. Three. Three.*

"Please," I said again. "No." Thirteenth Birthdays are celebrated with enormous royal balls, a feast, a dance, silk dresses, a silver crown. Not with curses. Mine was already all planned. "No," I said again, trying to make it sound royal and right. "No."

I looked at my mother. She would know how to fix it. My whole life, she'd solved every problem that had come my way.

There hadn't been many.

I watched her body lean forward a little, her mouth form an O shape, about to say something wise and true to this young witch, ready to finally break her queenly silence. But before a word came out, before she could stitch things back together, make our world right again, she froze. A glass box appeared around her, trapping her inside.

She was Spellbound.

My heart spun right out of my body and joined her in that glass box. I didn't cry or scream or throw myself onto the glass. Instead I buried my face in my arms and bent at the waist, like if I could get small and hidden enough, I could disappear from the moment.

She was not yet done teaching me how to be a queen, and I was immediately lost without her. I couldn't think of words or find the right shape for my body to take. I ran through everything she'd ever told me about queens and witches and spells and How to Be. Queens don't beg witches to be kind. Queens don't let their eyes fill with tears or let their hearts beat out *three, three, three*. Queens don't wish they weren't the oldest princess; queens don't wish their sisters would be hit by the spell first; queens don't hate everyone who isn't cursed.

I closed my eyes and told my heart to shut up. Queens are quiet.

I knew enough about witches to know that a thirteen-year-old witch could only cast a Slow Spell, the kind that didn't have everlasting consequences. When witches turn eighteen, their spells turn True, permanent, everlasting, and damaging.

"How do we break the spell?" I asked, trying to find the right words for a queen to say, hoping my mother could hear me and be proud of me, even behind that layer of thick glass.

The witch's eyes were steady and wide and gray. Her skin

looked like mine—an uneven, patchy white. Her mouth was a surprising shade of red, like my mother's. It is impossible to pick out a witch by anything but the skirts around their waists. In every other way, they look like the rest of Ever. Their skin is every shade of white or brown or in-between; their noses and eyes and chins take different shapes. They are tall and short and round and straight. They are mostly women, but there are witches across the gender spectrum. The only thing they always have in common is magic and the layers of fabric in all colors and textures and patterns tied around their waists, marking them, warning us.

"I'll return in five years' time," the young witch said, repeating her earlier promise with no further details. It wasn't what I wanted to hear. I wanted a new answer, a better spell, an easier curse.

Alice's fingers found mine in the silence that followed. Nora drew closer to me. Mom in her glass box had a straight back and kind eyes. I tried to imitate her, but my knees kept buckling. *Queens aren't scared,* I told my knees, but they didn't listen. My mouth was dry. My head swam.

"Please," Dad said. I had never heard my father beg for anything. He was the king, after all. If queens weren't meant to beg, kings certainly weren't either. I wrapped my arms around myself, as if that could hold me together. We were all falling apart.

The witch didn't care about any of it. She didn't tell us why. She just looked at us, at all of us, like we already knew.

"How do we break the spell?" I called out to her again, a

question I'd already asked and she'd already answered. These were the only words I had. That, and three days. Three days. Three days.

"I'll be back when the spell has bound the last of you," the witch said again. With one more sorry look at me, the witch was gone and Mom was trapped, and three days later I turned thirteen and I wasn't able to lift food or drink to my mouth. I wasn't able to eat.

And finally, five years later, we are here. Eden's birthday. Chocolate-cherry scones. A dress that doesn't fit. A crowd of people across the moat, remembering or not remembering that we were not always Spellbound.

I don't know when the witch will turn eighteen, when exactly the Slow Spell could turn True, as all unbroken Slow Spells do. But I hope it's months from now, or maybe a whole year. We've studied the breaking of spells these past five years, and they can be complicated and dangerous to undo. Maybe we will be required to cut our hair and give up all our jewels or climb a mountain in another kingdom or solve a nearly impossible riddle. We may have to sit alone in a locked room for weeks or stand outside in the town square for a month without speaking. We might have to give up our castle, our attendants, our avocados, the summer months.

My stomach grips as I try to imagine what tonight will bring. I didn't know it was possible to look forward to something and dread it all at once, but it is. I am. We are.

"I hope—" I start, but I have no idea how to finish the

sentence. I want a hundred things I can't have. "I hope—" I try again, but there's no end; there's nothing to say.

"I know," Olive says. My father's voice bellows from downstairs. He's loud when he's happy, and it seems to startle Olive. Her shoulders jump. "I hope too."

My heart pounds, like it did all those years ago. My knees are weak again, weaker now, from lack of nourishment. And I want my mother more than I've ever wanted anything. I want her here, now, the way she should be. Smoothing my dress, suggesting hairstyles, telling me I look beautiful.

"I want to show my mother my dress," I tell Olive, and she escorts me downstairs and out the door. I don't go anywhere alone. Even when I'm sleeping, Olive checks in on me throughout the night, to make sure I'm safe and comfortable and the right temperature for a princess.

We don't stop in the dining room, don't greet my family. I don't speak with them when they're eating. It's easier that way.

"Your Spellbound! Good morning!" a girl with brown skin and braided hair calls out from across the moat the second we are on the Grand Yard. We aren't meant to speak directly to our subjects, and they know this. But they try anyway. I wave but say nothing.

"Your Stillness," her white, rosy-cheeked friend booms to my mother in her glass box. "We miss you!"

Subjects say silly things from across the moat. It's our job to let them. To smile and wave and say nothing. We stay on our side of the moat, and they stay on theirs. It's how things are and how things have been and how they will always be.

A long time ago, before I was Spellbound, I wondered aloud what it would be like to walk in the kingdom that belongs to us, to know its streets and its people. But my mother and father assured me I *did* know Ever. "You don't need to see every leaf in the forest to be the sun giving it the light to grow," Dad said, and now I know that he's right. Princesses stay in castles. Kings gives speeches from towers. Attendants say yes and bow their heads when the king enters and sometimes shake at the sight of him. We see Ever from here. That is enough, because it has always been enough.

What I don't understand, what maybe no one understands, is witches. "They keep us at rest," Mom said before she was rendered speechless in a box. "And we keep them safe. It's an imperfect thing. Witches are imperfect. We are too. A queen needs to know that." I nodded. She nodded back. Looked at me to make sure I was really hearing her. She didn't need to look so hard, though. I always listened to my mother. "Anyway, it's all we have. The imperfect agreement. It's all they have too, after the War We Won. We're all just waiting for the kidnapped princess to return." She looked like she had more to say. She was speaking more quickly than usual, repeating herself to make sure I understood. "The witches help us wait." She nodded to the candles across the moat, the ones our subjects keep lit at all times, so that the kidnapped princess can find her way back to us, someday. And she gestured to the rock carving of the kidnapped princess that Alice had made based on a photograph Dad had given her. She looks a little like me. Pointy chin, straight back, small nose, long hair.

I'm supposed to hope for the return of this princess, for solving the mystery of who took her, for knowing which kingdom, out of all the kingdoms, is actually the one that should be Banned. But I can't hope for anything but the breaking of the spell.

"Do you like my dress?" I ask my mother, holding up the corners of the gown that now more or less fits me. It's an icy pale blue and is embroidered with jewels. "I wanted something special for Eden's Thirteenth Birthday," I say. "Olive made it." Olive stands a few yards away from my mother and me. She knows when to be close and when to give me space. She knows what I need more than I do, sometimes.

What I need right now, though, is my mother's kind smile and her bright eyes. I want her to tell me I look like a queen, finally, because the last time she spoke to me, I was so young and so silly and so unstudied.

"The dress is fine, Jane," my sister Nora says from her spot on the lawn. I don't know when she joined me out here. She's sneaky, Nora. Quiet when she wants to be and never wasting time with things like saying good morning or asking how I'm doing. She has hitched her skirts up to her knees and is letting the sun freckle her skin. "Who cares what you look like anyway. This isn't exactly the party where you're going to meet the love of your life."

Her mouth sort of folds over the word "love," like it's a joke. And I guess for her it is. The same spell that cursed me with not eating cursed her with not loving. She can't feel any kind of love—not for princes or princesses or dukes or duchesses, which wouldn't be so unusual. But Nora can't feel any love for *us*, either, not for her family, or her subjects, or the small blue birds she used to feed bread crumbs to, and not even for herself. I suppose for Nora, love sounds about as attainable as a roast chicken does to me.

"Thirteenth Birthdays were Mom's favorite," I say. Nora and I remember her best. Alice, Grace, and Eden guess at who she is and what she loved and what she used to say. But Nora and I recall the specifics—the way her hair knotted in the wind, the way she held her hands to her heart when she was disappointed, the care with which she shrugged into a new ball gown like it was a second skin. "She said a Thirteenth Birthday marks the moment a princess becomes herself."

The day the spell was cast was so close to my own Thirteenth Birthday that preparations had been well underway. Mom and I had chosen the ocean as a theme. I've never seen one, but I was fascinated by the idea of an expanse of water so large you couldn't see the other side. My Thirteenth Birthday was going to have seafood entrées and waves of water beneath glass floors and the smell of salt in the air. The witches had agreed to help make it so. Olive made me an ocean dress in blues and greens, waves of fabric that swished and swayed with such force I could have imagined I was caught in a tide's pull.

But when it was time for my Thirteenth Birthday, I spent it in a corner, and I called Olive ridiculous for making the gown. I refused to eat a last meal. If I think too hard now, I can still feel the pain of it. How good it felt to topple a tray of bonbons. How I wanted to punch my hand through a window or kick a prince.

It's there even now, deep down. A simmering rage I'm barely holding back.

Nora knows it too. We are both thinking about last year's party for Grace. And two years before that when Alice turned thirteen. A royal Thirteenth Birthday used to be a joyous moment, introducing a princess to her future. She'd meet princes and princesses from other kingdoms. She would be given a silver-and-emerald crown. She would be given a title. Princess Mara the Clever. Princess Emily the Listening. Princess Betsy the Strong.

Now we are given our spell and nothing else. Princess Jane Who Can't Eat. Princess Nora Who Can't Love. Princess Alice Who Can't Sleep. Princess Grace Who Can't Remember. Princess Eden Who Can't Hope.

"Who cares about Birthdays and dresses?" Nora asks. "Who cares about any of this?"

I'd be better off ignoring Nora, but I can't. She's so present. Her body looks the way mine used to—thick around the hips, rounded at the breasts, at the belly. Sturdy and sweet.

I squeeze my hands into fists and wonder what it would be like to shove her, hard, against a tree.

What would a queen do? my mind interrupts. *Be a queen.* I pull my shoulders back and lift my chin and take on the pose of a ruler.

Nora raises her eyebrows at the way the lace of my dress drapes, clings, tries to thicken me up, fails. Because the spell is a

Slow one, I can't waste away entirely, I can't die of starvation, but I can't imagine getting any skinnier than I am right now. I suppose that makes sense. One way or another, we are near the end.

I push the thought away. *You will be queen.* I will not die from this spell.

"Mom loved the food at the Thirteenth Birthdays," Nora says. I can't tell if it's meant to be cruel or matter-of-fact. I don't think Nora knows either.

"The only taste I remember is apple," I say.

"Apple, huh?" Nora says. She stands up, and her dress falls down around her, a mint-green cloud.

"It's sweet," I say, licking my lips like some phantom taste might still be there. "Tangy. Watery. A pinch of a taste. The kind of thing you could eat for hours and never feel full from. Is that right?"

"That's about right," Nora says with a sort of smile. "The Prince of Soar loves apples. Dad told me. The chef will be making them baked with cinnamon for him."

"He's the redheaded one?" I ask.

She shakes her head. "No, that's the Prince of Nethering. The Prince of Soar is the tall one. Glasses. Dimples. Soft voice."

I nod. It's hard to keep track of these things. When I was allowed to eat, names and faces and locations felt like distinct, graspable ideas. Now it's all hazy, and my anger keeps rising and rising, obscuring things even more.

Be a queen, I tell myself again. I try to stay still and silent. It's harder than it sounds.

I remember reciting the Royal Rules with my mother

before bed every night. I loved the rules. If I could follow them, I would be queen, and all would be well. At rest. The way it was meant to be. I can almost hear my mother's small voice singing its way through the long list of things I was supposed to be.

Then the moment's over, and she's just a woman in glass again, just a trapped queen, just someone I used to know.

Once upon a time.

2.

REAGAN

I run all the way there.

Magic brings me across the ocean, from my banishment in AndNot to my home of Ever. But my feet have to do the rest, taking me from the edge of Ever to the moat. I want to see my bedroom with its mauve walls and thick blankets. I want to see my cousin Willa and my mother and grandmother and my best friend, Abbott. But first I have to see the king in his castle.

Sometimes at night, these past years, I would think about those people, my home, the long afternoons spent learning spells that we had to promise never to use, the work of protecting a kingdom that had lost a princess. Sometimes I would think about Willa's smile and Mom's layers of skirts and the view of the castle from our Home on the Hill.

But mostly I would think about him. The king. His suffering.

I would sit on the edge of the shore, letting ocean water lick my toes, and I'd imagine a hunch in his shoulders, the way they must shake when he cries. I'd convince myself that he was awake too, staring out at his kingdom, wishing he could undo all his mistakes, knowing that he couldn't. I want to see the dark circles under his eyes and his slow shuffle as he moves from one room to the next, regretting everything he's ever done.

I wonder if he'll find his way onto his knees, to beg me to help his daughters break the spell.

Abbott will like to see that. I will too.

The last mile of my run is the hardest. The kingdom of AndNot, where I was banished to five years ago, is supple. Warm and muggy with oversize flowers growing out of everything. They grew inside the small cottage my mother had brought me to. There were no floors in the spare space, just dirt, with orange and blue flowers sprouting like a blooming carpet beneath my feet.

It's not like that here. It's hard to run in Ever. The air is dry and cool, there's a breeze that stings my arms, and my heart is racing with excitement. My skirts tangle up in my legs, the one heavy layer from the Spell of Without slowing me down the most. When I was a child, I said I'd never cast such a heavy spell. I didn't want to have to carry it with me. But it was worth it. It will all be worth it.

Five years is a little like forever, but I still know the paths that take me from the place I began to the place I want to be. A patch of shore that is shaded and a little hidden, tucked around a corner, not where all of Ever gathers daily to watch their royals across the water.

By the time I make it there, to the edge of the moat, where

I have a perfect view of the king's tower, I'm breathless from the run and from the thrill and from the anticipation of finally seeing what I've been dreaming of: a broken king.

The castle looks the same. The queen in her box does too.

Yes, five years is a little like forever, and it's a long, long time to be alone with your thoughts. But I worked hard not to think of the queen. Seeing her here, now, stops me and maybe even stops my heart for one half beat before it resumes thumping again.

Another long look and I see two of the princesses next to their mother and an attendant watching them from a different part of the yard. The princesses are in gowns. I try to see their faces, but they are turned away from me, looking only at the queen.

It doesn't take much waiting for him to appear. He has always loved watching his kingdom, standing in the fresh air and reminding them he is there. His white hands grip the balcony wall, and I start to smile. His head is lowered. There's the hunch. I think I maybe even see a tremble.

I surge with pride. I did it. I fixed the kingdom of Ever. I punished the king. I will be carrying the weight of my spell forever, a heavy burlap skirt, but it will feel light as air now.

Except.

His shoulders unhunch. His hands ungrip. What I thought was a tremble was a laugh.

The king is smiling. He is waving.

And then he is speaking.

"Good people of Ever! Thank you for gathering to wish

our Princess Eden a happy Thirteenth Birthday. Our youngest child, we are so proud to celebrate her today."

There is a cheer from the subjects of Ever. They aren't far from the small part of the moat I've claimed as my own. They are in their best clothing, which isn't very nice at all. And they smile at the king.

My heart twists, and I tell it to stop, that it's fine, that everything's fine.

"We hope you will celebrate with us, across the moat, and as a special treat I've sent champagne for you to toast with. We are in this together. One kingdom. One Ever."

An attendant appears next to the king with a flute of champagne. I watch her body for signs of fear, and it's unmistakable. *She* is the one with the hunch, the tremble, the worry. She bows her head. She doesn't look up.

I wrap my arms around myself, holding myself together as hard as I can.

A team of horsemen travel the length of the moat, handing out bottles of champagne to whoever reaches up to take one. The sounds of corks popping and fizz pouring fill the air.

The king raises his glass. "A toast!" he says. His smile widens.

"No," I say to myself. It's a whisper. I have been whispering words to myself for five years. I have been quiet in my waiting. Patient. There's no magic in AndNot, no other people around, no visitors. I have only had one companion: my hatred for the king.

"To the Spellbound princesses of Ever!" the king says.

"To the Spellbound!" the crowd bellows back.

"No," my voice says, louder than a whisper, so loud that people yards away turn and look at me.

I run.

I studied the royal family for five long years, preparing for the perfect way to have them break the spell. I know what fruits Alice is allergic to and how many freckles Eden has. I know their father is from Farr. And I know, like everyone knows, the story of the taken princess eighty years ago. I tell the story in my head now, to distract myself from the other thoughts trying to push their way in. The princess was stolen, the kingdoms fought over who took her, the witches tried to stop the fighting, and ten of us vanished in the process. No one ever learned who took the princess, but our magic eventually ushered in peace, and we were given the Home on the Hill as thanks for our work. We promised to keep the kingdom at rest; we gave them Enchanted Candles to help the princess find her way home; they promised to leave us to ourselves up on the Hill, to protect us from other kingdoms; and mostly everyone kept their promises.

Until five years ago, when I learned what the king had done.

They had told us the other kingdoms were who we needed to fear.

They hadn't told us to fear our own kingdom, our own king.

He has to pay, I think for the thousandth or millionth time. I look back again, hoping to see some hidden pain on the king's face. There's only a grin. *No,* I think. *This is all wrong.*

And: *I was all wrong.*

Before I cast the Spell of Without, I could run easily, light silks and sheers flapping against my legs. Now the burlap skirt leaves me breathless.

My grandmother is even less able to move. She is so weighed down by her impressive collection of skirts, each layer the result of a spell cast. Velvet, wool, and dozens of layers of cotton and linen encircle her waist and pin her to her chair in the living room.

A kind of throne, if witches were to have thrones.

Sometimes it looks more like a prison.

My skirt today reminds me of her, reminds me of what I'm afraid of becoming. The weight of a spell is only worth it if the spell works. I didn't even notice the heaviness of the burlap until right now, this very instant, seeing my spell fail.

When I finally reach the door of my home, I stop outside it. They should be expecting me, but there's no fanfare, no cousins peering out the window looking for me. Even my own mother isn't at the door, doesn't feel me nearing her, isn't eagerly sitting on the lawn, open armed and grinning at being reunited with me after all these years.

Eighty years of the people of Ever waiting by enchanted candlelight for a princess who will never return, and no one has been waiting for me.

It hits me hard, the pain of it, the loneliness. But there's nothing else to do, so I open the door and let myself in.

"Hello?" I call to the empty foyer, the familiar wooden floors and beams and heavy curtains and strange mix of magical smells. "I'm here."

There's a scurry of footsteps that I hope are my mother's, but I quickly see they belong to my cousin Willa, who thrusts herself onto me. She wraps her long brown arms around my white shoulders. Non-witches have been surprised that we are cousins—maybe because of our skin or maybe because Willa's energy is so light and bright and mine is heavy and twisty and wrong. Her happiness at seeing me after all this time is real and easy, and it feels so good I want to fall into it.

My mother is behind her, a little less exuberant but smiling warmly and letting her eyes fill with tears. "My girl," she says, pulling me away from Willa and into her arms. I hug her gently. It's the only way to touch her.

"My mom," I reply, and it makes her laugh a little, or at least smile bigger. She takes me in, and there's no hiding anything from her.

"You saw him," she says.

I nod.

"It hasn't been good," she says.

"You warned me it wouldn't be," I say. "I was so sure—" I look for the end to the sentence, but that confidence, that assurance that I had ruined the king, made my point, and was returning to victory, feels so childish here and now.

"You have a chance to make it better," Mom says.

"I want to make *you* better," I say. We are whispering. I wish I could have come back weeks earlier, spent time on the roof with my mother figuring out what to do, how to feel, who to be, before telling the princesses how to break the spell.

But all we have is this moment, right here.

"Well, what you did—that was never going to fix me, Reagan. I'm not the only broken bit of this whole mess," Mom says. Her hands flicker in and out of visibility. I want to hold on to them, make them stay right here. "Ever is broken. Ever has to heal, for me to heal. That's what I wanted you to— that's what I tried to explain—there's so much more than one witch and one king."

I want to tell her that may well be, but I only care about her and him and the terrible things that happened in his castle.

But before I can, there's a clatter in the kitchen, and more aunts and cousins wander to the front door to say hello to me. If everything were different, I'd be hugging and gossiping and taking in how tall this one has grown, how many skirts that one is now wearing.

Instead I can only see my mother and the way she still winces at loud noises and unexpected movements.

The day I cast the spell, she and I were startled by Willa dropping a heavy cast-iron pot from the counter onto the floor. My hands squeezed at the fleshy part above my mother's elbow. I always reach for her when I'm scared.

But the place I touched was the wrong place to touch. The sound of the pot, too, was the wrong kind of sound. And my mother lost her breath. She curled into a ball. I ran for someone, anyone, to help us.

My grandmother couldn't move from her chair, of course, so it was my aunt Idle who heard my screams. She whispered *Breathe breathe breathe* into my mother's ear and told me to list everything I saw in the room. I couldn't imagine why, but

Aunt Idle sounded confident, as if she'd done this before, so I followed her instructions.

"There's a blue carpet," I said. "There's a wooden chair. There are five cast-iron pots. One of them is on the floor; the others are lined up for Willa and me to practice our spells. Willa is hiding behind a thick gray curtain. The Enchanted Candle is on the long wooden table, just like always. It's gold. All is well in the kingdom of Ever."

"Don't say 'king,'" Aunt Idle whisper-yelled. But it was too late. My mother, who had been breathing in time with my list, snapped back into panic. She bellowed. She brought her head to the floor. I listed more things in the room: Grandmother's book of spells, the vegetables hanging from the ceiling like an upside-down garden, my discarded shoes, Willa's cape. But it didn't help. Aunt Idle asked me to leave, and I did, huddling myself with my little cousin right outside the kitchen door.

The house shook with magic.

I don't know what spell Aunt Idle cast to bring my mother back to herself, but whatever it was draped them both in the thickest, itchiest wool skirts, now permanently wrapped around their waists. Some spells aren't meant to be cast. Those spells are the heaviest, the most cumbersome. The price for casting them is eternal.

Witches carry their spells forever. And Aunt Idle hadn't wanted the burden of this one.

When Willa and I reentered the kitchen, Aunt Idle told us why my mother had crumbled like that. My grab of her elbow, perfectly timed with Willa's dropping of the pot. The touch, the crash, it brought her back to the worst moment in her life.

And upon hearing the story of the worst moment of her life, without thinking a single thought, my fury drove me out of the Home on the Hill and to the castle moat, where I cast the biggest spell I could muster.

Mom is remembering it now too. Her hand grips a handful of my burlap skirt. The heaviest kind of spell.

We both take a deep breath, and the smell of roasting pig fills the air. The witches roast a pig whenever a witch is invited to the castle. They are expecting me to be invited tonight, but no one has handed me a thick silver invitation, engraved with my name. I suppose the roasting pig is like the lit candles out in Ever. A way to mark the waiting. A way to hang on to hope.

"You're back just in time," Mom says. Her voice is a sigh. I want her to sound different than she does.

"She certainly is," my aunt Idle says, coming in from outside, carrying the smell of the pig, the fire, the salt, the woods with her. She doesn't smile. "You look older," she says.

"I am older."

"And wiser?" she asks. She hasn't forgiven me.

"I don't know," I say, because witches tell the truth.

"Mmm." Aunt Idle would have banished me forever if she could have. *We are trying to prove we are not who they think we are,* she said the day I cast the spell. *What have you done, but shown them their stories of us are right? And now you've gotten rid of the queen, too? A kingdom with no queen? What were you thinking, Reagan?* Her voice had gotten louder and louder

25

with every impossible-to-answer question. *We're supposed to protect our magic, not hurl it at young girls.*

"It's up to them to break the spell," I say. "Hopefully, they'll—"

"You've learned nothing in your time away," Aunt Idle interrupts. "They'll do what they can do to break the spell. But it's you who has to Undo it. The real work is yours." I have an awful feeling gnawing at my insides. A hollowness carving me up. I don't think regular humans can be filled with emptiness, but as a witch it isn't an unusual sensation. To be absolutely bursting with absence. Sometimes parts of us even vanish: a finger, a shoulder blade, a foot—gone until the feeling passes.

In worse circumstances, if the kingdom itself is in unrest, a whole witch might vanish. Forever. After the princess was taken eighty years ago, a great battle broke out between the witches and the royals. Ten witches disappeared. First their feet. Then their hips. Their hair went last.

It's a detail they never leave out when they warn us about what could be.

Ten witches. Gone. Because of a war that went too far. Because of a kidnapped princess who was never found and kingdoms that all blamed one another. Because of unrest. It's why we watch the Enchanted Candle on the kitchen counter. It's why we keep the peace. It's why my aunt Idle looks at me the way she does now. The only way for us to be safe is for the kingdom to be safe. So we protect them, and that protects us.

"I needed the king to suffer," I say weakly, "so I hurt the princesses. You all taught me about justice, and that was—"

"You didn't just hurt princesses," Aunt Idle says. "You think of spells as small. But they are huge. A spell is like an infection, Reagan. It gets to everyone nearby. It can spread through an entire kingdom. Making the whole place diseased." Aunt Idle sighs. I'd forgotten about the force of her sighs. They are hurricanes of disapproval. It's awful to be caught in one.

In the distance, there's the melody of the song the townspeople sing whenever a princess comes of age. It's a rollicking song about princes and princesses and royal weddings and beautiful babies and growing up. Willa and I used to sing it to each other, as a joke. Now it sounds sinister.

The empty feeling grows, and I watch as my pinkie finger vanishes.

A new smell wafts in, covering up the roasted-pig smell. Aunt Idle's nose wrinkles from it. My mother's, too. My grandmother's. A too-sweet, dense smell. Royal fear.

When it's from the king, the smell of royal fear has hints of coffee. With the queen, back when she was not in a box, there would be an undertone of pine. And when the princesses are afraid, we can smell a touch of the ocean.

Without princess fear, we'd never smell the ocean all the way in Ever.

And there it is. It's the smell I lived with for five years on the shores of AndNot. It's faint, but it's there. The ocean.

"The princesses," I say. "The princesses are afraid."

"But not the king," Aunt Idle says. "He hasn't been afraid a single day since you cast your spell. Not one moment."

"That can't be true," I say. "His wife is—and his children are—"

"Yes. Well. It's quite a disease, your Spell of Without. The men, they simply love it, most of them. Even the king. He pretends not to. But we know. It's smelled of nothing but burning wax and dead fields and the ocean for five years."

Aunt Idle doesn't blink. She watches it all sink in. My failure. My other pinkie vanishes, and a part of my knee. Gone, just like that. She watches my invisible parts, satisfied. They'll come back. They always do. But it's never the same.

"Ever has always loved keeping people in their places," my aunt says. "Witches on a hill. Princesses in a castle. And now a queen in a box."

My heart sinks further and further down. A thousand skirts wouldn't be as heavy as my heart right now.

"Anyway, I suppose it's time to celebrate," Aunt Idle says in her least celebratory voice. "Fried berries for breakfast." It's her way of dismissing us all, and it works. My aunts and cousins go to the kitchen to prepare the food. They don't say another word to me.

The Home on the Hill is chilly in the mornings. At noon sun floods the place and warms up the floors and the walls and the air itself. But right now, without the help of the sun, our home is the temperature that witches manifest—forty degrees on the dot.

I am missing the warm breezes in AndNot. And a hundred other things that made the last five years bearable.

It's only Willa who stays beside me. "You know Aunt

Idle," she says. "Always cranky." She shrugs, like it's nothing, what I've done, and I love her for it, but it's bullshit. Still, I give her another hug. She has a few more layers of chiffon skirts around her waist than when I left. They are featherlight and lovely. She's been busy in my time away, but only doing small, gentle spells.

I'm jealous without meaning to be.

"Let's have a picnic!" she says, like no time at all has passed, like we are just two witch cousins making our way in Ever. We used to have an enchanted picnic every week, sitting underneath a tree on a blanket made and Spellbound by our grandmother, who invented a picnic blanket that creates the picnic for you after you lay it on the grass.

It's a flawed spell, because the only picnic the blanket knows how to make is bread and pickles and jam.

But Willa and I like bread and pickles and jam. We make pickle-and-jam sandwiches and tell secrets in the moonlight. We used to pretend we were princesses too, ordering the littlest cousins around as if they were our attendants, picking out stars to name after ourselves, the way princesses do. We gave ourselves titles, pretending to have royal Thirteenth Birthdays. Willa the Whimsical. Reagan the Ravishing.

"I can't," I say. "I have to come up with the spell-breaking." First the princesses will have to follow my instructions. They'll have to perform a feat or gather some objects or make a sacrifice. If they accomplish what I demand of them, I'll perform the Undoing, and that will require its own magic, an even heavier skirt around my waist.

Willa's face changes. It turns serious, and I have never seen Willa serious. "Make it easy," she says. "Make it easy for them to break. Make it kind. Please, Reagan. Be kind."

Willa has a soft heart, and her magic reflects it. The spells she casts are gentle and sweet. She's good with wishes and love and food. She can cure the ill. But she never could have cast the Spell of Without like I did.

Maybe no other witch could have.

Maybe no witch should have.

3.

JANE

Nora and I aren't alone with Mom for long after Dad's toast. Our sisters come out one by one. Alice's gait is slow and practiced. She hasn't slept since she turned thirteen two years ago, so she is prone to falling. Alice is taller than the rest of us, and she talks the least, but when she does speak, it's always clear and sturdy. When she was born, it was assumed that she was the first and only royal son. But after a few years it became clear to everyone that she was actually their third daughter.

Grace walks without paying any attention and sometimes loses her way from the door of the castle to the glass box, a mere fifty paces away.

Eden is the only one who bounds out of the house. She runs toward me and throws her arms around my waist. She holds on tight.

Eden has not yet turned thirteen. She is hours away from it now, and the spell is attached to her like a shadow we can all see. She hugs me tighter, and I give in to it. Dad doesn't hug me anymore. Neither do my other sisters. I think it has to do with the jab of my bones, the smell of skin that hasn't been nourished.

There's a surge of love when Eden crashes into me. Then it hurts. Because it could be gone forever.

Nora scoffs. Things like a hug from her baby sister mean nothing to her now.

Dad is following behind my sisters. He has his red robe draped around his shoulders. It is trimmed with white fur, and Mom used to call it *a little much*, but Eden loves it, so he wears it every day for her. She hides in its folds; she snuggles against the fur; she hangs on to the fabric, attaching herself to Dad for hours a day.

Sometimes the rest of us do as well. My favorite mornings are the ones when Dad and I hole up in the library, talking about the kingdoms. I have a passion for the history of our world, and Dad knows more than anyone else about our past. He and Alice spend long nights outside doing stonework. He tried to teach us all the ancient trade, but she's the only one that took to it. The backyard is covered in enormous slabs of marble that he and Alice chip away at, turning lumps of stone into works of art. He'll tell Grace romantic stories for as many hours as she wants of princes meeting princesses and falling in love. And when she presses him for stories of two princesses falling in love, he tells the few of those he knows too. His patience with her is endless. She asks over and over if she can marry a princess someday, and every time he answers yes with the same wide grin, the same gentle voice, the same clarity.

Even Nora wants to be in his glow. She'd deny it, but she sits next to him at every meal and walks the grounds with him in the evenings when they both grow restless and sad. It isn't love, but it's comfort, which is maybe as close as it gets for Nora.

His subjects would do anything to have access to him the way we do. "Your Majesty!" a chorus of voices call out now. They want even one second of his gaze on their shoulders.

But that's not how it's meant to be. We are royals. We are not meant to speak to our subjects like they're our friends. We were chosen for this and they were chosen for their lives, and they can yell across the moat as much as they'd like, but it won't change that simple truth.

"Hello!" Eden calls out to the subjects. Dad stifles a smile at her precociousness. Mom taught the rest of us to keep what she called a Royal Distance between ourselves and the people of Ever. But Eden was too young for that lesson, and she wasn't built for distance anyway. I'd put a stop to it, but the spell will take care of that by the end of the day, so what's the point? If we survive it, if we break it, Mom will be here to explain the ways of Ever to Eden. She'll teach her how to be royal, how to be distant, how to live in a castle and care from a tower.

It's unimaginable that sometime before midnight Eden will be without hope. Right now she's brimming with it. She hopes to travel the world over and barter peace. She hopes to bring her light to other kingdoms, other people, other universes if she could. I'm not sure any of that will be allowed, but we let her dream it. I've only ever wanted to be the Queen of Ever, but Eden wants to help the whole world.

"Dad?" I try. "Do you think it will be a hard spell to

break? Do you think she'll tell us why she did this? Do you think she feels bad?" I tried to ask just one question, but the rest came spilling out. I've been counting down days to Eden's birthday for five long years, and these last few hours are proving to be the hardest. My whole body is on edge. I want to do something now, immediately, but we haven't been given instructions, so I can't do anything but invent ways the spell might be broken.

Dad looks out over the moat, at his kingdom. I've noticed he doesn't look at Mom often. I think it must be too painful for him, to see her trapped there. He has his red, fur-trimmed robe and his crown with diamonds that glint in the sun. He is the Gentle King. The Good King.

But still, he can't save her.

Or us.

I go to him and hold his hand. Maybe I'm the only almost-eighteen-year-old in the world who still holds their father's hand. But I'm also the only one with this man as my father. He holds my hand back, gives it three squeezes, which is an unspoken language between the two of us. *I'm here,* his pulsing hand says. *We've got this,* his strong fingers beat out.

The townspeople have caught sight of Dad and me holding hands. I can see them pointing to the place where our fingers interlock.

"Such a kind king!" they yell. "Such a good daughter!"

"They're louder today," Grace says. "Why are they so loud?" She has taken up Dad's other side.

"They're excited for Eden's Thirteenth Birthday," I say.

"They love Thirteenth Birthdays, just like Mom used to. Remember?"

Grace looks at me blankly. No, of course she doesn't remember.

"It will be loud the next few days," I say. "Will you be okay?"

"Do you think I'll be okay?" she asks.

"You might get scared."

"Why?"

"You get scared sometimes."

"Why do I get scared?" Grace asks.

"Because you don't always understand what's happening," I say.

"Why?"

"Because you can't remember anything, Grace-bell. You're Spellbound with the Spell of Without. You are without the ability to remember." It always ends exactly here—the place where I remind her of the spell, of her particular curse.

Her little brown eyes fill up with tears. When those tears fall, they will be huge and heartbreaking. They will wreck me. They will make Alice scream, desperate to be allowed to sleep and escape the pain. She has made stone sculptures of Grace's face, made holes where the tears are. Eden will wipe them away. Nora leaves us to deal with them.

"We know you try," Dad says. "We know, honey." He is gentle with Grace. With all of us.

Not remembering won't kill Grace, though.

There's the rage again, accidental and shameful and aimed every which way when it should only be aimed at that witch.

I clench my jaw and will it away. Queens don't get enraged. They aren't jealous of their sisters. Their insides don't itch with desperation at the thought of a slice of buttered toast.

The people of Ever call out to us from across the moat. Dad gives us a look, reminding us to be kind about it. It is our job to be kind even when they are making us dizzy with questions we can't answer.

"Which prince do you most want to meet at the Thirteenth Birthday?"

"When you are allowed to eat again, what will you eat first?"

"When you can sleep again, what will you dream about?"

As I look at each face in the crowd, I can guess at what they ate for breakfast this morning. It's something my brain does now. That one had oatmeal. That one toast. Eggs. A cup of coffee and nothing else.

"Will the kidnapped princess return this year?" an extra-loud voice asks. One of them always asks. Will the kidnapped princess return? Is our wait over? Will this old pain finally come to an end? Can we find out, once and for all, who to hate for taking her?

The kidnapped princess would be well into her nineties now, if she returned. And we are right here. We are alive and trying to survive. I want them to worry about *us*, the way they fret over their vanished royalty. If I die, will they light candles for me the way they do for her? Will they fight for us, if we need them to?

I'm scared of the answer.

"You girls have to start getting ready," Dad says. "The day's escaping us. And it's a very big day."

He leads us back into the castle after waving at his people. He lifts another glass of champagne in their direction. "To the princesses," he says.

"To the princesses," they call back.

But we stay quiet, as princesses are meant to.

Once we're inside, our attendants line up for us. They are from a dozen different families, and they look nothing alike except for their clothes. Every gender of attendant wears gray pants with a white shirt and a gray apron. At twenty-two, Olive is the oldest. She isn't as pale as my sisters and me but maybe would be if she wasn't outside all the time. She has honey-colored hair that she wraps into a high bun every morning. I know only a few things about her: that she lives with her father and her half brother, who was offered a job in the castle that he refused to take. Before she died, Olive's mother had also been an attendant, her grandmother and grandfather, too. Her brother's mother was a schoolteacher who taught the history of Ever to the older children until her death ten years ago, right after the beginning of the Famine.

When I asked how it was possible that both of their mothers had died, that her father had lost two wives, Olive looked at me like my question was sad and silly.

"A lot of people die," Olive said. "Just not people like you."

"We're all the same," I said. My mother taught me that. Olive let out a sound that could have been a laugh or could have been a sigh or could have been a cough and didn't say another word. We never spoke about her family again.

We princesses tuck our hair behind our ears, smooth our

37

skirts. Dad won't notice, but Mom loved those little rituals. "It's what makes us royalty," she used to say. "Holding on to tradition." She'd give Nora a heavy look when she reminded us of this. Nora's knees were always bruised, her hair never brushed, her whole self entirely out of order, uninterested in the old royal ways.

This is something that hasn't changed. Nora's elbows are skinned from who knows what, and her bangs stick this way and that, unkempt and unclean. Her attendant presses them down against her forehead, brushes dirt from her dress, shakes their head at the impossibility of making Nora look like a princess.

I don't think I'll care enough about tradition if I ever become queen. I don't want to disappoint my mother, but I like the way Nora's face shines with sweat, and I think the lining up of attendants is silly. They fidget and cough and seem to hate it.

Also: the silence. I'm not sure I believe in the silence in front of our subjects.

"A big night tonight," Dad says to all of us.

"Can I skip it?" Nora asks. She must know the answer. The attendants do. I hear one of them gasp, another giggle. There aren't really skippable family events. Especially not Eden's Thirteenth Birthday. But Nora has never liked things like Birthdays and Feasts and Banquets and Ceremonies. She likes wading in the moat and catching fish with her bare hands. She likes sleeping outside at night, under the stars, with nothing but a single wool blanket to keep her cozy. She likes spending time in the stables, coming up with dirt under her fingernails and the smell of horse in her hair.

Still. She won't be allowed to skip the party. It would be the talk of all the kingdoms for weeks. For years, even. The Princess Who Skipped a Birthday. It would be taught in school. It would, in a century, be in storybooks. Everything we do or don't do eventually turns into a story spun from tiny threads of our actual lives. Dad's voice is even gentler, his robe longer, in the stories they write about him. Mom's glass box is larger. We princesses are suddenly beautiful. Even the kingdom is fancier, with more towers and bigger stones, and the moat is filled with dragon-fish and mermaids, instead of tadpoles and cool water.

"Your mother loved the Birthdays," Dad says.

We are quiet in the awful absence of her. I miss the length of my mother's arms. The there-ness of her face. The sound of a voice I no longer know the pitch of. A mother is simply one more thing we are without.

"Mom cared about a lot of things before she ended up in a box," Nora says. I try to remember the other Nora. A Nora who snuggled into me at night, the one who knit scarves for the horses and planted flowers for the attendants and let me kiss her knees when she inevitably scraped them all to hell.

It's hard to picture Nora that way.

"It's where we met," Dad says, pretending not to hear Nora. "I was a visiting prince at your aunt Gloria's Thirteenth Birthday. And your mother was—well. Spectacular."

"She wore yellow," Eden says. We all know the story. It was

told to us at night by our starry-eyed mother; it was told in the town square during speeches; it was told on their anniversaries and their Birthdays and by townspeople and other kings and queens and of course by our own parents, who told the story like it was the only one that mattered.

Grace still asks to be told the story when she's bundled under the covers, pulling at the too-long sleeves of her favorite peach nightgown, brushing out her short, curly hair so that it morphs into a kind of cloud on top of her head. She won't listen to us when we remind her that you can't brush curly hair into straightness.

"She wore yellow," Dad repeats. "Yellow and silver. Two colors you don't see together very often."

"And that's what you noticed first," Grace says, happiest when we are talking about love. She remembers old stories like these, but nothing we've told her since the spell bound her.

"That and her eyes. Gray eyes. Long lashes. A quiet sort of beautiful." Dad smiles, so we all smile. It's exactly the right way to describe Mom.

"I like quiet," Alice says. She's only really half-here, only half listening to the things we're saying.

"Your mother was meant to marry the Duke of Soar at the time. Preparations were already being made ever since her own Thirteenth Birthday three years earlier. But the duke showed up, and your mother couldn't stand the way he shook her hand. Like she was delicate. Like she could break. She went to her father and informed him she would not be marrying someone who didn't think of her as strong."

We all smile. It's the best part of the story.

"And when you approached her, you practically broke her hand," Eden says.

Dad nods. "I was so nervous I squeezed her hand much too hard. I swore I could feel her bones cracking. And she took it as a sign that I was meant to be hers."

"And she was meant to be yours," Alice says, her voice emerging from her dreamy state.

"No," Dad says. "No. She was only ever her own person. She didn't belong to me. She didn't belong to her subjects, either. She doesn't belong to that witch. She doesn't belong in that box." He shakes his head. This part of the story is new. I lean in, waiting for more, for some new shade of something to hold on to. But that's all there is, I guess. "Anyway, it's a big night," Dad says. "You need to get ready." He starts walking toward his library, but I stop him. I have to.

"Dad?" I call out. "Will it be hard? I've never broken a spell."

I have been holding down these questions for years. It's always seemed so far away, Eden's Thirteenth Birthday. It's sounded like a fantastical moment in time that might never come. Now that it's here, everything I've been holding back comes pouring out.

"You'll do your best," Dad says. "Witches are—well. They're evil. That's clear now. They're manipulative and cruel and unreasonable. They're liars most of all. If we'd known what they were capable of, we never would have given them the Home on the Hill. But you girls are smart and strong. You're good and pure and true."

Grace lights up from this, and Eden nods, brimming with hope. Even Alice makes a sleepy, content sigh of a noise. But they haven't heard what I heard.

He didn't say we'd be able to do it. He didn't say it would all be okay.

He didn't promise I wouldn't die from this spell.

I watch him go and try to will him to turn back and tell us we'll be fine, we can do it, we *will* do it, things are about to go back to how they were before. He doesn't turn around, though.

"What time do you think the witch will get here?" I ask Olive. It isn't the precise thing I'm dying to know, but it's close enough.

Olive looks at the ground but doesn't answer.

"What time did the invitation say?" I ask. The witch can't come to the Thirteenth Birthday unless we send her an invitation. Hers should have been the first one engraved, the first one delivered.

"I'm not sure she's received an invitation yet," Olive says. She speaks carefully when she doesn't want to get in trouble.

"How is that possible?" I ask. The other attendants are leading my sisters behind me; all five of us need our hair done, our faces painted, our dresses smoothed, our bodies covered in something that smells the way a princess is meant to smell.

"I suppose your father . . . forgot?" Olive says, turning a statement strangely into a question.

"Forgot to invite the witch?" I ask. Sometimes, speaking to Olive, I feel like there's a conversation underneath the one we're having. But I'm always too hungry and tired to unearth it.

42

"I suppose maybe he did," Olive says.

There's a pause. It's a terrible pause, filled with things I'm too scared to look at.

"Well, good thing we've remembered," I say. My stomach turns. It isn't like my father to forget anything at all, let alone something so important.

Olive and I are eye to eye. "Good thing," she says.

"Nora's attendant can help me while you deliver the invitation," I say. I don't have time for a conversation under a conversation. I need to have it right here, on the surface.

Olive nods. I nod back.

Outside, the people of Ever light candles and wait for their kidnapped princess.

I am only waiting for the witch.

4.

REAGAN

I would have gone to him, but he comes to me.

He's at the door and Willa answers it, but I recognize the knock. Two softs knocks, a pause, then two louder knocks.

Abbott Shine.

By the time I get to the door, Willa is practically dancing around him, saying she's missed him and he could have come by even with me gone and he looks good and how's his half sister, the one who works in the castle, and how's Ever and did he miss me and does he love me.

"Okay, that's enough," I say when Willa asks this last thing.

"It's a joke!" Willa says, and maybe it is, because witches don't fall in love. My grandmother reminds me of this constantly.

"It's a joke," I repeat with a special smile just for Abbott.

"That's what you have to say to me after five years?" he asks. Abbott Shine is handsome in the heartbreaking way. Light brown skin, dark hair that turns gold at the tips, eyes so big and brown I forget myself at the sight of them.

"You're here," I say to Abbott. "Like you promised."

"It's the birthday," he says.

"I'm back," I say.

"You guys are just stating facts," Willa says. "Hug or something." She giggles and skips off the way she always does after causing her kind of trouble.

So we do. We hug, and it's familiar and not. He's taller and broader and something else, too. I lean back from him, look at his face, and stop thinking about the beauty of it. He's sadder. I look for his wrist, to see if all is lost. And I blush when I see tied there a tiny gray pebble on a string. He sees me see it, and in that moment we are in it together again. Remembering the past, facing the future.

Abbott Shine came to the Home on the Hill when we were ten and declared himself a Friend of the Witches, and said he'd do anything to help us fight the royals. I'd never heard of such a thing.

"We protect the royals," I said.

"You stay away from them," he said.

"Because magic needs its own space," I said, repeating a thing I'd heard my grandmother say when my cousins asked her about our arrangement.

"What if there was more to it?" Abbott Shine asked me. "What if the royals do terrible things, and you're the only ones who could stop it?"

His family was struggling, his sister had been recruited to be an attendant, and he wanted to fix things. He thought they were broken. He thought the royals were the reason. He believed witches were the way out.

Maybe he made me believe that too. We thought we could make things better, Abbott and I. We had the kind of grand plans twelve-year-olds have. But I cast the spell before we had a chance to use my magic in some other way.

We used to meet by the moat, and he'd tell me about Ever, and I'd tell him about the Home on the Hill, and it felt like we were the only two people in the world who knew about both places. He used to talk quickly, listing all the things we could do to change the kingdom, all the spells I should cast, all the people who wondered, like he did, why the royals and the townspeople lived such wildly different lives.

I'd nod my head, but I didn't really know what he meant. I had five years to think about it, I guess. But if I'm honest, I didn't. Not much. I thought about the king. The king's pain and humiliation and regret. How good it would feel to see him broken.

Now with Abbott here in front of me, it feels shameful.

"I can't believe it's been five years," he says.

"Five years is a long time. Something in Ever must have changed," I say, desperate to feel anything but this sinking feeling that keeps bringing me impossibly lower and lower. Abbott looks at me. Somehow I'd forgotten that he would grow up, that when I returned, he'd be older just like I'm older. I'd been picturing twelve-year-old Abbott with his full cheeks and impish grin. I'd been picturing a child.

"They've still never crossed the moat," Abbott says. I'm so lost in thinking about the king that it takes me a moment to catch up.

"The princesses?" I say. "They're not allowed."

Abbott rolls his eyes. He never rolled his eyes five years ago. Things have gotten worse for him, or Ever has gotten worse, or maybe everyone gets angrier the more time they spend on this side of the moat.

Now he's pacing. "They don't care about us. They don't know us. If anything, your spell made it worse. They have even less time to think about our lives. They get to be victims again. Just like when their princess was kidnapped."

"I thought—" I start, but it's hard, right now, to remember exactly what I was thinking. The image of the smiling, waving, straight-backed king is so distracting, so present, it's obscuring the past.

"You thought . . . what?" Abbott says.

I don't remember exactly how to navigate space with another person. I'm awkward around people now. Even ones I've known forever. I don't know what my body means in relation to theirs. I don't know how my voice is supposed to sound. I settle on a shrug.

"I was young," I say.

"We were both young," Abbott says. He stood behind me when I cast the spell. I heard him say *Reagan, no, think,* but the words were like the wind—sharp and there and then gone so fast I could forget all about them. Besides, my magic isn't the kind that can be stopped by a boy and his worried words. "But I knew enough to wait and think. You were selfish."

I don't like the way the word sounds. "I was protecting my mother," I say. "That's not selfish."

Abbott closes his eyes for a moment longer than a blink. "You're like them, sometimes," he says at last.

"Like who?"

"Royals." It makes my spine prickle.

"I have to break the spell. I made a mistake. I know that. I get it." And I do get it, but I also haven't let go of my anger, my need to see the king in pain, my sureness that punishing him matters. Abbott and my grandmother and my aunt Idle and my mother and everyone else in Ever want me to have done everything differently, but all we've ever done was wait around and be careful and worry about a kingdom at rest, and that isn't good enough for me.

"You only care when it happens to you, to your mother, to your people," Abbott says.

"She's my *mother*," I say. I am willing to apologize for a lot of things, but caring about my mother more than anyone else isn't one of them.

"It's like the kidnapped princess," Abbott says. He shakes his head back and forth. He is so grown-up now. He doesn't feel like he's my age anymore. He sounds like a teacher or a parent. A father, if I had any idea what a father was like.

"This has nothing to do with the kidnapped princess," I say. I'm tired of the old story of why things are the way they are. Why we live here, why we protect Ever, why we want the kingdom to be at rest.

"Do you know how many people were kidnapped that month?" Abbott asks. It's starting to feel like he's having one conversation and I'm having another, and I've never felt so out

48

of synch with my best friend, even when we were an ocean and many years apart.

"The month I cast the spell?" I ask, squinting at him like that will help me make sense of him.

"No," he says. "Eighty years ago. When the princess was kidnapped."

"Are you saying more than one princess was kidnapped?" I ask. "Because a lot of witches vanished too. We all were hurt by that—"

"Nineteen people," Abbott says.

"I don't know what that means."

"Nineteen people were kidnapped before the princess. Nineteen people. Some from my mother's family, but no one cared about those girls. They had brown skin and worn shoes and no jewels. Other young people were taken too. Ones no one cares much about. Poor kids and kids without parents and kids who have never been in a castle *or* a Home on the Hill."

Abbott's speaking quickly, like he has to get this out before we have another minute together, and I don't know why it's so urgent, I don't know why he needs me to care about this right now, but I try to listen—I try—and I try to care as much as I care about my mother and how much I hate the king.

I try, but it's hard.

"It was eighty years ago," I say. "This is right now."

It's the wrong thing to say.

"Right now, we're all hurting," Abbott says. "And it's because of them. But it's because of you, too."

"If you'd told them why—if you've told them what kind of king—"

"You don't listen, Reagan," Abbott says. "And I did try, once, to tell them why I thought the spell had been cast. But we barely—my family barely survives. *Barely.* My sister works in that castle. We need her to work there. My father can't think about— You think I can go accusing the king of—and be okay? And survive? You think that would be worth the risk for us? My family—my mother's family—has already lost so much." He keeps shaking his head and staring across the moat. When I was in AndNot, I dreamed about his bright eyes and the way he made me feel. I wished he could live in my AndNot cottage with me. I thought he'd like to see the ocean. That we'd learn how to swim together.

I never imagined the look on his face, rage and dread and sadness and frustration. My heart flip-flops between anger at him and at myself. And then back, always, to the king.

The thing about Ever is, we're all just trying to survive.

"My family has lost a lot too," I say. And again, it's wrong.

"You have your Home. You have food. And magic. You have—"

"Okay," I say. "Okay, okay."

He's saying things that are true, but I don't want to hear them. Not now. I want us to be angry about the same things, the same injustices. I thought that's what we had together, but now it feels like something else. I reach for the way we used to be.

"Do you still dream of oranges?" I ask. "And . . . what was it? Peppers?"

"Bell peppers," Abbott says.

"I still believe my spell might—" I start, but Abbott does that awful laugh again, the one that is more a dismissal than a laugh, and I stop myself. It's all wrong. I put a hand on his arm. It's strong in places it wasn't before. "Tell me how to fix it. Tell me what needs to be done."

"Reagan."

"I messed up. I know I messed up. But there's still time."

It gets so quiet I can hear Willa breathing. She only disappeared into the next room, and she's still listening to us. An old part of me wants to tell Willa she's not old enough for this talk, but she is now—of course she is. I'm turning eighteen in a few days; she'll be fourteen not long after that.

"You think you have it worst of all," he says. "And the royals think they have it worst of all, because of their missing princess. Their curses. But you and those princesses look the way you look and live where you live and have all this power, and all you do with it is—"

"I tried to fix things," I say, the words straining, because even I don't believe me right now.

"That's not how to fix anything," Abbott says. "If you can't hear how things really are, you might as well just stay in AndNot."

"You'd miss me," I say. It slides out, all slippery and warm and accidental, and I blame his eyes and my own thumping heart. *Witches don't fall in love,* I remind myself. I thought all these years that it was a truth, a spell we were under maybe, a part of our makeup. But I'm starting to wonder if witches not falling in love is just a rule.

A rule is easier to break than a spell.

"I did miss you," Abbott says. He doesn't look at me, though. Those eyes of his are hitched to the ceiling.

"And now?" I ask. It feels like something is going to happen, but nothing does. Abbott doesn't so much as shrug. Abbott isn't lost in the same moment I am. I've been alone for five years, thinking about him, and he's been right here, thinking entirely different thoughts about me, I guess.

"The breaking of the spell," he says. "It's your choice, right?" He's all business, so I try to be the same.

"It's my choice," I say.

"I want them to leave the castle. I want them to see us. Can you make them see us?"

I think about the queen in her box. *I did that,* I think. A strange blend of power and regret mixes me up. My insides rock and shudder and pulse with it. *I put the queen in a box. I froze her in time. Me and my magic.* It's exactly the kind of thing Grandmother doesn't want me thinking. *There's no glory in magic,* she used to say. *There's no thrill in it. It's for protecting. Your magic is something to hang on to and stay quiet about and have control over. It's for maintaining the peace. For keeping us safe by keeping the royals safe. That's it, Reagan.*

She had to say this to me over and over, because my magic was never quite in my control, and I always smiled too big at the way it ricocheted off me, turning pansies into palm trees, turning golden hair green, making rivers from puddles, princesses into Spellbound beings, queens into frozen trophies.

I'm thinking about what my mother said, that Ever needs to be healed, and what Abbott said, that he wants to be seen. There's the voice inside me too, that wants the king to suffer. Wants him to be small and useless. To be wrong.

"I can make them leave their castle," I say. "I can bring them into Ever."

"They say it's their kingdom. But they've never walked among us. Maybe if they left the castle—" Abbott doesn't finish the sentence. He doesn't want to hope. I can see his grown-up face fighting against it. But right below that, right underneath the ridges and stubble and sweat of an almost man, I can see the still-boy of him. Hoping. Believing.

What I can't tell Abbott, what I can't tell my mother, is that all their talk of fixing Ever is fine, but my anger isn't subsiding. The idea of fixing Ever doesn't feel as good as the idea of making the king suffer.

Anger in a witch is a dangerous thing, Grandmother has told me again and again. *What we are protecting is so much bigger than your anger.*

She said it to me a hundred times, like she knew my anger would one day overpower me, like she knew what was coming.

And maybe she did.

But isn't anger better than fear, when you get right down to it?

"Think about it," Abbott says. He has it all. Anger, fear,

53

and other things too, things I don't understand.

"I will," I say. "I am." And I do; I try.

"Okay," he says, turning to go.

"That's it?" I ask.

"I don't have anything else to say." There's a space between us making my body awkward again. I lean into the space, then out of it, like I can't decide what size and shape it's meant to be.

He leaves before my body makes up its mind. Before I can say goodbye.

An hour after Abbott leaves, there's another knock at the door. A young woman in gray is on the other side. She's holding a silver invitation, engraved with the royal crest. A century ago, it used to be a fruit tree with a crown wrapped around its center. But since the princess was taken, it is now a candle with a flame sitting atop the king's throne. A kingdom waiting.

"The invitation!" Willa says, so excited she seems to startle the young woman.

"It's for a witch named Reagan," the woman says. "I'm Princess Jane's attendant, Olive."

"That's me," I say, stepping forward.

Maybe I thought the royal invitation would come with something spectacular—a three-piece band, a parade of horsemen, a shower of rose petals. This woman in gray seems sad, nervous, not very royal at all.

"It's tonight," she says. She turns to go, then changes her mind and looks back at me. "You should have asked us," she says. She sounds like Abbott. Not just in what she's saying, but the cadence of it.

"I'm sorry?"

"We would have known what would hurt him. We would have told you what we needed." Olive's voice breaks. Her shoulders hunch. The hunch and shudder and pain I wanted to see on the king—it's right here, on this attendant.

"I thought—" I'm so tired of trying to explain what it is to hear your mother has been hurt and to know you would do anything to fix it. I'm tired of trying to find words for the kind of anger that is built from love. For the fury that means you will either tear off your own skin or someone else's to survive the feeling.

"No," Olive says. "You didn't." She bows her head. There's the sound of a pot hitting the floor in the kitchen, and Olive jumps, holds on to herself, as if pieces of her might fall off in a moment of fear.

She scurries away before I can tell her that my mother hates the sound of a clanging pot too.

I eat dinner and sit with Mom in the kitchen, waiting for time to move, waiting for the moment when I can go to the Birthday. The invitation sits between us. We are both looking at the Enchanted Candle. It is gold. The kingdom is at rest, though we are not.

"Why is the flame gold if Ever is broken, like you say it is?" I ask.

Mom sighs. "That candle only tells us if things are the

same as they've always been. Calm. The royals are happiest with us when things are calm."

I should have asked these questions five years ago, when I had all the time in the world to understand Ever.

"So Ever at rest means Ever remaining broken?" I ask.

Mom closes her eyes. She's thinking. "The War was a terrible time for us and for Ever. And how things are now—it's not perfect. But it's how we are surviving."

I think of Abbott and his gaunt face. The worry etched on it. I'm not sure that he is surviving. I'm not sure any of us are.

"Have you come up with their tasks?" Mom asks.

"I'm working on it," I say, even though the truth is more complicated. I try to make my anger small and unnecessary. It won't be shrunk.

"Your heart will tell you," Mom says, and it's not entirely a platitude. We've learned since we were babies that magic isn't just academic. It's also in our hearts. That's why Willa's spells are a little messy and very sweet and a little unexpected. It's why my spells are too strong and stubborn and Mom's went from powerful to fearful. It's why Grandmother's spells are far-reaching and deep, and Aunt Idle's are orderly and neat. The tasks the princesses will complete will reflect my magic. It's probably why they're all so scared. Willa could break a spell with cotton candy and a kiss, but my magic isn't like that.

Magic is powerful and should be used sparingly—that's why we get a new skirt attached to us every time we cast a spell, so that we carry the weight around with us forever. It's a delicate, balanced thing—and we need to work together with the Spellbound to break spells.

The skirt, however, never leaves. I told my mother this was unfair once. "I'm sure they think it's unfair we have magic at all," she said. "A heavy spell changes things, whether or not the spell is someday broken. At least a spell is a choice you make, Reagan. At least your burden is one you choose."

I should have listened more carefully to the lessons in between her words.

"What if together we can't break the spell?" I ask.

"You have to perform the Undoing." Mom pulls at her clothing. She hates talking about my spell. Her neck strains; her hands twist themselves together into a knot. "You have to, Reagan."

"They say it hurts," I say, "the Undoing."

"It's meant to hurt," Mom says with a nod. "You caused hurt, so you will hurt."

"The king caused hurt," I say. "And he seems just fine." Mom sighs, like it's ridiculous that I'm so focused on that one fact, but it feels like the truest, clearest, most important thing in the world to me.

"He's not a witch," Mom says. "You have to let it go. You have to just— We are here to keep Ever at rest. For their protection and for ours. It's what's safest for everyone. That's it. That's the whole thing."

"I want to do more than that," I say. As soon as the words are out of my mouth, I know Mom will hate them. Grandmother, too. "I want to be more than safe."

Mom warned me about being a Seen Witch. A Seen Witch isn't a humble witch. A Seen Witch wants to be glorified and appreciated. They want their magic to be celebrated. "This isn't the time for Seen Witches—" Mom says now.

They speak of Seen Witches like they're a common occurrence, but I've never heard of one. Unless, of course, I am one.

Grandmother interrupts my mother. "It's barely time for magic at all," she says. "The less magic the better. Magic is to be saved and stoked. We don't need glory. We need simply to stay here, every one of us." She speaks loudly, so that the whole Home can hear her. And I did; I heard.

"This is our home," Grandmother says. "We want to stay at our home. We've been safe for a good long time here." I turn the words around in my head and try to understand them, but they're wrong. And they make me feel like I'm trapped in my own glass box.

We look at the candle. It's gone from gold to rose gold to silver gold. It's a smoky gold now.

Gold means things are fine. Gold is how Ever is meant to be.

I wonder what it would look like without a flicker of gold in it. I've never seen the flame go to blue and black and deep, deep purple. I'm not supposed to be curious about it. The kingdom at rest is all we are supposed to want.

The kingdom unchanged. The kingdom unchallenged.

I shiver. A not-small part of me wants to return to AndNot, where I can do nothing but bathe in ocean water and think about the sun's place in the sky. This isn't how I thought it would feel to be back. I thought I would be a different, braver, better version of myself. Not just the same old Reagan, more confused than ever.

"Sometimes I don't understand what it is that I'm protecting," I say.

"Us," Mom says. She shows me her hands. They are almost all gone, just palms and pinkies right now. If the kingdom isn't at rest, we could all vanish, the way witches sometimes do. If the kingdom isn't at rest, our magic is threatened.

But if the kingdom *is* at rest, the king stays in that tower, grinning.

"She's so much like you, Bethly. Too much. It's dangerous," Grandmother says. I've never thought of myself as much like my mother at all. She's quiet and nervous and cautious. I've never been any of those things for even a moment. I almost correct my grandmother, but contradicting her would be unheard of. "You need to protect us," she goes on, turning to me. I wonder, for a strange, unsettled moment, if that's what the king would say too. "Don't be rash again," she says. "How will they ever have time to break the spell? They'll have, what, five days?"

"Four," I say. "I turn eighteen in four days."

Grandmother rubs her face. She's right. I didn't think it through. It is nearly impossible to break a spell in four days. I didn't know how few days were between Eden's thirteenth birthday and my eighteenth. I bow my head. "I'm sorry," I say. "I'll do what I can." It doesn't really mean anything at all, when you get right down to it.

59

Mom nods, because she knows I can only do magic my way. That's all any of us can do.

She knows that if I fail, tea will keep steeping, wrists will keep flicking at the end of a spell, arms will raise, capes will get hemmed, chants will be practiced under the breath of the youngest cousins, a few words always missing so that they don't accidentally start an earthquake, end a battle, freeze the sun in the sky.

Princesses will die, but the witches will go on.

Unless they vanish from unrest. A thought I pretend we aren't all thinking but that is written on Grandmother's wrinkled face.

Still, I will do it. My way. From my broken, brave, too-stubborn witch heart. It's the only way I know.

5.

JANE

As the party begins, we stand in order of our age. It wasn't always this way. Mom told me once that the princesses used to stand in order of their beauty, from most to least beautiful. "Your father put a stop to that," she said, smiling the way she always did when she talked about him. "He insisted that practice was wrong. He refused, and the kingdom was outraged. But you know your father."

"Stubborn," I said.

"Determined," she corrected me. For all her talk of rituals and tradition, my mother loved the way my father turned things around, made the kingdom more vibrant, more fair, less strict.

"How did they decide who was most beautiful?" I asked. Mom always skipped the parts I found especially interesting. She'd tell half the story, but miss the strangest details. She never told the in-between.

In my experience, the in-between is the part that matters.

"A spell," Mom said. "They'd make the witches cast a spell that would simply move the princesses into a line, placing them where they were meant to be."

"The witches must have hated doing that," I said.

"I imagine they might have," Mom said.

"But we made them do it anyway."

"It was one of the spells they gifted us every year."

"In exchange for us gifting them their safety."

"We keep each other safe," Mom said. Her voice was solemn. It's serious business between witches and royals.

"Couldn't they cast a spell to tell us who took the princess?" I asked, knowing the answer was no. Though we have our suspicions, we don't know which kingdom stole the princess all those years ago. I wish we did. Then we'd know for sure which one to be suspicious of, which to not marry into, which to ban from our Feasts.

When the princess was first taken, Ever accused Soar and Soar accused AndNot and AndNot accused Farr, who said it was certainly Nethering, who said they had evidence it was Droomland.

In the end, when it was clear that the princess wouldn't be returned and that everyone was suffering from the War that ensued, all the kingdoms agreed that it must have been some mysterious person acting on their own.

Except, when we were taught this, it was with an eyebrow raise and a tiny shake of the head, like no one actually believed this convenient lie.

But, like Dad says, we do what we need to do to keep peace. So do the witches.

"Peace is the most important thing," I said then, repeating a dozen textbooks and my parents.

"You certainly pay attention in your history lessons, don't you?" Mom laughed.

My favorite part of school isn't learning about peace and princesses, though. It's learning about the witches. Pieces of them can vanish, and in bad circumstances, if the kingdom is in a state of unrest, the whole of them can disappear entirely, and I wonder sometimes if the witch that cast the spell on us was trying to punish me for that reality. If she and her family have to lose fingers and feet, we have to lose bits of ourselves, too.

My father tells me not to look for logic when I float these ideas by him. He says witches don't need reasons to cast spells, but my lessons tell me the exact opposite is true.

I wish I could ask my mother.

"Where were you, in the order?" I asked her when I couldn't stop thinking about the beauty ranking between her and her sisters. I knew my mother was more beautiful than any other person. I didn't need a witch to tell me that. She had strong hands with long fingers and kind eyes that were never the first to look away, and she always smelled like she had just finished baking, even though my mother rarely went into the kitchen.

"Oh, who can remember?" Mom said, but there was a grimace sneaking onto her face that told me she did remember. Her body remembered being moved like a chess piece from one place to another. I didn't push her to answer.

But I knew from the way she looked out the window and commented on a flock of geese making their way from one side of the kingdom to the other that she had been last.

Since that day, I'd wondered where the witches would place me, if given the chance.

I do it now, by accident, as Dad moves through the crowd to take his place at a crystal podium. I put myself dead last, hating how fragile my body is, the way my face can't hide anything without some fullness in the cheeks, my stringy hair that falls out in tiny clumps every so often, desperate for nutrients.

A Slow Spell can't cause permanent damage, so even though I can't eat, I won't starve to death. I'll just slowly droop. But when our Slow Spell becomes True, there won't be any slowness keeping me alive. I will die, the way anyone who doesn't eat will die.

It will be quick.

When I look in mirrors now, I see that promise of death looming in my eyes and along my jawline. A sort of shadow that no one else sees. The royals from faraway kingdoms look at all of us with the same leer, the same interest, the same calculating stares. I hate them for ignoring what seems so obvious to me.

I'm dying. Right now, right here, right in front of their eyes.

I wonder if this is how they looked at the princess, before one of their kingdoms took her.

And I wonder, again and again, which kingdom it was. And why we ask for her return, but not for answers.

Tonight I look everywhere for the young witch who cast the spell, who will any minute now tell us how to break it, but instead all I see are princes and princesses, dukes and duchesses, royalty from our kingdom and other kingdoms, waiting to talk to us. Royals from other kingdoms look nothing like our family. My sisters and I all have the same white skin and the same brown hair and the same freckles in the same pattern marking our faces. Nora's cheeks are higher, and Alice's nose is bigger. Grace's hair curls, and Eden's lips are thin. But we all look like our mother, more or less.

Families from other kingdoms mostly don't look like us or even like one another. But we recognize them anyway in their fancy gowns and heavy furs and entirely unnecessary gloves covering them from fingertips to elbows.

As promised, the party looks like the night sky. And if this party is the night sky, I suppose Nora, Alice, Grace, Eden, and I are planets floating about in the darkness.

"My beautiful princesses," Dad says when the music pauses and the food stops its endless parade through the hall. "I'm delighted to introduce the esteemed royals of our neighboring kingdoms to my marvelous girls. Not only are they lovely and kind, we have also seen over the past five years that they are brave. And strong. Stronger than the rest of us. So strong they are enduring the worst spell our kingdom has ever seen."

Dozens of people bow their heads at this. But not all of them. I see an errant eye roll, a scowl, a smirk.

The Prince of Soar raises his eyebrows. He takes up a lot of room, this prince. He's tall and broad, and he's wearing a thick brown fur that only adds to his mass. He is big enough to grab a princess around her waist and run her out of the castle before anyone has a chance to hear her.

And that's about to change, I want my father to say. *They are here to break the spell,* I want him to proclaim. *We are celebrating the end of the Spell of Without.*

"Every Thirteenth Birthday is important," Dad goes on. "But this year, more than ever, it is a celebration of my daughters. For what they have endured. For what they insist on surviving. For their unusual circumstances. We won't ever truly understand them. We have tried to solve many mysteries over the centuries. Where our princess went and when she will return. How the candles in our windows have never-dying flames. How to coexist with the witches themselves. But the biggest mystery of all, it turns out, is these five princesses."

He raises his hand and sweeps it through the air, gesturing toward us. I look to my left, past Nora, at Alice, whose eyes are closed. Her body waves back and forth in a state I call Alice's Near Sleep. This isn't the way Dad has ever spoken about us. I don't need him to think we are magical and enchanted and mysterious and unknowable. I want to be his daughter, the way I've always been. Last year, for my birthday, he carved a bird in stone, with Alice's help. Usually a carved bird is sitting and still, but this one was in flight. It was beautiful and simple and somehow exactly what I needed. A reminder that we are moving even when we feel trapped.

I want *that* father, the father who whittled a soaring bird in the backyard so that I wouldn't catch sight of it until the morning, when he served it to me in bed, like he used to bring me breakfast.

When Dad's done talking, the royals rush at us once again, but it's Grace who reaches my side first. She taps my elbow.

"Why'd he say those things?" she asks. "Why did he act like we're girls from a story?" Her brow is furrowed, the way it always is when she's trying to unwind the world. "We're real girls," Grace says, sure at first, then doubting herself immediately. "Right?"

I hold her close. I want to tell her we aren't girls from a story, but of course we are. We are written into books every day, the tales of our lives shaped and sharpened into something for students in Ever to memorize.

I can't explain that to Grace.

"Right," I say, because a queen gives hope to those who need it. Alice opens her eyes for a half second, like she needs to hear the answer too, so I say it extra loud. "We are the realest girls."

The Prince of Droomland approaches from behind me and puts a hand on my shoulder. "You sure are real," he says, turning something sweet into something awful. He has broad shoulders and blue eyes and thick dark hair that girls probably think about running their fingers through. I'm sure I used to have those thoughts. But today I find him repulsive.

So does Grace. She runs away, to a tower of cheese and bread that I've been avoiding.

The prince stands closer than I'd like. Closer than feels entirely proper. It does not feel like an accident.

"Your Spellbound," the Prince of Droomland says. He doesn't sense the way my body leans back, the way my eyes dart to other places I'd rather be.

Or, worse, he does sense it and stays anyway.

I have never liked Droomland and its tall men and smirking prince and king with a very young wife and castle that's rumored to have a suspicious number of locked rooms.

"I won't be Spellbound for much longer," I say. "You can call me Jane."

"Just Jane?" It's all slippery and wet coming from his mouth. I hate it.

"Princess Jane." I hope it sounds like a line drawn in the sand. His fingers touch my arm, the place in between my elbow and my wrist where my sleeve stops and my bare skin emerges. It could be an accident, but it's not.

"Well," he says. "You can call me Felix."

"Prince Felix," I say.

"It's a bit much, isn't it?" he says. "The prince business?"

I watch Dad introduce Alice to the Prince and Princess of Soar and Nora to the Prince of Nethering and Grace to the Princess of Farr. Alice is already stuck in a chair, too heavy with tiredness to move but maybe in the back of her mind planning her nighttime sculpture of this event: stars and eager faces and princesses looking around for a witch to appear. Somehow, Alice will be able to capture it all. When Alice was six, she chose her name. I wanted her to pick something that would tell everyone what an artist she is. Maybe Elna, which means "creative." But Alice chose her name, which means "of the nobility." I understood. Being noble, being royal, is the most important thing that we are.

Tonight, though, it's hard to be anything but desperate.

Nora has a wrinkled gown and narrow eyes. Eden won't

move from the door, she's so desperate for the witch to arrive and tell us what to do. I wonder if in this strange, topsy-turvy world, I am the most desirable girl here, if Dad is proudest of me.

For the first time in five years, I wish my body were even more slight, more invisible. Unseen.

"It's all a bit much," I say at last.

"Especially for you, I guess," the prince says. He takes my wrist in his hand. Looks at it like it's made of glass. I haven't been touched by any royal man but my father. Not ever. My flesh prickles. He circles his fingers around my wrist, and they go all the way around and then some.

"Look at that," he goes on. "Tiny."

I pull back, but he doesn't let go. His fingers are dry, and his mouth is wet. He is measuring me.

They don't tell you, when you are a young princess, how very often men will take stock of you, the size of your parts and the way they fit together. What they might do with each bit of you. We used to believe we were whole, but the witch and these men know that we are only a collection of parts. A witch can take a part away. A man can decide he wants one bit of you but not another.

"Not one crumb in five years," the prince goes on. He doesn't see what's happening inside me. For all his assessing, he's forgotten to care about the expression of my mouth, the loud, fast beat of my heart. It doesn't concern him, I guess. More parts to discard.

What he's said isn't a question, so I don't answer. I wait

for my father to come by and save me. It is the kind of thing my father would do—swoop in and direct me somewhere else, giving the prince a stern look or a talking-to.

But my father is speaking to a queen from another kingdom, and I can't catch his eye. I have been having trouble catching his eye lately.

"It's alluring," the prince says, still handling my wrist. "Is that wrong to say? It is, though. Intriguing. So many princesses—they're all the same. You girls. You're different, aren't you?"

The hall is filled with delicious smells that normally would be haunting me, but right now that pain is better than this shame. I inhale the scent of everything I used to love and focus on how much it hurts to know I won't be eating any of it. Roast garlic. Melting cheese. Thick cream sauces. Ginger. Strawberries. Shrimp.

I watch ten roast ducks with whipped parsnips and pomegranate seeds be wheeled by on a gold tray across the room. Prince Felix hovers over me. Watches my wanting, pairs it with his own.

"Anyone could marry a regular princess," Prince Felix says. "Practically anyone. Anyone of note. But there's only four of you. Five now. That's—well. I'm honored to be here. Honored that I might deserve something different than a regular princess in a castle, pecking at pastries and sipping champagne and waving at peasants." He considers my waist. My face. The slump of my shoulders. "I bet by the end of the day you can't even wave your hand. I bet you can't stand at all.

Can you even sit? You must be on your back every evening, no fight left in you."

I check my arms, my legs, rub the back of my neck to make sure I'm still there, that I'm a whole person, and not just the idea of a princess. My skin is hot. Sweating. Usually, at the Birthdays, they kiss our hands and compliment our hair. From time to time they've whispered a question about the spell. But this is new. This is base and terrible and wrong.

I wonder if this is the way they spoke about the kidnapped princess. No one knows where she ended up or if she's alive or why she was taken to begin with. But right now, with the prince finding me perfectly weak and takeable, I think I know more about that princess than I ever wanted to.

It turns out I'd also forgotten that she was a person, and not just a bit of lore. My grandmother's sister. My great-aunt. It's hard to think of her as anything but a story we've been told, though.

I'm as bad as he is, this awful prince.

I must blush. It feels like rage, but I think it shows up on my face as modesty. I want to tell him that I won't be this way for much longer, that tonight is about the hope for the future, is about breaking the spell. I want to tell him to get away from me, to stop looking at me with those awful eyes. I want to tell him that the way he's talking to me only makes me more determined to break the spell.

I try to make him see I will be queen. But he doesn't see. His gaze is fixed on my waist.

"You must simply fall to pieces at the slightest bit of trouble," he whispers in my ear. His breath is hot against my skin. It is worse than hunger. It makes me even emptier. I lift my shoulders to my ears, but of course it's not enough. "I'm here to catch you," he says. "You can collapse anytime. I've never seen a fainting princess."

I hate the way it sounds, but I don't respond. Sometimes that's better. Easier. Princesses aren't meant to respond to every little thing. *It's okay to be quiet and still,* my mother told us years ago. Except now those words feel like an awful premonition of what was to come for her.

"Can you dance?" the prince asks me.

"All princesses have to learn how to dance," I say, hanging on tightly to the rules I've always followed, the way I'm meant to be.

"I know you *could* dance," he says, putting a hand on my waist. His thumb grazes my ribs. Once it finds them, it moves back and forth, like it's found the very spot it's been looking for. "But are you able to dance now? Can your body . . . handle it?"

No one ever taught me how to say no to a prince. It seems like it would have been an important thing to teach princesses of Ever. It's strange, eighty years after a princess was stolen, that we wouldn't have been shown how to not be taken away.

But that's how it is. So I dance.

Prince Felix ends up practically moving my body for me, and I let him. It's easier than considering my feet, his hands on my waist, my body in space, the smell of the meal, the smell of his skin, the way my skin feels too thin to be touched like this.

Instead of being in my own body, instead of being in the dance, I watch my sisters.

Alice is in the Prince of AndNot's arms. Her head is on his shoulder, and he's grinning like it means something, like she wouldn't rest the weight of her head on any sturdy surface. My feet are making remembered patterns on the floor, and Nora looks at me with pity, but they're coming for her, too, and I can't do anything to help her.

Grace is dancing as well, with the Princess of Thorner. The princess is exceptionally tall with brown skin and big brown eyes, and she dances a little out of beat with the music, but it looks good on her; it looks like an awkward elegance. Grace's nose has found its way to the softest part of her neck, and because I know Grace as well as I know myself, I know she is imagining this is her moment of falling in love.

It wouldn't be the worst thing in the world, Grace falling in love with the Princess of Thorner. I've never considered that the kingdom of Thorner could have taken the princess. It is a small, friendly place, and there wouldn't be anywhere to hide her anyway.

Grace won't remember any of this tomorrow. She won't remember the princess's sharp chin or the way her neck smells. She could fall in love a hundred times tonight and not remember a moment of it.

It might be sadder than my want for a bite of an apple or Alice's long, rock-carving nights. Grace deserves to remember the good things.

I'm exhausted from the dancing, disgusted by the hands on my waist, and I am still waiting for my father. For a moment, I think he sees me. His hand nearly waves. But when I try to mouth something over Prince Felix's shoulder, my father turns away.

He turns away. I tamp down the worried feeling, the almost anger, the panic at this break from the script of our relationship. He must not have seen. He must have misunderstood. He's right there. I'm safe.

I look for the hundredth time to the door, wishing the witch would appear and put a stop to whatever this night is. Olive promised she delivered the invitation, said the witch seemed to know it was coming. I look for Olive now, though, and she's nowhere to be found. She's been my shadow for years, but when I need her, she's gone. I'm alone.

"You need special care, don't you?" the prince says, his tongue practically touching my ear. I tense. I shudder. He doesn't care. "It's a good thing. It's a beautiful thing. Your need. Don't be so quick to let it go."

He holds me closer. I can't find the phrases to explain that hunger isn't the same as desperation, that tiredness isn't the same as surrender. I can't find any words at all.

Or breath. I am losing my breath, too.

With each spin I re-search for the witch, and she is never there.

"We won't be this way forever," I tell Prince Felix at last, when my mind emerges, as it sometimes does before dulling again.

"Oh?" the prince asks. He smirks. He could rival Nora with his snide expressions.

"Of course not. We're going to break the spell."

Prince Felix lets his hand wander to my hips. For a moment I'm thankful for how little of my body is left. There's not much of it to press against him. I'm easy to keep close but hard to hold.

"You're the only ones who want to go back to the way things were. The rest of us like you this way. Special."

My stomach turns. I put a hand below my ribs to calm it, but it doesn't work. Nothing works. I wonder, when he says this, if he likes my mother where she is too. Frozen. A statue forever, if the spell isn't broken.

"Spellbound," I correct.

"Enchanted," he says. The word in his mouth sounds like a delicacy.

I break away from him when the dance is done. "I'm going to sit down," I say. Prince Felix follows me to a table, and Dad finally, finally approaches.

"I see you two have found each other," he says. The whole room stops to watch us. They love seeing the king with his daughters, and I can understand why. He is a perfect father—calm and kind and knowing. I imagine he can tell just from cupping my shoulder how I feel about this prince, this night, this Feast. I'm so relieved to have him next to me that I lean against him a little. I wish the night were over and we were in the library, reading aloud the best parts of our books to each other.

Soon, I tell my heart. *Soon,* I tell my tired limbs.

"Your daughters are truly something to behold," Prince Felix says. His hand grabs mine. A roomful of people hold back gasps.

"They're much more than that," Dad says. He smiles at me, and all is right. I'm not alone. I'm never alone. My father is right here, always protecting me, always the Good King, always there for us.

Prince Felix gets up from his chair. "I suppose," he says, "I should pay my respects to the other princesses. See what is so exceptional about each of them."

"I suppose you should," my father says.

I want to hold him back, to keep him from them. But I don't know how to protect myself, much less my little sisters, and he can move so quickly and speak so surely, and I am having trouble holding my body upright, walking in a straight line, breathing through my mouth.

"Your Spellbound," Prince Felix says with a half bow to me. Dad nods and continues his walk through the room, but as soon as he's out of earshot, the prince leans down and whispers into my ear. "The cheeses are salty and soft. The duck is succulent. Even the bread is perfection. Soft. Comforting. With a swipe of butter it's truly something to—"

"Shut up," I try. Words I have never said. Not together. Not *to* someone. A queen would never tell a prince to shut up. I move my head, working to get his lips to leave the place where they keep hitting my skin.

"Fine," Prince Felix says. "But I brought you a gift. I'll leave it here." He reaches into his pocket and pulls out a tiny parcel. It's wrapped in red paper. I don't open it. I don't need to. I can smell it. Sweet and rich and poking at a hundred happy memories.

Chocolate.

I keep it in my hand and do what I never let myself do—imagine eating it. I imagine a first bite, over and over and over until I can't even see the rest of the room, until the Thirteenth Birthday doesn't exist anymore, until all there is in the world is my mouth and the darkest kind of sweetness on my tongue and the desperation I feel at not being able to have it.

The Prince of Soar approaches next and hands me another small packet, a hard chunk of cheese. The Princess of Nethering folds a tiny parcel of coffee into the palm of my hand. It smells the way being awake feels. I almost remember energy and verve and the brilliance of a morning that doesn't feel so hopeless. Every royal in the room drops off raw almonds, ripe strawberries, a slice of salted ham.

My hands are filled with everything I've ever loved to eat, but I'm too hungry to move from this chair, from this moment, from this horror.

My father doesn't notice, and I'm too ashamed to tell him we need him again and again and again. We are princesses. I am meant to be queen. I need to be stronger. I need to need less.

So I let it happen.

And the rest of the guests let it happen.

They let it happen. And I think maybe they even enjoy it.

6.

REAGAN

I mean to walk to the castle alone, but Willa appears beside me when I am halfway there. She's faster than me, my young cousin. She has more skirts, but none are heavy. Mine from the Spell of Without never lets me move quickly, doesn't let me run ahead.

"You don't want to go to this," I tell Willa, who moves as easily as any subject of Ever. "It's depressing."

"I've heard it's beautiful. The princess coming of age. All the kingdoms gathered to celebrate."

"I guess," I say. I can't imagine the castle being beautiful. Nothing in Ever looks beautiful to me anymore.

The walk to the castle isn't long. We're almost at the moat, which we will easily wade through without a problem. Witches aren't scared of water. I take a look around for Abbott. Maybe he's waiting by the moat to see me off, to wish me luck. Maybe he has more suggestions, more things I need to know about the Ever that he lives in. I'd like to see him here and now, just to get a glimpse of someone beautiful and true and real before I change everything.

"You must be glad I'm here with you," Willa says when I stall outside the door of the castle. I am, but I'm older and should be wiser and braver and able to do this on my own. Instead I'm some silly girl looking for a cute boy, clinging to my fourteen-year-old cousin like she's a life vest, an anchor, my mother.

"I'm fine on my own," I say. I have said some version of this a thousand times over the years. It's practically my mantra, words whose rhythm match the beat of my heart. *I'm fine on my own,* I've told my mother and my aunts and my grandmother and now, finally, my little cousin with wobbly knees that aren't so wobbly anymore and a pretty pout that only ever gets prettier. I say it again, for good measure. Willa doesn't always hear every word that's said to her. "I'm fine on my own."

"I promised your mother," Willa says with a shrug.

"You promised?"

"She said you couldn't go alone. She said it wasn't safe. She said she knows that better than anyone."

"Oh." There's the shiver of a memory that isn't mine but lives inside me all the same. Popping up, tall and strange and awful and mysterious, like the castle itself.

We are in front of it now, more quickly than we were prepared for, and though it's where we knew we were headed, it feels surprising. A place we came to but somehow never really meant to arrive at.

"You're not scared?" I ask Willa. I don't look at her. My eyes don't move from the castle door.

"I guess not," Willa says. And like that, my heart surges

for her and the way she is both clumsy and brave, a combination that seems impossible. I'd do anything to be more like her.

I haven't been here for five years. I'd forgotten she would greet me. The queen in her box.

I bow my head. Even *I'm* not sure if she can see, if she knows we're here, if she knows *she's* here.

Even I don't know what I've done.

We use a Spell of Above to cross the moat, and when we're on the other side, we show the silver invitation to a horseman at the gate. It is addressed to the Witch of the Spell of Without, so he knows who we are when he looks it over. In a breath we see him go from bored to scared. A man trained to fight other kingdoms, trained to protect the king, scared of two young witches.

It feels a little bit good. Willa and I are both in our black wool capes with large fur-lined hoods. I've seen royalty with similar garb—the king in his robe, the visiting princes draped in fur. We fit in, dressed like this, and I tell Willa to keep her hood on until it's time.

"When will it be time?" she asks.

"I don't know," I say. "I guess when I say it's time."

Once inside, the party is bigger than it was in my head. More absurd. My first breath is one of rage. That they live in this opulence while their subjects beg us to cast spells that would allow them to grow three potatoes instead of two, a spell that would fix their broken shoes, a spell that would rid their children of lice. The subjects don't know what's in this castle. They guess at it, but they don't come close. Abbott never came close. He wouldn't know what to do in this grand hall, surrounded by delicacies and jewels and laughter.

He'd hate them even more. I know I do. It's hard to feel bad for princesses who have everything except the one thing I took from each of them. It's hard to want to fix the only thing wrong with their perfect lives. My magic would be better spent giving Abbott's family a cherry orchard, a herd of cattle, a home in a different kingdom.

But he'd never take it. Abbott wants to fix Ever, not just himself. Probably *he* should be king.

"Let it turn True," I say under my breath. Words that escape before I've had a chance to think them through. But Willa hears. Of course she does. She hears nothing that our grandmother asks her to do; she hears none of the details of how to cast this spell or that. But she always hears when I show my worst self.

"You're going to let the Slow Spell turn True? Without giving them a chance?" Willa asks. She grips my arm, and her voice shakes. "Did you ask Grandmother if that's okay?"

"Give me a second, Willa," I say. I need to take it in without her fluttering next to me. I need to let myself believe, for a moment, that I could let them suffer forever. My gaze flies over attendants adjusting napkins and candles and princess hair. There's something in the way their eyes flit to the king, the nervous energy of their hands, even how close they stand to one another, like they're safer that way, that makes my palms sweat.

I keep my warm hood on, though. I need time to see them without them seeing me.

The scared movements of the princesses and attendants and a candle flickering by the throne are the only familiar things in this whole room aside from heaps of fabric hanging from every surface. So many different weights and textures and colors, just like our skirts. Fabrics and colors and patterns that they'd never wear but have crowded their castle with. Chiffon hangs from the windows; silk lines the tables; even the throne is draped in a thick velvet.

"It's even prettier than I thought," Willa says. She has always loved princesses and castles and silk gowns.

"It's exactly how my mom said it would be," I say.

"Why was she ever here anyway?" Willa asks. She knows what the king did to my mother; she found out when I did, that awful day when I cast the spell. But we've never spoken about it.

"What do you mean?" I ask. At first glance the question feels like an accusation, like my mother is to be blamed for the king's actions. But after a breath I know what she means. Witches don't go to castles. There would be no reason for her to be here. Not ever.

It's funny how what he did was so big my mind didn't ask any more questions aside from *How can I hurt him?* and *How will he pay?* I never asked how it happened.

Not funny, actually. Enraging. Impossible. Exhausting.

My fury is rising again, taking up too much space for me to theorize with Willa, shivering my insides, making my fingertips itch with the desire to cast another spell, to try again and again and again to make the king suffer. I want to care about the things Abbott and Olive and even my own mother told me matter. But remembering what the king did nearly wrecks me. Willa must notice the change in my temperature. She puts her hand in mine.

"Look," she says. She points across the room to a figure so slight I barely see anyone at all. "There she is. The oldest." Her voice falters with heartbreak or surprise or some combination of both. My body reacts to Jane's body with a stumble.

She is not spindly or slim or small or skinny.

She is dying.

The look of her is unbearable.

"Oh," I say, a breath more than a word. "Oh." The second "oh" is the sound of my heart dropping to my feet. It feels wrong. Cruel. I'm not a cruel witch. My magic isn't cruel. But Jane's ribs, the way her head looks too heavy for her neck, the collapse in her shoulders, is cruel.

I did that, I think. *My magic did that.*

I scan the room for the king. He is the same as he was this morning. Smiling. Strong. His head sometimes leaning back in a laugh, his shoulders carelessly low. I look back and forth between them. The king and his dying daughter.

Already essential parts of me are shifting into new, awkward spaces. My heart in my throat. My fear twitching in my fingers. My thoughts racing up and down my arms. My memories rolling around in my stomach, giving me wave upon wave of regret.

"He doesn't care," I say to Willa. I try to keep my voice a whisper, but it's hard to get a hold of. "Look at her. *Look.* And at him. He's—he was supposed to be—look at all of them. They like this. They like her like this."

Willa doesn't say anything, but her hand stays in mine. I fight back a retch.

In AndNot I imagined a hundred ways this would all go, a thousand ways to break the spell, a million glorious moments where I would be heralded as the witch who fixed everything. I dreamed of my mother, reborn as someone calm and fine and healed, and the king as shamed and regretting and wanting me to save his children. I imagined maybe the vanished princess might even return to see her glorious kingdom restored. I dreamed a fairy tale that was never real. Not this king. Not this kingdom.

I make myself look at Princess Jane one more time. I know this is it, the moment I have to come forward and take the next step. I look at her head. It hangs, like her body can't quite hold it up. And her eyes, which stare somewhere else entirely.

If the king doesn't suffer in her suffering, if even her slow, magical death doesn't make him collapse, I know nothing will.

All that's left is to make them all see what I see. What I should have seen when I was thirteen and thought I knew everything.

I can't make him see his daughters; I can't make him care about their pain or this spell or the hurt he's caused.

But maybe I can make *them* see *him*. Make them see their kingdom, their king, their truth. And mine.

There's a change in the music, one song ending and another beginning. A transition into a new melody, a new beat underneath it all.

"Now," I say to Willa. I walk her to the center of the room. I'm sure the king would like me to stand off to the side, but I won't stay there for another second. This will not be a party any longer. There will be no more dancing or feasting.

I am a witch. I have magic. I don't need to ask permission. I didn't need his last-minute invitation. My mother came here without permission, and I am her daughter, a witch with even bigger magic. I didn't need a piece of silver to tell me to be here.

We are in a room dressed up to be the night sky, and he has forgotten that we are the moon and the stars and the black of night itself. We are it. The witches of Ever. And we are here.

When we get to the center of the night sky, we let go of each other. Our hands move to our hoods. We pull them off our heads, slip the cloaks from our shoulders, revealing our magical gowns, layers of skirts, the sign of witches. Of spells cast.

It takes no time at all. Our skirts make us unmistakable. Princesses and duchesses and royalty from every kingdom wear sleek gowns in dull colors that hug their waists and slink around their legs. Only witches walk around bell shaped and draped in color.

The room turns our way. Princes. Princesses. Queens and kings. Then our princesses. Then our king.

"I'm the witch," I say, my voice as strong as I'd hoped it might be, my words as sure. "I cast the Spell of Without." I look at all of them in their dresses and unsettling joy. Then I look at Jane. At Nora. At Alice and Grace and Eden. And finally, finally at him. The king. "I'm back," I say.

7.
JANE

She doesn't look the way she has in my head all these years. In my head, she is tall and sharp faced. In my head, her hair is thick and wild and her eyes are narrowed and her chin points and her hands grip. In my head, she hates us.

But she is looking at me from across the room, her white face soft featured, her hair straight and almost blond, standing next to a smaller witch with brown skin and worried eyes and wearing layers of light, airy skirts. They don't look like they hate me. They look like they pity me.

I know the look well. It took some getting used to. For years I was looked at with honor and respect and envy. Then, all of a sudden, it was there. On Olive's face. The other attendants'. Sometimes a subject. Always my own sisters.

Pity.

"It's going to be hard," she says, the whole of her facing me and only me. Her gaze doesn't drift to my other sisters. Her body doesn't shift toward my father's place at the head of the longest table. "My magic is stubborn."

I swallow what I want to say, which is that someone with

stubborn magic shouldn't be casting spells that could kill a person. One that could kill princesses. But the fight in me is fading. I've spent so much of the night hating Prince Felix that there's not much left to hate this witch.

"We're ready," I say. "We've been ready. We're stubborn too." I pull my shoulders back and imagine a crown on my head. Queens say things simply, if they say anything at all.

"We're ready," Eden says. She is still shining and light. She is still filled with hope on her Thirteenth Birthday. The spell will hit the second she turns thirteen, and Dad couldn't tell us when exactly that was. *It's hard to keep track,* he says each time we've asked what to expect. *Your mother would know.* "Just tell us," Eden goes on. Her chin sticks out. Her hands are on her hips. There's a giggle traveling around the room at her precociousness, but people underestimate moxie.

People underestimate Eden.

"We're not scared," she says, and it's not true, but it sounds true, the way she says it. "Right, Dad?" We all look to my father. He gives one silent nod. He doesn't cower at the sight of the witch who broke us. He doesn't rage at her either. He doesn't do much of anything in her direction except shake his head a silent no and rub his chin in thought. I've seen him take that stance before, a shape his body finds when he's waiting for the next thing to happen, when he's being patient with something terrible.

Don't make decisions quickly, he's told me during our talks in the library about what it means to rule Ever. *Don't let anyone tell you who to be and what to do. If you are queen, you'll know, if you wait and listen.* I loved the advice. And the idea that Dad's decisions come from a place of patience and searching. A place we can trust. A quiet place. *Silence is powerful,* he told me when I asked why queens weren't allowed to talk to their subjects, why kings gave speeches but not queens and certainly not princesses. *Silence is more powerful than any of the rest of it.*

I see now how true it is. His silence is hurting her. She rises up on her tiptoes, which is exactly what she did before she cast the Spell of Without. I take a step back, then another, as if a few feet could protect me from her magic.

Eden doesn't shift. She rises up on her toes too. "We're royalty," she says, and it sounds a little silly, the way she says it, but it's true. I asked Dad once if being royalty made us better than everyone else. *Of course not,* he said in his slow way. *But it makes us know better.*

Reagan's witch friend grabs hold of her hand and says something into her ear. It changes Reagan, who takes a deep breath, brings her heels back to the ground, and turns to me again.

"You'll need to bring me a collection of objects," she says. "You'll need to gather them up and deliver them to me. Before I turn eighteen, of course. Because of the True Spells. Because of—"

"You don't have to tell us," I say. I do not need a reminder of how close to death I am. "We know about Slow Spells and True Spells. We know about witches."

"Do you?" I can't tell if it's a real question or a challenge.

"We know everything about Ever," I say, bringing my shoulders back.

"Well. You certainly know the inside of this castle well."

"We go outside."

"That's true. You know as far as you can see." She raises her eyebrows like a challenge, but I can raise mine, too, so I do. Princesses aren't meant to wander streets and farms and Barren Fields. She's welcome to traipse through Ever doing whatever her heart desires, but I take my job seriously.

"The queen always said that with distance comes wisdom," I say. I look to my father, who smiles with pride. "She'd say it now. If she could."

Reagan looks at the witch next to her, and that witch shakes her head. Reagan plays with a heavy burlap skirt. She seems to consider its weight, its texture. She clears her throat. The witch next to her grabs her elbow. A look passes between them that I know from the way I gather strength from my sisters. "I turn eighteen in four days," Reagan says. She's looking at her friend, but the message is for us. She simply isn't brave enough to look at us while she says it.

"Four days," I repeat. My whole body starts to shake. It's just a tremble at first, but quickly it is a rumble, an earthquake of bones. I can hear Nora breathing next to me. Her inhales are quick, and her exhales are coming out heavy. Little gusts of angry wind next to me. "It can take months to break a spell," Nora says. "It can take years. *Years*. And we have *days*?"

Alice sits down. She rests her head on a table. Grace whispers questions in Alice's ear that she's too tired to answer. But

I can't stop looking at the witch. She is so many things at once: wobbly knees and strong shoulders and nervous fingers and certain words. It's confusing me, because I've been told she is only one thing: cruel. No. Two things. Cruel and hysterical.

"I'm sorry about the timing," Reagan says. "If I'd known when I cast the spell that Eden's birthday was so close to my own—I didn't—back then I didn't have time for—"

"Thinking?" Nora sputters.

"Math," Reagan finishes.

"Can you—" I start, but there's no point finishing the question. The earthquake moves to my throat. A thousand tears gather there. A thousand screams. There's no end to my question.

"There are rules," Reagan says, answering the question I know not to ask. "There have to be rules. That's what makes it magic. I don't know how much you know about witches and the way we—"

"We know," I say in the lowest, meanest voice I can find. "We know about witches. About Ever. We know plenty." My sisters are all stiff beside me. We have waited long enough.

"We've taken classes too," Reagan says. She doesn't go on. I know what some of the books say about us. There are books written about royals that tell tales of our cruelty, of the way we have taken wealth from our subjects. That we have abused witches to draw us to power, that we do nothing for Ever, that we are silly.

And there is the story of the kidnapped princess, the question of whether or not she maybe deserved to be taken away, and the theory of some people on the fringes who think we got rid of the princess on purpose. Questions about whether it was worth it, to battle over that one girl. Questions about why we don't fight as hard for others in the kingdom.

Without definitive answers, some people are sure to make up stories. *Don't worry about why she was taken,* Dad told me when I asked why we still invite all the kingdoms to our Birthdays in spite of all we don't know about them. *Worry about how to keep our people filled with hope that she will return.* I don't know exactly what the witches believe. I know we are supposed to be grateful to the witches for enchanting our candles with the Spell of Return and for restoring all the kingdoms to peace. And they are meant to be grateful to us for giving them a place to call home after the wars and battles between the kingdoms.

But maybe none of us are truly grateful, none of us are safe from one another. The balance is so tenuous it's very nearly not there at all.

Certainly not now, not in this ballroom, with this witch and her four days and tasks that I imagine will be impossible and my limbs that are ready to give up.

I'd like to sit in the library with my father and ask him a hundred more questions about how Ever works, what witches are, why we're still waiting for the princess to return, why we let the witches live among us, why we let kingdoms who might have kidnapped royalty party in our castle. I'd like him to talk me through it slowly, calmly, the way he talked me through what he knew about the Spell of Without, what he knew about Slow Spells and True Spells, what he knew about what happened to women frozen in boxes for years at a time.

Sometimes I'd fall asleep on his arm in the middle of his explaining, and he wouldn't move a muscle all night, wanting me to enjoy my dreams the way I could no longer possibly enjoy waking life.

But right now we don't have time for libraries or catnaps or lessons about Ever.

We don't have time for anything.

I look closely at Reagan to see what she believes about us, how much she hates us, whether or not she thinks a princess deserves to be hated or kidnapped or Spellbound. I try to see the truth of her heart, but she is stony.

I asked my dad once why, if the witches are supposed to protect us, this one would have cast a spell that hurt us. I asked when they cast the Spell of Famine, and I asked when she cast the Spell of Without.

"Cruel creatures," Dad said. "Vengeful. Unhinged, honestly. Our protecting them is a great kindness. No one else would take them in. Not for how little they give us. They're supposed to be protecting us. But what do they do for us? Cast spells. Bewitch us. Undermine us." He shook his head. I wanted to know why we kept them around if the arrangement was so fractured. But he straightened his back and reached for his crown, setting it atop his head, as he often did when he was done with a conversation. "But still, we persevere," he said. It sounded very royal.

But it didn't really answer all my questions.

I have so many questions, still, always, and not enough time to ask them all.

Four days. Fine. *Fine.* We will persevere. We will survive.

I will survive. I'd yell the words directly into her ear if that was the sort of thing a future someday queen could do.

"There are four objects—" Reagan begins.

"Louder," Dad interrupts. "Say it louder." He crosses his arms and walks over to us at last. He hovers over the witch. He is too close, and she angles herself away from him but can't seem to make her feet move. This is a rare side of my father, but one I've seen before. He's towered over kings from other kingdoms who have tried to work with our witches. He has stood close to gardeners who stole enchanted tulips and a horseman who stared too long at Alice.

So of course he's doing it now, trying to protect us from this witch, making sure she knows who's king.

She knows. She doesn't seem confused.

"Four objects," Reagan says. She holds her hand up like we are children who need to see four fingers and a folded down thumb. Four days for four objects. We can do it. We have to. Grace takes out her little silver notebook. It's where she writes the things she wishes to remember. It's already brimming with information so simple it squeezes my heart to think about it. She's written down sweet things Dad has said to her and reasons why Mom is in a box. The name of her attendant and her own bedtime. The reason she's mad at one of her sisters and the color she's decided is her favorite. And now, the way the spell will be undone, little by little, as spells always are.

Her hand trembles as she writes. She doesn't want to get

a single word wrong, doesn't want to leave any room for her own confusion.

Grace doesn't understand that we don't need her to remember the things that are impossible to forget.

"The princesses have to gather them. They have to do it on their own. They can't send attendants and horsemen. The objects have to be given willingly. They can't be forced." Reagan's eyes flit to my father. He doesn't even blink. "The objects are as follows." She clears her throat and looks to her friend, who is wide-eyed and slack-jawed at all of this. "A clock from the oldest person in Ever. A lock of hair from the most beautiful one. A thimble full of tears from the saddest one. And a crown of jewels from the richest one."

Reagan stops. That's it. That's the list. We look up, expecting a crack of lightning, a flurry of snow, something to mark the occasion. We know how to break the spell. We have four objects to gather in four days, and we'll be free. Surely the ceiling should open up for that.

But instead there's stillness.

"Only four objects," Eden says. She grins. It's eight in the evening, and she still hasn't officially turned thirteen yet. It can't be far off. I hang on to that grin, that spirit, the shrug of her shoulders that says *It's fine, we've got this, no problem.*

"That's it?" Nora asks. She squints at the witch, looking for something to be skeptical of. But there's a simplicity to the way this Reagan talks that makes it hard to imagine trickery. She's too nervous for fooling us, and her words are too basic to be twisted up.

"That's it," Reagan says. "Then it's my turn to do my part. We unbind spells together. The Undoing. Magic is a collaboration. That's what my grandmother always says."

I wonder if her grandmother's voice is in her head the way my mother's and my father's are in mine. All of us following age-old ideas of how to be.

I almost like her for a second.

Before I remember to hate her.

Alice lifts her head and doodles on a napkin, ideas for a new sculpture, I'm sure. Maybe, unmagicked, Alice won't have time to care about pressure applied to stone to make it beautiful. Maybe she will abandon her late-night projects and become someone else entirely, when she doesn't have long nights to herself.

I'd miss it, but she would probably trade a hundred sculptures for one night of sleep. The spell has changed us, and I don't know what to do with the things I have come to love about my Spellbound sisters. I don't know if that makes me the same as the royals from other kingdoms, loving our pain.

There is nothing to love about my mother trapped in glass.

And there's nothing I love about my Spellbound self, either. I can't be a queen this way. I can't rule Ever wisely, like my mother, and surely, like my father. Not if I'm so hungry.

Not if I'm dead.

And then there's Eden.

She is looking at Reagan now, with a half smile that turns to a half frown. It happens in an instant, the way magic sometimes does.

There it is. 8:07 in the evening. The exact moment Eden turns thirteen. A fact we would have happily gone our whole lives without knowing.

"We'll never be able to do it," Eden says, her voice an entirely new one, her hope lost.

She is one of us now. A Spellbound princess.

I miss my hopeful sister the moment she's gone.

"Look what you've done," I say to the witch.

Reagan and her friend look around, following my instructions, I suppose. It's their first time inside a castle and probably their last, and maybe they're soaking that in too.

"Look what *you've* done," Reagan says. She has a thing for echoes, this witch. She keeps repeating us, throwing back everything we say. "Look what you've done," she says again, quietly.

She is looking at only one person.

My father, the king.

8.

REAGAN

"You have to want it," Mom says. We are on the roof of the Home on the Hill the next morning. From here, we can see all of Ever. The Barren Fields, where so many used to live and thrive, where now there is only an expanse of dust and memories. The town, bustling and impoverished save for a few brick mansions by the moat. The houses of the residents: small shacks with gardens that only grow potatoes, carrots, parsnips, turnips. Avocado trees that don't bear fruit. Lemon trees that don't have lemons. Apple trees missing any sign of an apple. A land ravaged by royalty. If only they all understood it that way. "You have to want them to break the spell."

Then the castle, rising up above it all, filled with everything the rest of Ever will never taste. Filled with riches they'll never understand and people who don't deserve a lick of it.

"What will they think of their kingdom," I say, "once they actually step out into it?"

"Don't worry about that," Mom says. "We don't worry about what the royals think and feel. We worry about them

97

staying away from us, letting us remain here. We worry about keeping ourselves strong, keeping our magic safe."

"Other kingdoms would take us in," I say, because after yesterday I know it's true. Kings came up to me, said they had homes on hills and homes on mountains and homes on islands and homes in the woods. Any kind of home we wanted.

"Other kingdoms aren't our home," Mom says.

"What makes Ever our home?" I ask. I stumble over the word "home." I don't know exactly what it means anymore. I think it's supposed to have something to do with safety and stability and a promise of forever, or at least a long while, but I'm not sure Ever has any of that for us.

"Your grandmother grew up here," Mom says. "And as the oldest witch, her home is our home." The way she says it, it sounds simple, but it doesn't feel simple.

"That's it?" I ask. With witches, there's usually more than what seems to be there at first.

"Sometimes you choose a patch of uninhabited earth and declare it your own, and that's enough," Mom says. "Your grandmother is trapped in a chair from spells to let us keep this patch of earth as our own. We're not going to desert it. Certainly not because of some shiny offer from a greedy king. And not because you made a rash mistake. Witches stay. We stay and we keep our word. We promised to keep Ever safe. That's what we've always done. That's what you are meant to do."

It sounds noble and loyal, coming from her. But she's not saying the truest thing, which is that witches are scared. It's been true my whole life. When Willa and I snuck out to use the magic picnic blanket, we'd come inside to a fretting house, our cousins and aunts asking if anyone saw us, how far we went, if we remembered to hide our skirts. We don't use all of our power, just in case there's a magical deficit someday. We gather around the Enchanted Candle at night and mix up spells that bring peace, always peace. We don't talk to non-witches. We are careful. Once a year we magically raise the hill one more inch, slowly moving farther and farther away from the rest of Ever, but not wanting them to notice. In case the king gets mad. In case our magic fades. In case we lose more witches. We won't leave this Home on the Hill, because we're too scared to do much of anything.

Except I'm not so scared anymore, and neither is Willa.

"I want them to see things as they are," I say.

Mom sighs. "You'd have to see things as they are first, Reagan." She looks out at the castle. Even now, even here, safe on our roof, my mother is missing her elbow, her ear, her knee. She's missing pieces that keep her connected. There's nothing between her shin and her thigh, just a patch of invisibility that tells me she is hollow inside, too. That she isn't whole.

I wonder if the princesses would care, seeing her. I try to guess at what they know and what they don't know, but judging from their party, I'm not sure they know a single thing. Not about me, not about Ever, not about their father or my mother. Not even about themselves.

But maybe I don't either. I thought my mother would be happy with the way they are meant to break the spell. But she seems as nervous as the king did. The only people who want the princesses to leave their castle are Abbott and me.

"I've never seen your joints go," I say to my mother, who is waiting and waiting and waiting for me to be a better kind of witch. The right kind of witch. It's harder than I thought when I was little. I don't know the rules.

"They go sometimes," Mom says. "On hard days."

"And it's a hard day."

"You're not whole either, sweet girl," Mom says. She doesn't often use pet names for me, so when she does, they go straight to my heart and make it ache. She nods at my hand, which is missing a pinkie again, and my shoulder, which is missing a patch of skin that creeps close to my heart.

"It's been happening since I returned," I say. Mom nods. She's thinking all kinds of things she isn't going to tell me.

"Your heart needs to want things to go back to the way they were," Mom tries again. She wipes her brow. The heat is heavy today, the sun extra bright in the sky, the air extra still. I reach to try to remember some perfect Before that we are striving for, but my mother has always been hurting and the king has always been smirking and the princesses have always been tucked away and their queen always silent.

"I don't know if that's what my heart will ever want," I say.

"I used to be that way," Mom says. "It didn't do much. Wanting to fix things. Wanting to make some better, different Ever. We're hurting. They're hurting. We're all trying to survive." She says the words like they are rules from a book that she memorized but maybe doesn't fully believe. I search her

face for clues, but she's so hard to read, aside from her shaki-
ness, her big-eyed sadness, the worry that keeps her shoulders
hunched and her lips bruised from anxious biting.

"The king isn't hurting. The princesses weren't hurting
until—"

"Ever hurts everyone," Mom says. She's sure on this fact.
So sure that I don't remind her that Ever hurts some people
more than others, that there's a difference between the way the
princesses are hurting and the way Abbott's family hurts and
the way we hurt.

Below us, the kingdom rushes around, readying itself for
the Spellbound princesses. The king appears in the tallest tur-
ret of the castle, as always. We can't see his face from here, only
the form of him, the glint of his crown, the red of his robe.

I wish I could cover my mother's eyes. I would do anything for a spell to make her blind to him.

"I hate him," I say. I've said it a hundred times before.
Down below, the people of Ever think he is good and gentle
and kind. The Gentle King. Because he throws a spring fes-
tival and gives the children of Ever candy and the people of
Ever turkeys to eat. The Gentle King because he lets dogs
jump up and lick his face, because he asks his impoverished
subjects about their lives, looks them in the eye when they
speak. The Good King because he hired the families from
the Barren Fields to work for the royal family when he saw
how much they were suffering after my grandmother's biggest
spell. Former farmers no longer able to farm. Fertile land gone
dead. The Good King because he lets the attendants stay in

adorable cottages next to the castle. The Gentle King because he can be seen having tea parties with his daughters and their dolls on the Grand Yard.

"Hate doesn't break a spell," Mom says. "Hate doesn't make for good magic."

I cross my arms over my chest and shake my head at it all. "We're the only ones who see it the way it is," I say. "They're just wrong. About everything. You should have seen the party. Their dresses. The food. And him. He still doesn't care. He isn't paying for any of it. For what he did. For who he is. Princess Jane—if you'd seen her—she's—it's awful. And Alice, barely able to keep her eyes open. They're his children and they're suffering and he's smiling at other kings, rubbing his chin, smirking at my list of objects. And the princesses, they're in pain, but they don't know anything about their people. They have attendants bringing them everything they want; they are draped in silk and eating cake like it's nothing. It's all so ugly. If you'd seen—"

"I've seen it," Mom says. She looks directly at me. She is entirely visible. Every bit of her full. She is talking about the king and the castle and the time she was inside that awful place, but for the first time she is entirely *here*. I lean against the sudden sturdiness of her and wait for her arm to encircle me. I wait for her to shake her head at the king in his tower, the girls in their dresses, the people of Ever toiling away in their potato gardens.

"Of course you have," I say, remembering all of a sudden Willa's question: *Why was my mother there in the first place?*

I know what the king did to her in the banquet hall of the castle, twenty years ago, and I know how it lives in her bones, lives in the Home with us, makes us all whisper and tiptoe and try not to clang or break or grab too swiftly at anything. But I don't know the whole story. "When you were there—" I start, but that's not the right way in. "Were you there at, like, a ball or something? Like I was?" I don't want to say it the way Willa said it, so blunt it felt like a bludgeon. I want to ask in a way that will make her happy to tell me the rest of the story we all live with.

"Something like that," Mom says. I try to imagine her getting a silver invitation, walking through the doors, tasting the delicacies, dancing with a prince. None of it makes much sense.

"Why were you invited to a ball?" I ask. But it's a question too far, and Mom starts shaking, her hands vanishing, her skin turning blue around her lips. Her breath is gone, and I have to find it. I list off everything I see on the roof, except for the castle. "There's the flower patch," I say. "Blue violets. Orange pansies. Herbs I don't remember the names for. There's our dining table. It's brown. Willa and I painted on it when we were little and snuck up here alone, so it's got paint all over it. Remember? Red paint. Purple. We told Grandmother we'd magic it back to normal, but she said magic wasn't for making life perfect. I loved that."

My mother's breathing normally again, even though I've done a terrible job listing what I see. I am listing what I remember and what I feel about what I see, and I'm thinking about what I want to see. I need Aunt Idle, to make things clear and crisp and black and white.

I list what we're wearing and what we're sitting on until my mother tells me she's fine, I can stop. We sit in silence for a while, with me looking over every few seconds to make sure she's still here, she's still breathing, she's okay. It's what she said she used to do when I was a baby.

"Him being wrong doesn't make you right," she says after a great long while. I don't have a response, and she lets me stay on the roof alone. She goes downstairs, and I watch my hands fade into nothing.

I don't come down at all. I watch and watch and watch and wait to feel something else.

Instead my toes vanish one by one.

Hate is hollowing, it turns out.

My invisible feet take me back to the moat. To Our Place. A strip of land that is mostly hidden by trees. It might not be safe, but Mom has left me alone and my cousins are lost in lessons that don't interest me, and I want to be near someone who doesn't think I've failed.

Abbott is my only hope.

He's there. I wasn't sure he would be. I thought maybe I would take the journey and end up alone, watching the castle from a new angle for no reason at all. But Abbott's right here, leaning against a tree.

"You're the talk of the town," he says by way of a greeting.

"Always have been, always will be," I say. We used to be

able to joke, Abbott and I. Five years ago, we'd go back and forth for hours, but now he doesn't even respond when I try to make light of this moment.

"They're excited to meet the princesses," he says. "The Spellbound." He nods toward the town, the whole of it. Most of them are still tucked in bed, and those who aren't are tending to their tiny patches of garden.

"And excited to help them?" I ask.

"They want to know why."

"Why what?"

"Why they should help. What good it will do." Abbott shrugs. "I guess I'm wondering the same thing."

"They'll die," I say. My voice screeches a little, by accident. I thought this is what Abbott wanted. To be seen. "Maybe not all of them. But Jane. Alice. They won't just be Spellbound princesses if the people of Ever don't help. They will be dead princesses."

It's the first time I've said it out loud. It's a thing my brain has known, but my heart has kept quiet.

They will be dead princesses, my heart repeats. *They will die.*

Him being wrong doesn't make you right. I hear Mom's voice over and over, saying a thing that is true even though I hate it, and Abbott would hate it too.

"The people of Ever are starving too," Abbott says. "I'm starving."

I conjure up a pie. It's hot. It's apple. It smells like cinnamon.

"Fuck, Reagan, that's not what it's about," he says.

"I did what you told me to do," I say. "They're going to leave their castle. They're going to see Ever. They're going to see you. And the kingdom. And their father. The real one. The one we see. I was very careful choosing—" Abbott shakes his head, stopping my words. His face might as well be my mother's. The two of them disappointed in whatever I try to do. The two of them wanting some indecipherable and impossible *more* from me. Abbott won't even look at me. His arms are crossed right over his chest, and he shakes his head at his own feet.

"I thought—you get invited to the castle and you just hand them a list of objects. You didn't even try to tell them—"

"I thought we were friends," I interrupt because I am tired from a day of being told that what I did wasn't enough. "I thought we were in this together."

"You sat on a beach for five years," he says. "And we went on. We go on. The best we can."

"I know that," I say. I want to argue with him, but I'm not sure what part isn't true. It *feels* untrue, the way he says it, but I did. I sat on the beach in AndNot, and I thought about waves and how they roll and palm trees and how they wave back and forth in the wind. I ate oysters and crabs straight from their shells. I missed Abbott and my mother and magic.

But that missing wasn't enough for anyone.

"Maybe if we break the spell—" I say.

"You," Abbott says. "You and the princesses will break the spell. It will be like it always is. You try to protect the royalty. The royalty tries to protect you. And the rest of us sit around hoping for something better."

"We can't do it alone," I say. "We need the people of Ever to—"

"The people of Ever are tired," Abbott says. "We're so fucking tired."

"I can conjure more pie," I say, but the second it's out of my mouth, I hear how unbelievably stupid it is. How small. An apple pie. For a starving kingdom.

"Reagan," Abbott says. "You have to tell them. The princesses."

"Tell them what?" I ask, but I know.

"Who their father is. They deserve—they should know. That's what you wanted me to do, isn't it? I thought you were going to tell them last night. I thought you would tell everyone as soon as you got back. Isn't that what you wanted this whole time? The kingdom should know."

"Look at us," I say. "Who's going to believe the two of us?" There's something else, too. Something I know Abbott won't understand. He cares about the big picture, the good of Ever. And I care about my mother more than anything else. I've never asked, but I don't think she wants anyone to know what the king did to her. She wishes she hadn't even told me, I'm sure. "We can't tell them," I say. "It was probably a good thing that you didn't end up telling them when I was gone."

"They deserve to know," he says. I don't know how to explain to him that I agree that Ever deserves to know who their king is, *and* my mother deserves to have her story kept to herself. I don't know how to insist that both things are true.

I don't know how to say it, so I don't even try. "They won't believe us," I say, which is truer than the rest of it anyway.

Abbott's clothes are worn, and I am a mess of skirts and a thick sweater borrowed from Willa that is too big for me in some places and too small in others.

We are a farmer and a witch. Not the kind of people Ever wants to hear from.

Not the kind of people who are believed.

"That's for them to decide," Abbott says. "They'll believe or not believe. But it's up to us to decide to tell." He pauses. Shakes his head, because what he's said is wrong. "It's up to you."

9.

JANE

When I wake the next morning, it's later than I intended to sleep. Eden's Thirteenth Birthday lasted deep into the morning hours. I should have woken at dawn, to get the most hours out of our three days to break the spell. But it's past noon. I nearly yell at Olive, but I'd told her not long ago to never ever wake me, since my dreams are the only place I sometimes don't feel so hungry.

I'm surprised to find my sisters just getting to breakfast, everyone but Alice. We finally find her outside.

"We have to come up with a plan," I say. The dark circles under her eyes have turned heavy and black. Her head bobs, trying to right itself and failing over and over again.

"That's what I'm doing," she says. "It's not ready."

"We've already lost time," I say. I can tell I'm speaking quickly. Alice hates when people speak quickly, when they lead with their nerves, when they rush through sentences that are impossible for her to keep up with.

I check her hands. They're covered in stone dust. The gray

stuff is packed underneath her fingernails and smudged all over her face. She's been working.

"I have to finish," Alice says. It's impossible to argue with her when she's in a state like this. So we wait, even though time is ticking away. We wait, because we trust Alice and we need her, we need all of us, to break the spell.

An hour passes. Two. The boat is set up; we are dressed and brushed and powdered by our attendants. Three hours have passed. The day is getting away from us, three days turning to two in the time it's taking Alice to finish what she feels she needs to do. When we are ready to go—a snack packed, our attendants given instructions on how to keep us protected, our shoes shined, the boat checked for safety—we join Alice again on the lawn.

She's done. "Drum Drascall," she says, the answer to a question no one actually asked. "Turner Dodd. Abbott Shine. And our father."

"What are you talking about?" Grace asks. Alice sighs. She's used up all her energy on a list of names and doesn't want to explain. Nora goes to her side to hold her upright, to give her a place to lean. Even without any love, Nora has moments of kindness. I would have thought the two were inextricable, but it turns out there can be one without the other. This is kindness without love. It pains me to imagine what love without kindness might look like.

I shove the thought away.

Alice gestures to the stone she has spent the evening and the morning and much of the afternoon carving. There are four faces. A tired old man. A young boy with an exaggerated frown. A heartbreakingly handsome face. And the face we know best, our father's. "Drum Drascall. Turner Dodd. Abbott Shine. Our father," she says again, like it's a chant, a prayer, a call to arms.

There are 537 residents of Ever. When I first told my mother, years ago, that I wanted to be queen someday, she said that to be queen you have to know your people. I told her I would be the very best queen Ever had seen. She laughed, because I hadn't realized that meant I thought I could be better than her. "Let's go meet them!" I'd said.

"No, we don't meet them," Mom said. "That's not how royalty knows its subjects."

I had a hundred questions about how we were meant to know people without meeting them, but she said it so simply that it sounded easy. So instead I took my mother's words as an assignment and set out to learn something about all 537 residents of Ever. I put their names on flash cards and asked Olive to go out into town and take photographs of everyone she saw. "I want to know one thing about each of them," I said, giving Olive a notebook. She came back after that first day with one hundred photographs.

One of them was Drum Drascall.

One was Abbott Shine.

One was Turner Dodd.

I reach for the facts I once knew about them.

"He used to grow spinach," I say. "Drum Drascall. Lives on the edge of town. The one thing he wanted me to know about him was that he used to grow spinach. He's the oldest man," I say. "And Turner Dodd. He's the saddest. Wanted me to know there hasn't been one day in his whole life that he hasn't cried. And Abbott Shine." I reach for the fact about him. What I mostly remember is that he had one of the most beautiful faces I'd ever seen. "He misses his mother. He loves his sisters."

My heart pounds in recognition. I miss my mother and love my sisters too.

"You could have just written down their names," Nora says. Her nose turns up to the sky, and her eyes roll. "What a waste of a day."

But Alice is Alice. She has to process through stone. Her brain is a foggy mess, but stone is clear and sturdy and strong. I go to her side and sit with her under Drum Drascall's chin. These sculptures make our goal clear, our journey solid and doable. Nora would rather rush through things, but Alice knows we need a map carved into stone if we're going to do the unthinkable and venture out into our kingdom. She knows that to break the spell, we need to be durable and sure and committed. Maybe it seems like a waste to Nora, but to me, it's a bit of hope.

"We'll do it," I say. "Maybe we'll like it. Being out there. In Ever." My heart pounds. I wonder if the air is different across the moat. If there's a stronger breeze. Maybe the ground feels shakier, maybe there's a magic that could hurt us more, maybe the witch is luring us into a trap. Princesses aren't meant to wander the kingdom, and perhaps there's a reason for that.

We all turn to the moat. The thing we've never crossed. The places we've never been.

We linger by Mom in her glass box before getting into the boat our attendants have tied to the shore for us. I want something from her—permission, maybe.

Queens are meant for castles, she always told me, and it feels wrong to be disobeying her when she can't argue her side. The words sound even sadder now, though, with her trapped like this. Queens may be meant for castles, but they can't possibly be meant for glass houses.

We don't get permission from Mom. Or Dad. But our attendants start rowing, and we wave goodbye to the castle we've never left. It isn't a long distance, but our boat is the only way to get across. A moat without a drawbridge. It's always felt like the way things are, but now I'm wondering if it's the way things have to be.

Mom and Dad talk about Ever like it is set in stone, the rules already decided and unchangeable. But Alice can carve up stone, shift it into something else entirely.

My heart thumps as we chip away at the things we thought had to be. *We are crossing the moat,* I think. *We are princesses going into our kingdom.* These are facts that I was told weren't possible. Those thoughts rock me more than the boat.

"Are boats safe?" Grace asks. "What are they made of? Has anyone ever been hurt in one? Why are we going in one?"

I close my eyes. Her questions are too much for me today. It is taking every bit of energy I have to be on this boat, swaying toward Ever. "It's just Ever," I say at last.

"They won't know how to be with you," Olive says. "They might be—they're not—you know different things. They know some things. And you know other things. And they might be angry. Or strange. Or kind. They could be kind. Some of them."

"I'm a princess," I say. "They're obsessed with princesses. They've been waiting for the vanished one to return for eighty years. They light their candles. They tell her story. They wave at me from across the moat and tell me I look just like her and—"

"It's complicated," Olive says. She's never interrupted me before. I don't know what to do with the words I was going to say, so I swallow them down.

"We're royalty," I say. "It's simple."

Olive sighs. I've never heard her sigh. "Try to forget the things you've learned. The books you've read. Your father's words. Try to . . . put it aside."

We hit the shore. Olive looks past the people waiting at the moat, strains to look past the brick buildings on the shore where dukes and duchesses and the elite live. She looks for something else. Someone else.

"You lived here once," I say, which is true, but I've never given much thought to it.

"Of course I did," Olive says. Maybe I should have considered it before, but no one ever told me to. She's Olive. She's my attendant. She's kind and easy to be around and smart and pretty. I never thought to learn more about her. But there's a bite to her voice now. A new sound.

"You're angry," I say. "You're one of the angry people of Ever."

Olive blows a slow breath up to the sky. I wonder if she's seen what or who she wanted to. I wonder if she's caught sight of her home. Her family. Her half brother. Her father. A used-to-be farm they must live on.

"Aren't we all the angry people of Ever?" she asks before taking my hand and leading me to shore, where the ground feels exactly the same as the ground outside the castle, except also completely different.

"You're here," Reagan says when we are all unloaded onto the shore. Olive and the other attendants have gone off to see their families. We're alone with the witch and our kingdom.

"We have to be here," I say. "Why are *you* here?"

"We perform the Undoing together," she says like it's all so simple. "I thought you might be nervous, seeing Ever for the first time. I thought you'd get an early start. I've been waiting."

She is something else, this witch of ours. She is not one thing or another. Sometimes I am only Princess Jane Who Can't Eat and Alice is only ever Princess Alice Who Can't Sleep and we wander our tiny section of the world being the Princesses of Without, the Spellbound, the Enchanted Royals of Ever.

I want Reagan to be this way too. Reagan the Evil. Reagan the Bad Witch. Reagan the Jealous Liar. Reagan Who I Hate.

But she is refusing to be one thing.

"You have to tell us—" I start, before stopping myself. I want to ask again why she cast the spell, what we ever did for her to punish us—punish our poor mother—so cruelly. But I stop the question before it has a chance to leave my lips. Her face makes me stop. It's so bare and gentle. It's kind.

A strange, unsettled part of my heart doesn't want to know what could make her turn so cruel.

I'll ask later. I'll ask when the spell is broken, when we're done. There is already too much to take in, stepping foot into the town of Ever.

Walking around out here, I don't understand anything. The trees are sometimes tall and sometimes short. The homes are squat and sad. The gardens are mostly empty. This is not the Ever of my textbooks.

No one swarms us. No one blows kisses or sneers or says much of anything at all. They just watch us. Warily.

"This can't be right," I say, walking past a row of houses so small I could fit two of them inside my bedroom.

"They should really build bigger houses," Grace says. "Prettier ones. These ones aren't good."

"I thought we were supposed to like our own kingdom," Nora says. "This is—it's ugly. And quiet. And—"

"Sad," I say, looking at brown dresses hanging from clotheslines and what must be the Barren Fields in the distance. "Are we almost there?"

"Yes," Nora says, pointing at the smallest house, the ugliest part of the road. There aren't leaves on the trees. There isn't growth from the earth. There's just a wooden shack and a man outside it who is sallow and sorry and sagging.

Drum Drascall. He smiles. He has a long beard and a

thousand wrinkles and beautiful hands. I notice them right away, because I am always looking at people's hands to avoid looking at their mouths. Mouths make me jealous and hungry. Drum's hands are slender with long fingers and freckles near the wrist. They are familiar.

The oldest man in town. I wonder how old he actually is.

"Princesses on my lawn," he says. "I never thought I'd see the day."

"You're our first—all I've ever been told is not to talk to—princesses aren't supposed to—" I wish I wasn't the oldest, so I didn't have to be the first to speak.

"Hello," Drum interrupts, saving me from myself. He bows. Then catches himself and puts out a hand to shake. This is wrong too, so he bows again. "You're more beautiful up close."

"Oh," I say. "Okay. That's—thank you." I'm not even sure it's a compliment, but I'm as nervous as he is, and my sisters aren't stepping in. Reagan leans against a tree and fidgets. I thought witches were still and sure, but she is all tapping fingers and sweaty forehead.

"You're the oldest man in town," Nora breaks in, seeing that I've lost my way. Drum's eyes light up with shock; then he laughs. It's a big laugh, the real kind.

"I suppose I am."

"Well, then we need something from you."

"Nora—" Alice says. She puts a finger to her lips. "You have a lovely home," she says, staring at the saddest pile of wood we've ever seen. "It's very nice to meet you." Alice did the best job studying the ways of the people of Ever. We took classes on the rules of polite society and how the people we ruled live. But it never felt as interesting as studies about witches or our own royal aunts and uncles and pasts.

Drum cocks his head. He's trying to figure us out and is moving through a dozen feelings in the process. Awe, confusion, amusement, fear—it's all there. "I don't have a very nice home at all," he says at last. "None of us do. As you must be seeing. Finally."

We learned how to dance waltzes and wear our hair and how to recite poetry and play the violin. We did not learn how to stand face-to-face with this old man in our apparently rotting kingdom and have a conversation. I want a violin and a pair of dancing shoes. I want a ball gown and a feather-filled chair to sit in. I do not want to smell barren dirt and this man's skin.

Then I remember how many days are left until Reagan's birthday—three—and I swallow down everything but my own need.

"It's the spell," I say. "You can help us break the spell."

"Ah," Drum says. He clasps his hands together in front of himself, lifting his fingertips and placing them back down over and over again. He looks at each of us greedily, taking in more of us than we want to give. He lingers on Alice's hair, on Nora's breasts, on Eden's tiny little-girl legs. "And how can I do that?"

I look helplessly at Reagan. If she's going to sit there watching us, I wish she would do something witchy and powerful, letting Drum know we aren't to be messed with. But Reagan doesn't even look up from the ground.

"Do you have a clock?" I ask.

Drum smiles. "Lill?" he calls into his home. "Do we have a clock for the princesses?"

A woman joins him on the stoop. She has the look of a person who used to be beautiful, used to be happy, but is now too worn out to be either. She's as familiar as Drum's hands. The woman is in an enormous black overcoat, buttoned all the way from her neck to her toes with silver buttons. It's a strange outfit, a startling one, but then I don't know much about the things the people of Ever wear.

"I'm so sorry to interrupt you," I say. "We just need a clock. Do you have a clock? I think any clock is fine. Maybe even a watch? Reagan, would a watch be okay?"

I want to leave. I'm sure it's written across my face. I want to leave so badly my body turns a little bit away from Drum and Lill. I don't want to see them and their home and this part of Ever.

"We do have a clock," Lill says. "Why don't you come inside and take a look?"

"Oh, that's okay," I say. "I'm sure you can't fit us."

Reagan closes her eyes. I've said something wrong.

"I'm sure it's not convenient," Nora tries. This is better. She's got more of her senses about her. I should shut up.

"We used to go to your home all the time," Lill says. "It would be our pleasure to have you here." She holds the door open, and in our confusion we walk through it.

"Our home?" I ask. That can't be right. Subjects don't come to the castle. Certainly not often. We follow her into their tiny home. Inside, there's a long wooden table decorated with burlap and dried leaves and, yes, a clock. There's a cake in the center of the table, next to the clock, and plain unglazed ceramic plates set up for us. They are all different sizes, as if not a single set of salad or entrée plates has survived, so they make do with bits and pieces of what's left. They knew we were coming. Of course they did.

"You were young," Drum says. "Some of you weren't even born. It was a long time ago. Things were—well. Things were different."

I squint at him, then at her. Scan the room for clues. The outside of their home is like every other one we walked by, but inside there are the trappings of old wealth. Velvet curtains that have gone threadbare. Floral carpets now covered in footprints and stains. A silver vase that hasn't seen polish in a decade. And the clock. It's fancier than anything else I've seen so far in Ever, a relic from another time, maybe, a more prosperous kingdom.

"Who did you used to be?" I ask.

"Sir Drum," Drum says. "And Lady Lill. And now, I suppose, we're the difference between you breaking the spell and not breaking it." The look on his face frightens me.

Lady Lill pulls out a chair for each of us. Starts cutting into a sad cake that won't taste anything like the cakes we're used to eating.

It's that motion—the cutting of the cake—that brings

them back to me. I remember Lady Lill in our dining room, back when I could eat, when I was very small and she seemed very tall. I remember her speaking with my father in hushed tones that stopped when I entered the room.

I remember Sir Drum playing the fiddle for me, and all of us eating a thick potato soup that we never ate any other time.

"It's what they're used to," my father said when I asked him about it. "We want to make them comfortable. They're used to different foods than we are."

It sounded kind, back then.

I hear it a little differently now.

"Maybe we should come back another time," I say, because the smell of cake is lemony and strong, and every part of my body is telling me to go.

"We hoped your father might come with you," Lill says. "We were looking forward to seeing our old friend. Showing him our home."

"He's busy," I say.

"Busy," Drum repeats, laughing.

"He's king," Grace says.

"He is," Drum says.

"I'm sure he sends his regards," I say. I'm drawing on all our old lessons about the ways of the people of Ever, but it's coming out stilted, speaking a language aloud that I've only ever read about. I've never practiced for this moment. I could have used some practice. I can stay perfectly still; I can be quiet; I can wave when people are calling my name and smile when they ask me questions. I can keep my distance and bow my head when my father speaks. I am an excellent queen in training.

But they didn't teach me about this.

"The king would like you to help us," Nora tries.

"If that is what the king wants, why isn't he here?" Drum asks.

Maybe the clock stops ticking, or maybe it's my heart.

It's a question so good we don't have an answer for it. I want to tell them again how busy our father is, but he isn't. This morning when we were piling into the boat, he was sleeping in. He spoke of having some of the visiting kings over for lunch. He talked about taking them on a horse ride around the moat.

Everything that seemed normal starts to twist. *If my father wanted to help us, he would be helping us.*

I try to unthink the thought. I try to shrug it off like a sweater that itches, like a pair of shoes that pinch.

But it stays. I'm sweating like Reagan now. Thick sweat that I've never felt before.

Where is he, our father? Why is the witch here and our father up there? Why, at the Thirteenth Birthday, did he not save me from the prince? Why did he look away? Why did he say the things he said?

My father has always been a solid thing to hang on to, and now that solid thing feels wobbly and wrong. I try to hold on to it, I try to make it be what it's always been—concrete, stone, safety—but it wants to be something else. Something slippery and new.

My sisters, too, look like they are struggling to stay afloat in this current moment.

Drum waits for us to respond, and when we don't, he shrugs his shoulders. "I think I'll wait for the king to ask me," he says. I swear there's a smirk there too. A knowing look. "That clock is enchanted. I bet you didn't know that. Keeps me alive. Counts down the days until I die. And I have another five years left, as long as I can hang on to it."

"I don't—magic? Out here in the kingdom?" I ask.

Even Reagan tilts her head at the thought of it. Magic, floating around Ever, not just locked up in the Home on the Hill where it's meant to be.

"More magic than you think," Lill says. She sounds a little sad and looks extra long at Reagan.

I glance at the clock. Its golden hand is almost the whole way around the circle, lingering on today's date, moving toward a day five years from now, marked by a tiny, brilliant diamond. It scares me, being so close to something that could tell me what I don't want to know.

Except: I know where my end is too, if we can't get this clock. And it's much, much closer than five years away.

The time on the clock suddenly looks like a luxury to me. A luxury that fills me with rage. When you are so empty from hunger, things like rage and jealousy and fear can fill you up fast.

"You've Spellbound the whole kingdom, haven't you?" I say, turning to Reagan. "That's why it looks like this. That's why everything's so awful. You've come out here and cast spells over everything and come up with some impossible list of tasks for us. It's not fair. We don't have magic. You can't just come and enchant the kingdom against us—"

"Jane," Reagan says. She doesn't deny or explain. She doesn't apologize. She just *is*. She always just is, and maybe that's what being a witch is like, or maybe that's what being not a princess is like, but either way it's making me want to scream.

"Ever is under some awful spell from you and your family. Look at all this sadness, all the hunger. You cast spells on everyone, didn't you? The Spell of Without isn't just on us— it's everywhere."

"Jane, no," Reagan says. She picks up the clock. "This is enchanted, yes. I didn't know that. I knew they used to be friends of your father, that's it. I didn't know I was asking you to get a clock like this one—I didn't know a clock like this one could be in a home like this."

"There's so much we all know," Lill says. "And so very much we don't." She looks sad. Like she wishes things could be different, but knows they can't be. "It's not easy, being a subject. Being a witch."

"Being a princess," I say. Lady Lill does not nod in agreement. Neither does Reagan.

Reagan wilts and I rage, but Drum doesn't care about any of it. He picks the clock up out of Reagan's hands.

"If your father asks for it, I'll happily hand it over," he says. "Even knowing what it means. For the king, I'd do that."

"It's what he would want," I say. But I can't possibly sound convincing. I'm too seeped in shock and worry.

"Well, then I'm sure he'd be happy to come and tell me that," Drum Drascall says. He shrugs his shoulders and moves out of the kitchen into a back room, the conversation over.

Outside Drum's home, Ever has turned from quiet into something else entirely. The sun is starting to set, and night is coming, even though we've only just gotten started. The subjects are in their homes, but we are greeted with royalty. Princes and princesses, dukes and duchesses from other kingdoms. They've been waiting for us.

"Empty-handed!" Prince Felix of Droomland calls out, and the rest of them cheer. My sisters move closer to me. Reagan, too, drifts to my side.

"I love you," the royals say.

"I must have you."

"Marry me."

"Choose me."

"You are goddesses."

"Stay just as you are. Forever. With me."

They are holding, each of them, a goblet of water and a basket of white feathers.

In the kingdom of Ever, marriage proposals come with water and feathers, to symbolize the simplicity and softness of love. My father brought my mother a teacup filled with water and a dove in a birdcage. This is very different from that bit of romance.

"We should go," Reagan says in a strong whisper.

"We love you," the Prince of Soar calls. "Just the way you are."

"I don't want anyone else but one of you," the Princess of

Farr says. Her voice cracks, and I hate her for not even choosing one of us to love most.

"Why are you here?" Grace calls out. Her voice sounds at once panicked and proud. She hates not understanding everything, but all Grace has ever wanted is a princess with a goblet of water and a feather asking for her hand in marriage.

And now she has a dozen princesses, two dozen princes, clamoring for her.

Or at least for *someone* enchanted.

"The world needs you," the Prince of Nethering says. He reaches into his basket and pulls out a single feather, waves it like a flag. "We want the Spellbound princesses. We don't want you taken from us!"

"Don't let them break the spell!" the Princess of Thorner calls out to Reagan.

I look at the witch, expecting to see a smile, maybe, an agreement. She hates us. She's against us. She doesn't want us to break the spell either.

But she isn't smiling at the royals. She isn't nodding in agreement. She's looking at me.

"I'm sorry," she says, her voice spotted with the same shock I'm feeling. "I'm so sorry."

And with the words comes something else. A flutter of a feeling in my hands and my feet and my heart. A shiver on my skin. A funny sensation that I can't seem to place.

It stays.

And so do the royals.

10.
REAGAN

All I can smell is the royal fear. The princesses are in a cloud of it, the smell so strong it almost chokes me. It seems impossible that the royals from other kingdoms, Drum, Lill, even the Spellbound themselves can't smell it. But they don't seem to notice.

I walk fast, and the princesses follow. So do the royals from the other kingdoms.

"I want one in a box," the Prince of Farr says. "Like the queen. I'd like a princess in a box. Hey, witch, put one of these girls in a box, why don't you?"

Next to me, Princess Jane shivers.

"Don't listen," I say. "Tune them out."

"How?" she whispers back. I don't have an answer for her. She doesn't know how to be outside the castle, and I don't know how to be off the Hill, or far from my cottage in AndNot.

"Just move. Fast," I say, and it doesn't answer her question or any of mine, but we keep going.

"How the hell would you fuck her?" the Prince of AndNot says. I didn't know princes say "fuck." My heart jumps. Princess

Jane's shiver runs through all of them, as if they've been hit by an icy gust.

"Get in the box with her!" the Prince of Nethering says. He cracks himself up.

"I like the tired one," the Prince of Droomland says.

"Nah, I want the one who looks like she's about to break. All bones and knees and hunger," the Prince of AndNot says. "She'd look good in a box."

I keep them walking, the princesses on their shaky legs with their shallow breaths. "Come on, come on," I say to them. They have never been scared. Not like this. They've never had to speak to anyone outside the castle, never been even this short distance from home. They keep wanting to stop, like little kids who think if they hide their faces behind their hands, no one will be able to see them.

"My father's talking about putting my mother in a box," the Prince of Farr says. "If we can find a witch of our own to cast a spell."

A witch of our own. The phrase chills me. I look all over, hunting for a way to escape them, but there isn't one.

"We could take one," the Prince of Nethering says.

"Caused a lot of trouble last time," the Prince of Farr counters.

"That's 'cause we weren't able to hold on to her. Slipped right though our fingers."

"Things are different now."

"Thank god."

Jane starts to cry. It isn't a sound I'd be able to hear if she weren't practically on top of me, squeezing my shoulder with one hand, grabbing Eden's arm and dragging her along with the other.

"We have to run," I say.

"I'm tired," she says, and she nods at Alice, who is even more tired. "I can't run. You should." She says it like she's used to being left behind. Like it's her job to be unimportant. I've been thinking of princesses as selfish—and they're that—but this one has also spent her life learning to be queen. And a queen is quiet and sacrificing and sweet.

A queen is good.

A good queen doesn't save herself.

Everyone likes a good queen. But it's rarely enough, to be liked.

I might have given the king exactly what he wanted with my spell. A wife he can stare at but never have to speak to. A literal trophy on his lawn. A group of daughters so broken down and fragile that they are somehow more alluring than the strong, healthy, unenchanted princesses in other kingdoms. Possibly even the beginning of another war, another kidnapped princess, another search for a lost girl.

Everyone loves a lost girl.

I created this group of foreign royals, even. I made them want women in boxes. I made them desire princesses who are too tired to say no. And now they want me, too. A witch to do their bidding.

Princess Jane clasps her hands in front of her and looks at her sisters, worrying about them. She walks as fast as she can, which isn't very fast, and then slows down when she realizes

Alice can't walk even at that pace. Soon she is walking only as fast as Alice can.

"Excuse me," she says when the princes get too close to her. "I'm sorry."

It's not a hot day, but I'm hot. I'm sweating. I'm flushed.

I could run. But I won't. I walk alongside her, as slow as Alice, as slow as the most tired person in all of Ever. It is not fast enough to outrun even their words.

"My family used to have a witch in it. That's what my father says. Generations ago. When there were more of them," the Prince of Farr says.

"When they couldn't all hide out in Ever," the Duke of Nethering says.

"There were too many in AndNot," the Prince of Soar says. "That's what I've heard. We took care of it."

"Are there too many witches, do you think, Princess Jane? Princess Grace?" a long-haired prince asks. "Do we need to take some off your hands?"

I'm stuck on what they're saying. It's some shared idea of a history that I've never heard of. I've never heard of witches in royal families or being *taken care of*. I try to go over our history, and it suddenly feels like I barely know it. The princess. The War. The ten vanished witches. The agreement for peace. The Home on the Hill. The kingdom at rest. That's it. Just a vague before and an urgent after and the tenuous now.

I'd like to go back to the Home on the Hill and ask more questions about the history I know and the history they're hinting at. But I can't leave these princesses, not cursed and alone like this. And there are a hundred things I could do to these people who are reaching for us, for me, leering at my chest and Jane's bony shoulders and Alice's sleepy eyes and Eden's face and Grace's long legs and Nora's way of holding herself, as if we're a thing for sale, a thing they are owed. But, for an instant, I forget every spell I ever learned, every Silencing or Disappearing or Invisibility spell.

A witch without her spells is just a girl alone in the woods.

And no one wants to be a girl alone in the woods.

"I know you," the Prince of Farr says. He's gotten close to us. They all have. They kept their distance and got to us with words, but I can see now they intend to let their hands find our skin. It's right there on their faces: the wanting. The not caring what we want. "I know you," he says again, the *oo* sound turning long and decadent.

Of course he means he knows *of* me, he knows *about* me, but it's all the same to him. He knows I am a witch and he knows I am the Witch and he knows that I am scared. They all know that. It's nothing special.

He grabs my arm. The Prince of Nethering grabs my other arm. They smell like meat and wine and diamonds. They smell rich and not at all scared. I hate them.

"What's better?" Prince Felix of Droomland starts, his eyebrows rising and his mouth curling as he looks back and forth between me and the princesses. "A Spellbound princess, or the witch that bound them up in the first place?" He rubs his hands against each other. He's enjoying how it feels to size me up. He bows. "Thank you," he says. "You brought us the princesses we never knew we always wanted."

Maybe I didn't know what fear was until right now. Not the kind of fear that is urgent. The kind of fear that could grab you and take from you, because spells come from your heart, and your heart doesn't seem to be beating.

They see the fear. Princess Jane sees the fear. It makes her more scared. Her sisters, too. All of us are stuck in this swarm.

"We won't hurt you," the Prince of Farr says, even though his leer says something entirely different. "Not if you keep our princesses the way we want them." Jane bows her head. Nora lifts hers. God, I'd love to be Nora right now and maybe always. "You won't be breaking that spell, right? Little witch? You wouldn't do that to us?"

I wonder if they realize I haven't spoken a word.

"She wouldn't dare," the Princess of Thorner says. She glares at me. I'd thought she and the other princesses would do something to take the men away from us. But she doesn't feel aligned with us in any way.

Prince Felix's fingers twitch in my direction, and I fold my arms across my chest. I'm the one with magic. I'm the one who could cast a spell and turn any one of them into a frog, a mouse, a blade of grass. But somehow, the truth of my magic is amping them up, exciting them, giving *them* power instead of me.

As the royals stand uncomfortably close to me and lick their lips at my magic, I think of my mother. I think of how the king must have made her feel in the moments before. I usually only ever think of the during and the after. But maybe the before was even worse. Knowing what is about to happen, hoping beyond hope that it won't. Dreading the very instant you are actually in.

I wonder if her mind raced through spells she could cast but came up empty. I wonder if, because he was king, she chose not to use magic. I wonder if he pretended to believe she wanted it. I wonder if she thought she had to.

I wonder which version of this I will be in, if this situation turns even worse.

I wonder if all he wanted was her magic. I wonder if we can be separated from our magic, or if wanting our magic is the same as wanting us.

I am wondering so much that I float above the situation, and it is only the Prince of Farr's hand on my ass that brings me back. "Not great," he says. He laughs. "Not magical. Let's see how it compares to royal ass." His other hand reaches for Princess Alice. He gestures at his friends to touch me, touch them, compare and contrast, as they wish.

"Guess you don't have beauty spells," the Princess of Farr says, watching as her brother, the Prince of Farr, kisses my neck.

It is that touch—warm, wet, awful—that raises up my arms and reminds me that I am a witch and they are mortals. Royal mortals, but mortals nonetheless. Spells don't come easily to me after having been out of practice for five years. And I've promised my mother and grandmother that I won't make magic out of emotion anymore.

But.

But.

"You know what happens, don't you?" the Duke of AndNot

133

says. I used to be able to see his home from my AndNot cottage. I thought it looked cozy; I hoped he might be kind. "I've heard your magic can leave you, that you could someday just be a human. I've heard you can vanish into thin air. I've heard you're not quite as powerful as you try to make us believe."

Next to me, Jane takes a sharp intake of breath. It sounds like it hurts, that's how sudden it is.

The Prince of Soar's hand reaches my chest. "Let's check the rest of them," he says, and his eyes are roaming over to tiny Eden and her stooped, hopeless shoulders.

Just as Willa's magic is always sweet and clumsy and whimsical, mine is always rash and large. A smarter witch would simply extract herself from the moment—Quicken herself to the Home on the Hill or magic them into frogs for an hour or two.

I am not that kind of witch, no matter how many years they locked me away in AndNot and begged me to be better.

I am not who they want me to be.

So I turn my fury on the kingdom.

I turn the woods to ash, and light the sky up with day. Maybe awful things can't happen between men and women, between boys and girls, between people with power and people without in the daylight, in the absence of trees and the shadows they cast. I beg this to be true. I turn Ever into an Always Day. The royals are startled enough by the ash clouds and the burst of light that the princesses and I can sprint to the moat, to their boat, to the attendants wringing their worried hands, wondering where we've gone, what's taking so long.

We pile in, and the attendants row us toward the castle.

Behind us, Ever is a mess of dust and sunshine. But in the boat, things are clearer.

We catch our breath, all of us. It takes time, and the attendants row slowly, then let us float right in the middle of the moat. They know I can't go to the castle. They also know there's more to be said.

"Why did you do that?" Nora asks.

"To save us," Grace says. She looks at me like I have answers that no one has. She looks at me like I could break a spell that she probably doesn't remember I cast upon her.

"Thank you," Jane says. She's saying "thank you"; I said "I'm sorry"; we are not following our old scripts; we are trying out new words with each other. She rubs her hands together, waves her fingers. She looks at me with wonder, then shakes them out again.

"My magic—I get emotional. I'm not supposed to do magic when I'm emotional. But I do."

"For good reason," Alice says.

"I'm sorry?" I ask. She's so succinct it is often mysterious. I can't read her tired face.

"You do magic for a good reason," she says. "In response to something. Only when it's called for."

"All witches do," Jane says, repeating words they learned in their castle classroom.

"Yes," I say. "But still." It sounds like the beginning of a sentence, but it's the end of one.

"And the spell you cast on us . . . ," Princess Jane starts.

"That was for a good reason too," Princess Alice continues.

Nora closes her eyes. Grace flips through her notebook like the answer is somewhere in there, something she's simply forgotten. Eden rolls her eyes and looks at the sun.

"There was," I say.

"You can tell us," Jane says. She rubs her fingertips against the palms of her hands. She is nothing like the princess I imagined her to be. "What did we do to you?"

I look at the attendants, as if they can tell me what to do. They hold themselves a little like my mother. There is a nervous energy around them, a pain they aren't speaking, a way they look at the castle's highest tower like it's somewhere they've been but never want to be again, a place they can't stop thinking about.

One of them, Olive, the one who attends to Princess Jane and visited me at the Home on the Hill, raises her chin. Her eyes flit to the tower, to me, to her charge. "It was the king," she says.

I hiccup out something in between a cry and a laugh. The sound of being seen after so many years. The sound of a shared hurt that you've been shouldering alone. "It was the king," I echo.

Princess Jane leans toward me. The boat rocks from every movement we make. It is precarious, the moment we are in. Her mouth is a straight line, her eyes are serious, and her hands are shaking. "And what did he do to you?" she asks. "My father. Our father. The king. What did he do?"

"It wasn't me," I say. The words are so small and jagged, and I wonder if she'll even hear them. But I say them. I do. I think of Abbott, and I know he's right. That I have to tell the truth, even if no one wants to hear it and no one believes me and none of it matters.

The truth is the truth, even if it doesn't do what we want it to.

"It was my mother. It was a long time ago. Before I was born." I touch the place by my chest where the royals touched me. I consider the way it felt, to have unwanted hands taking what was never given to them.

"He hurt her," Princess Jane says. I can tell she wants me to say that he hit her. That he said something cruel. In the grand pause she knows it's worse than a hit or a word, and I see her want it to be that her father killed someone.

Anything but what he did.

What she knows he did.

"He raped her," I say.

I didn't know what it looked like—the breaking of someone's heart. I thought maybe tears, maybe loud noises, but it turns out there is silence. The thickest kind. The sound of a heart breaking is the worst, most dizzying quiet. It is dry heaves and bodies crumpling as easily as sheets of paper. It is a rocking boat and the worry of the whole thing tilting over—the boat, all of us, the world on its axis. It is fingernails dug deep into palms, into thighs, into cheeks. It is bodies that don't want to be bodies anymore, skin that wishes it could be ripped off.

It is so much worse than a spell.

And all of it, now, is in the brightness of an everlasting day.

Suddenly, all I want is the cover of night.

11.

JANE

My body responds with a giant *no* before my mouth can.

I shove Reagan. It must be an awful danger to attack a witch. The light in the sky, the Woods That Were, tell us that. But I do it anyway, as easily as taking a breath.

The boat rocks wildly in response. Shoving her is bad for me, too, since we are sharing this space, this moment, this stupid boat that we don't even need because the moat isn't deep. It doesn't have to be. The people of Ever are as afraid of oceans as they are of puddles, because we asked the witches to enchant them to be afraid of water, so that the moat would truly keep them away from us.

Still, the push surprises her, and she grips the sides of the boat. Almost loses her balance. Almost falls out. But Olive doesn't let her. In the blink of an eye, I feel something between them, a promise to matter to each other, even though they barely know each other.

The boat evens out, and Reagan stays squarely inside it. We are stuck in the middle of the moat, and I would rather be anywhere else with anyone else. I can't stop shaking my fingers, trying to make the funny tingling feeling disappear from their tips. There's a new glowing feeling in my body that maybe means I am nearly dead, but it feels almost powerful. Not how I thought the spell turning True would feel.

Reagan looks as surprised as I am. "I'm sorry," she says. This seems to surprise her too, because she shakes her head and her hands and her shoulders and drags her fingers through her hair. "I shouldn't have told you. Or I should have told you five years ago. Or none of it matters because you don't believe me anyway."

"No," my mouth finally says. Because "no" is the only possible answer. "No" is the only thing that could be true.

"No," Alice says.

Grace grips her notebook and looks at each of us for more answers.

We don't have them.

Eden dips her hands into the water and draws disappearing circles onto the surface.

My mind rushes through every story I've ever heard about my father and mother. Every time anyone called him the Gentle King, the Good King. Every easy touch to my shoulder, every promise that he wouldn't marry me off, every perfect moment with the man I love so much.

All I have to weigh against that are Reagan's words and the last few strange days as things around the kingdom have started to shift. A few unsettling hours and the way Reagan looks broken. The way night turned to day and didn't let up. All these tiny details lined up against a lifetime of kindness.

"That's my father," I say. I try to sound like a queen. Calm. In control. Certain. "That's the king."

"That's *your* king," Reagan says. "Your father. Not mine." I am starting to hate her face and the way it shows nothing. Her limbs that shrug at anything I say. Her hair that can't decide what it wants to be.

"Why are you doing this?" I ask. My hands buzz. I want them to stop. It's making it hard to concentrate, and I need to be entirely present right now.

"I just told you," Reagan says.

"You know that's not true. My father would never—he's the Good King. Everyone knows it. There's something else. You haven't been around men much, so maybe you're confused. Or angry. Or jealous."

"Jane," Reagan says.

"*Princess* Jane." I am trying to hang on to the things that make me me, the things that are true and real and important. I am a princess. I am Princess Jane. I am the daughter of the Good King. I am Spellbound. I am hungry. I am trying. And I am still the princess.

"Princess Jane." Reagan clears her throat and lifts her chin. She isn't shifting. I want her to shift. I want to see the crack in her lies. Instead she looks more sure, more pointed. "I don't know everything about your father. But this one thing I know is true. It happened when my mother was younger. In your castle."

"This was a long time ago?" I ask. I'm flooded with a kind of relief. If it was a long time ago, the details could be hazy and shifty and wrong. If it was a long time ago, it must not have been him. "Decades ago? The kind of memory that can get all twisted up with time? I know my father."

"No," Reagan says. "*I* know your father."

Her eyes frighten me. They are so steady and sure. But I have to be steady and sure too. I am the future someday queen. And queens are certain.

My father told us we could marry a prince or a princess as long as we loved them. Or we could marry no one at all. My father let Eden run wild in the Grand Yard even though others in the kingdom thought girls shouldn't act that way. He let us be ourselves, whoever that was. My father brings flowers to weddings of young couples in Ever. He hired farmers hurt by the Spell of Famine to be his horsemen, our attendants. He reads to me aloud from volumes of history and taught Alice how to turn stone into art. He keeps us safe in the castle and teaches us how to rule from a distance, how to listen and hear and be present for Ever in the way royals do best. He sings under his breath in the mornings and smiles at every silly thing Eden does and says.

He is not a man who raped a witch.

Good and Gentle Kings aren't rapists.

I want to tell Reagan all of this, but I'm guessing she wouldn't be able to hear it. Whatever impossible story her mother told her is a part of her story about herself, and she won't let it go. She destroyed us because of it. She ruined lives because of this belief. She won't budge.

So, fine. I won't either. Reagan is a rash witch who believed a story about my father, and, instead of putting him under a spell, she stole vital bits of humanity from the rest of us. She's impulsive and reckless and unhinged.

"Ask anyone," I say, "and they'll tell you how much my father loves and respects women. I'd tell you to ask my mother. But of course you can't. Because you put her in a box. But she fell in love with him because of how much he respects women. He wasn't like the other princes who treated her like some lesser— he loves women. Those princes today were awful. The things they did—disgusting. Terrifying. But my father—he isn't like those princes. You don't know him. You don't know him at all."

Reagan's face doesn't move. Her eyes go dead. I wait for her to ask my sisters, ask our attendants, just like I've told her to. But she doesn't.

The boat doesn't move either. No one knows where we're going or what we're doing.

"I shouldn't have bothered," Reagan says at last.

A strange, impossible part of me wants to hug her. I try to shove that part away and focus on the part that hates her. That wouldn't mind shoving her again, harder this time.

It's easy, actually. Easier than I would have thought, to focus on hate and ignore everything else.

"I'm going home," Reagan says at last. Olive picks up an oar to row her back to shore. Reagan shakes her head. She stands up and the boat responds in kind, the rest of us gripping its edges to try to make things steady again.

"What are you doing?" I ask. It comes out as a yell.

Reagan looks me right in the eye and steps one foot, then

the other, into the water. Her skirts, the dozen or so of them, float to the top of the water. Even the burlap is buoyant, here in the moat.

"You can't go back there," I say, pointing to Ever and the royals who attacked us. "It's not safe."

Reagan smiles a terrible smile, like she knows so much more than I do, understands things I never could.

"Well, it's safer than up there," she says, jutting only the tip of her chin toward the castle.

She turns away, and her skirts float behind her, trying to pull her back to us. I swear I can still hear the royals in the Woods That Were, cackling about which of us has a better ass, whose face would look better on which body, like we are paper-doll girl cutouts and not solid people at all.

I think about the way she walked slowly, alongside Alice and me. That she didn't magic herself away. That she didn't leave us behind when it would've been so easy to.

She walks farther away from the boat, her shoulders moving back in a show of strength. She plows toward the shore.

My hands, which had been tingling and warm, go cool. It's sudden and strange.

I miss the warmth.

"Reagan," I call out. She turns around, her face weirdly hopeful. It's confusing to notice that I've stopped hating her. An impossible part of me wants to jump in alongside her. My fingers, my shoulders, my heart flicker with something. And Reagan just stands there in the moat, waiting for me. "Be careful," I say. "Please."

Light dances across the water. It surprises me, the look of it, how sudden and lovely it is. A shimmer of something that I feel in my heart as much as I see it on the water's surface.

For a second that is fast, that is found and swiftly lost, we are something like friends.

Then I remember what she just told me, and she remembers what her mother told her, and we are a witch and her Spellbound princess once again.

12.

REAGAN

When we were little, Abbott and I had a bit of magic between us. An enchanted pebble that I would use to alert him whenever I wanted to see him. And he could use it to summon me.

Leave it to a ten-year-old witch to enchant a pebble to tell a handsome boy to meet up with her.

Maybe I didn't even know he was handsome then. I don't know what I knew when I was ten. I barely know what I know *now*.

But I know the magic on that pebble was strong because it was mine, and I know he still has the pebble because I saw it on a string around his wrist when he came to my home. And I know he wants me to know I can use the magic, because he didn't hide his wrist from me; he didn't take the pebble off before seeing me. He wanted to tell me without telling me that as furious as he is, all my mistakes don't add up to me losing him.

So I close my eyes and think of Abbott Shine. His beautiful face, his adorned wrist. The things he said to me, and the things I wish I had said to him. The fact of his arms,

145

which I know could hold me right now and maybe make me feel better or at least less alone or maybe less scared of running into another pack of royals wanting to touch or harass or kidnap me.

He arrives in moments that feel like hours, and he knows something's wrong as soon as his eyes meet mine.

"What did they do?" he says, rushing to me.

"It wasn't the princesses," I say. His hand reaches for his heart. "Not the king, either." It's nice, to be able to read his mind, to speak in shorthand, after a day spent with girls who don't know me at all, or know only the worst and wildest parts of me. "Other royals. Well, and then I told them. The princesses. About their dad. And that was—they didn't believe me."

"They never do," Abbott says. And I think he's about to lecture me about all the ways the royals and the witches are wrong and all the ways we've failed Ever and all the things I did to make it worse. But he stops there and touches my arm, gently, like he's asking permission to be close to me.

I nod my head, and he shifts so that we are fully touching, his arm reaching across my back.

"I didn't want to be alone," I say.

"I'm not going anywhere," he says. His touch is certain. He understands things I don't about royalty, about Ever. He has been hurt by the king too, in different ways. We all have. The royals are the ones that touched me. But the king, the way Ever works, made it possible. "What did they do to you exactly?"

I think through the words I would use, a quick touch here and there, the sneer and leer of it all, the threats that could be jokes. I don't know how to make it sound as bad as I feel. I'm scared it will sound like nothing, in the retelling. It will sound silly.

"I don't want to talk about it." I want to tuck it away, like my mother did. Already I see how I could pretend it didn't happen, how I could treat it like a nightmare and not a flesh-and-blood thing. It's tempting. It seems so much easier.

"Let's walk," Abbott says. And I guess that's why I called him, to walk me home, to keep me safe, but that feels ridiculous, because I am a witch and I am strong and I should have been able to stop everything, and it makes no sense that I didn't.

I can't say any of that, either, though, so I follow him, and we walk in silence all the way through town to the Barren Fields.

Without the princesses, no one notices me, even with my layers of magical skirts. I could have walked home alone, and no one would have blinked in my direction.

Maybe I should go right back to AndNot today. Maybe I can give up, let go of magic and my home and Abbott and the spark of something I feel between Jane and me. I could give up, couldn't I?

I feel nothing like myself. Somewhere between the prince touching my ass and the other one touching my breast and the lot of them grabbing at me with eyes and hands and words, I lost myself. I shouldn't have told the princesses. Not today. Not like this. I shouldn't have come here; I shouldn't have called Abbott; I shouldn't be a witch; I shouldn't exist.

The places they touched throb. In the moment, I was fine; I was me; I was waiting for it to be over. And even in the boat, it was okay—what happened seemed small and quick, and it was over, so we could row away from it and that would be it.

But it's an hour or two later, and it has stretched out, a thing that is happening instead of a thing that happened, which makes no sense, because there isn't a royal anywhere to be seen. Only the smell of the princesses' fear making the air sweet and salty, but I've gotten used to that.

"I'm cold. Are you cold?" I ask, trying to put a name to this feeling. But no, that's not right. "Or, like, hot?"

Abbott pulls me toward him again, and it's good, but also not, to be touched right now. He knows the jerk of my body, and he pulls away, tries to be the exact right amount of close to me, but I don't know what that amount could possibly be.

I put a finger to my lips and try to make them belong to me again. They're drier than I'm used to. Like a lizard adhered to my face. I don't like it, so I jump my hand away and try to find something familiar to rest it on. My thigh doesn't feel like my thigh and my hand doesn't feel like my hand and my hair is in tangles and couldn't possibly be mine either.

So I sit down in the Barren Fields, and I plunge my hand into the earth. It's dusty and as dry as my lips. But it's more real than my body or face. I dig my hand into the soil, letting dirt gather under my fingernails.

"Abbott," I say, "am I here?" He looks at all of me, all the parts that I guess belong to me but don't feel like it.

"You're here," he says.

148

"List everything you see," I say, because it's what worked for my mother, and I need something real to hang on to. I wait, but there's nothing for Abbott to list. We are in the Barren Fields. There's nothing.

"Dirt," Abbott says. "You."

I dig farther down. My whole hand up to my wrist is covered in the dirt. Then my wrist is covered too. The ground has some give to it, so it's not hard to cover myself, to hide my fingers, to imagine my whole body sinking into the ground and staying there.

The idea sounds a little sweet, a little irresistible. "What if I left?" I say.

"We need you," Abbott says. He looks sure, even though mere days ago he rolled his eyes at the idea of anything changing.

"You said—"

"I saw you with those princesses, walking through town. I watched you go by. And it felt—"

"Like a shimmer of something?" I'm thinking of that last moment with Jane, when she maybe didn't want me to go, or at least didn't want me to die, and how it felt like a seismic shift, before feeling like nothing at all.

"Yes. A shimmer," Abbott says. "I don't know why. But I felt it. Maybe others did too."

He gets up, and the line of him is straight and narrow and a little delicate, too.

"The things you do matter," Abbott says.

"Same to you," I say, because I am certain that Abbott is

the most beautiful boy in all of Ever, and in a day or two, we are going to need a lock of his hair. I wanted the princesses to see this person I care about, to see the way he lives, and the way it hurts. And I knew that Abbott, at least, would give them what they needed.

"Hasn't been true yet," Abbott says with a shrug. "But maybe someday soon. Look. You're—tired."

It's not the word for what I am, but he knows and I know that I don't want to talk about what I am right now.

"Let me walk you the rest of the way home."

"I'm not ready," I say.

"So let's stay here," he says. He doesn't ask me how I feel about what just happened, or how it went with the princesses. He doesn't critique what I ended up doing with the spell, and he doesn't make any more suggestions. I know his brain is thinking, always, only, about how to make Ever better. But right now he sits with me like we are Abbott and Reagan who have always been friends. Who will always be friends.

It's the one thing that makes me feel the tiniest bit *here*.

My hand's still in the dirt. The rest of me has to sit in the sun; Abbott and I are the only things in this whole field that are alive.

But just barely.

13.

JANE

They are eating roast chicken with apple stuffing, and I am trying to make the air be enough. The smell stops at my nose. I work to inhale it through my mouth, but even that taste isn't allowed for me. Even that small almost-pleasure is forbidden.

But for once I don't care.

My father didn't do that, I think, watching him offer Grace an extra helping of potatoes.

My father wouldn't do that, I think as he asks about our day.

My father isn't like that, I think when he smiles at me with an unsaid apology for the food, like he does every night. A quiet moment between us that shows me he sees me; he knows my pain; he respects what I'm going through.

Not my father, I think, until he smiles at the newest attendant, and I watch her eyes dart to an older attendant, who makes a tiny *come here* hand gesture that I must be misunderstanding. The young attendant scurries to the older one, who grabs her elbow and doesn't let go.

My body aches from the day. The walking. Drum's wandering eyes. The hands that touched me. The words that were

151

said. It's all bruising me, and now I'm seeing things that aren't really there: looks and movements and elbow squeezes that are probably the hallucinations of a very hungry princess.

Except: there is also the tingling in my fingers, the glow between my shoulder blades. The first good feeling my body has been allowed in five years. I don't tell them about it. I barely let myself know it.

"To Ever," Dad says, raising a glass of wine to our four glasses of berry juice and one glass of nothing.

"To Ever," we echo.

And then there's silence. He hasn't asked us what we thought of the broken-down houses or the dirt roads. He isn't making conversation about the spell, about Drum, about the friendship they used to have and why it ended. He isn't seeing if we've made progress. It's as if he doesn't care. I make fists with my hands and try to squeeze that thought away, but it lingers. Repeats itself in my head until it sounds a little bit like the truth.

He is licking his lips from the chicken, a greasy sheen on his chin that makes me ill. I want to be outside with my mother, imitating her stillness. But Dad insisted we all stay together in these troubling times.

I look at my sisters, to see if they are thinking the same things I am, if they are working just as hard to remove Reagan's words from their heads, from their bodies. Because what she said is now making my legs twitch and my heart beat and my mind circle around and around, no matter how sternly I tell it not to.

"I remember my first time stepping out in Ever," he says as if one of us has asked. "It didn't look anything like my home of Farr. Farr is icy. Cold in temperature, but also temperament. Not a friendly people. Then I walked through Ever, and people waved hello; the sun beat down on my head so hard it got burned on the top; there were fruit trees everywhere, warm pears hanging off branches, begging to be eaten. I stole a dozen. I couldn't stop myself." He shakes his head and grins at the memory.

"Whose were they?" I ask. I want him to recount sitting in a garden with some poor people of Ever, sharing pears and stories and worries and hopes. I want an image of the Good King, not one who takes what he wants simply because it is dangling in front of him.

Dad shrugs.

The shrug is wrong, but it's also so small I can ignore it, it doesn't have to mean anything; I decide it is just a shrug, just forgetting the rest of the story, not a sign of something else, not the slow unwinding of my father.

"Mom loved pears," Alice says. Alice does not usually speak at dinner. She is too worn out to do anything but take slow bites and sigh after the effort of every swallow. She isn't really eating at all, in fact. She is frowning and playing with her napkin. She is glancing at the attendants and at the rest of us. She has also seen the shrug.

I look at Grace and Eden and Nora. They have seen the shrug too. Maybe they are chronicling every time he has shrugged. Maybe we all are.

"Good memory, Alice," Dad says, and even this sounds a little mean, given how bad Grace's memory is. It's a tiny carelessness that wouldn't have registered yesterday but today feels heavy and awkward in the room.

Mom isn't in the memory of his day in Ever eating pears, of course. She's never set foot in Ever. Only kings can walk through and steal sun-soaked pears from the trees. My stomach asks for a pear right now, and I close my eyes to remind my body of its reality. It happens from time to time. My body rebels, forgetting it's cursed, and I have to tell it to quiet down.

"There weren't any pears today," Nora says, and I love her for it.

"Well, no," Dad says. "Those witches took them away."

"Why?" Grace asks.

"The Spell of Famine," Dad says.

"But why?" Grace asks.

"Bitter witches, making life hard for all of us. Taking advantage of our kindness. Being vengeful." He shrugs. It's not a real answer. It's a list of things he says the witches are, but it doesn't say why they might be that way, what happened that led to the spell.

I wonder if my sisters hear the negative space in his sentences. Nora purses her lips in a manner that tells me she does.

"Have you ever—" I start, wanting to ask about Reagan's mother, so that my brain can put it aside and think of something, anything else. Maybe I want to hear him laugh it off or look confused at the idea of it, or tell me he would never do something like that. Mostly, I need him to say something that promises it isn't true.

But I can't ask the question. My lips won't let me. Neither will Eden, whose hand grabs my knee under the table and squeezes me into silence.

Dad serves himself another heap of chicken. His calmness makes me less calm. Time is passing, the spell is turning Truer, my fingers and shoulder blades and the moat are shimmering, and he's eating chicken and remembering the past like he has all the time in the world.

I tell myself that it's for us. He doesn't want us to get frightened. His calmness is meant to give us strength. For five years he has tried to be both father and mother, both king and queen. He knows how to fight and how to recede. He knows how to rile us up and calm us down. He knows how to braid hair, how to make the perfect cup of tea, how to sit on the lawn and talk, how to leave us alone when we need our space.

Still. I wish I saw a wavering of strength from him now. A little bit of worry. A wondering what will happen, if we can't break the spell.

Or an offer to help us.

"We have a lot to decide," he says, his voice still cheery. He tears into the chicken, the flesh surrendering to his large fingers, the juices going everywhere. A spot lands on my hand and I try to lick it off, but it vanishes before my tongue can touch it. I let my lips stay against my fingers and suck suck suck at nothing.

I know from the way they all look at me that I'm getting worse, I'm getting more desperate.

"Jane," Dad says. "That's enough. You're still a princess. A lady. You're still—you're *very*—desired. All of you."

I don't like the way he says "desired." It frightens me.

I look away from him in the hope that will stop my mind from doing this terrible new math, asking if a shrug and a glance and a tone of voice and a way of eating chicken can add up to something terrible.

My gaze finds its way to Nora's mouth. Usually the last place I want to look, a mouth eating, but right now it's better than looking at my father. Nora's mouth makes fast, definitive movements. It is Nora who can be brave and reckless and curious. It is Nora who can be calm when everything is in chaos. I'm jealous for a moment that she could be a good queen too. Because she's eaten. Because she's rested and fine. Because being loveless keeps her head clear.

The envy is a new surge, and it's ugly. I try to hold it back, but it's hard to stop. Time is vanishing. Nora is going to be queen. I am going to die in three days. My father—

Nothing is the way it was supposed to be.

"I think we need to talk about it," Dad says. "About all the possibilities."

"There's only one possibility," I say.

"Breaking the spell," Dad says. "I understand that's what you want."

"Need." My voice breaks on the word. I break on it. My mind keeps wandering into more and more places I don't want it to go. What it would feel like to die. How long it would take after the spell turns True. If dying from starvation hurts. I am used to the empty stomach and the tired limbs. Would there be some other, new feeling? An unbearable one?

"The spell isn't broken yet. And I have been asked for each of your hands in marriage. Every single one of you. More than once. Princes. Princesses. Dukes. Soar. Nethering. Farr. Wherever you'd like to go." Dad doesn't look at me. He'd see my terror if he did. It's probably why he's staring out the window instead of at any of us.

"Dad?" I say as gently as I can. "I don't think we're worried about that right now. Marrying. Princes. Duchesses. Whatever."

"People want to marry us?" Grace asks. Her voice is light and airy with hope and forgetting. I wish she could remember this afternoon. The things they said. The places they touched.

The thing Reagan said.

And then, just as quickly, I'm flushed with relief that she doesn't, that she never will.

"I'll explain later," I say. She nods as if she understands, but I can see the dreamy look on her face. She's imagining a royal wedding, the Princess of Thorner dressed in white, her legs long, her lips soft.

"You can say no to anyone you want to say no to," Dad goes on. Even these words are strange after what Reagan has said. I watch Nora fidget in her chair. Alice shivers with something. "But we still have to talk about who we are now. It's different. Things are— Eden's Thirteenth Birthday proved that things are now—we are now—we're powerful. After all these years, we finally matter to them. We are finally more than the place that lost a princess. And the kingdoms are ready to come together. Eighty years is a long time to wait and worry and wonder. A long time to try to rebuild trust and unity. And we are entering a new era now."

My father's face does something I've never seen it do before. There's a blush and a glow. He looks younger all of a sudden. But also like he's not exactly ours anymore. I want to grab him by the shoulders and force him to look outside, to look at Mom. I want to make him face her frozen features, her vacant eyes, the way the glass obscures her aliveness.

A terror snakes its way through my body. *Maybe he doesn't care.* I shake my head, trying to get the thought out of there. But it sticks. It stays. I can't shake it. He is talking about other kingdoms and power and respect and all these lofty ideas that are impossible to care about when you are watching your body wilt, your sisters suffer, your mother exist entirely outside of life.

It should be impossible for him, too, to think about our place in the kingdoms, the legacy we might leave behind, the power we could amass.

But it isn't impossible for him. Not at all. Above us are paintings of royals who came before us. Some are our relatives; some are from other times in Ever's history, when different families were in charge. Families with white skin and brown, families with two kings or two queens, families with big smiles and forced smiles and no smiles at all. The history of Ever is complicated and long and eclectic, but Dad wants it to end with us, for our family to rule forever.

It sounded so important, years ago. Days ago, even. It makes less sense today. And looking at all the portraits of rulers, I'm wondering why our family has been in charge for so many years, almost one hundred already. It's the kind of question I might have asked Mom five years ago or Dad five days ago.

But today I can't. I wouldn't trust the answer.

No one is eating anymore. Their plates are still full, but none of us can think about food.

"What would Mom think of this new era you're ushering in?" I ask, hoping that's enough to remind him of everything he's talking about, everything he's willing to sacrifice for his kingdom. He shakes his head, like I've misunderstood some vital part of what he's saying.

"Your mother loves Ever as much as I do. More."

"How can we know?" I say. "We can't exactly ask her. And you're saying—she'd be in there forever. She'd be a statue. Gone."

"I miss her as much as you all do. So do her subjects. What the witch did—it's terrible. But other kingdoms—we have spent years lighting candles the witches say are enchanted and hoping for things to be okay. And now, finally, because of you, because of your beautiful mother, things have changed." I am looking at his face, trying to see my father. I see a king who is worried about his kingdom. I do not see my father who lets me sit in the throne when I need to feel something other than hungry, when he can tell that I am losing my will to be queen. I do not see the father who cried when my mother froze, who sat next to her in the evenings right after the spell was cast, to tell her about our days.

It's been a while since I've seen him huddled next to the glass. It's been a long while. He hasn't answered my questions, hasn't even acknowledged that what he's suggesting destroys everyone he's supposed to love. He uses words that sound big and profound but have no meaning. He sounds like the narrator of a fairy tale about our lives, like we are already a story they will tell later, a legend about enchanted princesses who died, in pain, one by one, and their mother who still lives on the castle's lawn, a reminder of what Ever came from, like the portraits on the walls of other ruling families, other ways of being. Dad is talking about us like we are people they will light candles for, people they will paint pictures of to hang in the dining room, like we are already gone.

"Our lives have changed," he says with a final nod that means he thinks we're done discussing this.

"They've been ruined," I say. "You mean to say our lives changed when the witch ruined everything."

"We never had a Birthday like that before," Dad says. "We've never— I find you girls absolutely beautiful. Breathtaking. Since the moment you were born. Each of you."

He pauses. There's a "but." There shouldn't be one, but there is. "The world doesn't always see our children the way we do," he goes on. He is careful with his words, like this conversation is a recipe, and too much salt or cilantro or lemon peel could derail the whole thing. *He is often careful,* I think for the first time ever. I've never noticed the way he watches his words as they come out, how deliberate he is with his movements. "And now the world sees you the way I see you. As special. As the most deserving and desirable and important princesses the kingdoms have ever seen. That's a direct quote from the papers in Nethering, if you can believe it."

"I can believe it," Nora says. Her voice growls. She is looking for him too. Our father, the Good and Gentle King. I'd settle for even a glimpse right now. Instead, all I can see is Reagan, waist-deep in water, looking anything but deliberate or careful or calculating.

"And what did the papers in Nethering say back when a princess of Ever was kidnapped?" I ask. "Was she beautiful too? So beautiful they couldn't help taking her?"

"Jane. You're tired. I can see that. But you need to calm yourself. You're upsetting the attendants." I look to the walls where they are leaning their bodies. They are crowded together as always, their shoulders touching. He's not wrong. They do look nervous. But maybe they always look nervous. Have I ever noticed? Have I ever thought to look at them for longer than the length of time it takes to give an order?

"Can't you see what this all means for our kingdom?" Dad asks. He finally, finally looks at me. "Jane. You love Ever. You want to be its queen. You must see what I see. Look what you've inspired. Look how adored you've become. That must feel good. Before you weren't—well, and now you're—there are other princesses, in other kingdoms, that are beautiful.

But beautiful isn't as good as enchanted. We see that now."

There are a dozen things in what my father said that cut me. But the awful, vain part of me only hears that he doesn't think we're beautiful. I will die if we don't break our spell, my mother is trapped in glass, and I still fight the desperate feeling of wanting to be pretty. Wanting him to think I'm pretty. He said it like it's something we knew already, and I don't think I did. Not really. I knew I wasn't as beautiful as the princess from Thorner or the twins from Farr. But I thought my father loved my eyes and that I had my mother's cheekbones and that maybe I was a special kind of lovely that was even bigger and brighter than the royalty from Thorner and Farr.

Dad's words tell me that isn't true, though. What's beautiful about me is what I lack. It's a spell someone else placed on me. It's the thing I hate most about myself.

And here I am, so thin my bones show, and all I want is for my father to think I'm beautiful.

And finally, three days from the maybe end of everything, he does.

And they did too. The men in the woods. The women laughing alongside them. The people who wondered what my body felt like, who laughed at my fear.

"What are you saying?" Nora asks, except I think she knows. I think we all know. Even un-remembering Grace hears something wrong in the words our father is laying out.

"Sometimes it's our job, as royalty, to embrace the hardships placed upon our kingdom. To set an example. To confront something difficult with dignity. That's the lesson we learned from the War We Won. We fought back, and all it did was cause pain. We attacked other kingdoms, and they fought back. And after all of that, our princess never returned. We never found out what happened to her. Probably just some disgruntled person acting out. We were only safe when we let go, invited the witches to live in our kingdom, stopped worrying about our personal needs, and put Ever first."

"But the Famine—" I say. "And the Spell of Without. And the kidnapped princess who might still be in pain—" I keep cutting myself off, because the wrongness in his words is so wide. We haven't been safe. We aren't safe right now.

Except for him. He's safe, I suppose. He has always been safe. And fed. And happy. And beloved.

Dad puts a hand over his heart and gazes at the candle on the table. It does not so much as flicker. "We'll never stop waiting for that princess. For the spells to be broken," he goes on, "but Ever deserves a new story."

"What do we have to do?" Grace asks, her eyes, impossibly, squinting more.

"He wants us to accept our lives with humility and elegance." Nora says the words like they are jokes. "He wants us to be okay where we are. To surrender to the spell. To stop asking questions, like they stopped asking questions about the kidnapped princess. And, probably, to marry whatever fancy royal person comes along."

We wait for Dad to contradict her, to correct her. He pauses and plays with his hands, making his fingers into a steeple, then making his fists into balls, then settling on making a triangle with his fingers and thumbs, an empty triangle that floats in front of him.

"You can marry who you like," he says at last, careful again. A teaspoon of coriander. A quarter cup of dill. A half table-spoon of compromise. "That's always been the case. It always will be. But your role in the kingdoms—it's different now. We have a road to safety. You are that road. Because of what you sacrificed."

"What was stolen from us," I correct.

"There is nothing more queenly than doing what is best for the kingdom," Dad says, directly to me. He keeps skirting around the issue of my death, as if it's an uncomfortable detail and not the main event.

"I'm not getting married," Nora says.

"We're breaking the spell," I say, louder and stronger than even Nora.

Dad takes three long strides across the room, to the win-dow. I imagine our subjects are out there, watching our mother in her box, taking in the expanse of her without anyone to tell them to avert their eyes, without any threat of rudely lingering too long on a breast or a thigh.

"Ever is complicated," Dad goes on. "But it's still—people love you girls. They love everything you are."

"They love what we *aren't*," I say. My stomach rumbles. It's an earthquake of desire in there, and I know that's what they love—the emptiness. The desperation of wanting some-thing you can't have that everyone else needs. The allure of all the things we can't do, all the things our bodies refuse, all the ways that we've been made weaker and smaller and worse.

It just hadn't occurred to me that my dad liked that about us too.

"Why did the witch cast the spell, Dad?" I ask. I say the words clearly, crisply, so that there's no mistaking them. "Why would a witch cast this spell on us? There must be a reason."

"Witches are very unpredictable—" he starts.

"No," Eden says.

"Excuse me?" Dad turns his whole body toward Eden. As if she were the witch.

"Spells aren't random. They aren't arbitrary or thoughtless. Witches don't cast spells for fun. Witches are serious. They pay for their spells forever."

Dad shakes his head and looks for an argument. "You don't understand witches," he says.

Eden's right, of course. There isn't much to do as a princess, and even less to do when your sisters can't eat or sleep or love or learn. Eden had nothing but hours upon hours to read and study.

And what would a little girl whose family is Spellbound choose to learn everything about?

The witches who cast the spell, of course.

We know this, Dad knows this, and I'd bet anything even our frozen mother knows this.

The part of me that remembers the history of Ever nods and stands next to my sister. Every bit of magic a witch does results in a new skirt around her waist. They cast some small spells and get sheer skirts in exchange. Some of these spells might be frivolous. The payment for them isn't large. They might make mistakes along the way; witches aren't perfect, especially the young ones. But a large spell, like the one cast on us, would result in a heavy burden for the witch. Even a young witch would know this. Even a young witch wouldn't be able to cast a spell so large without a very good reason.

The tiny, uncomfortable part of me that heard Reagan today in the boat stands up straighter, more alert than I've ever been. I am waiting for something from my father. But I don't know exactly what.

"A spell is a lesson that there's no other way to learn," Eden says, quoting from a thousand textbooks we've read over the years. I hadn't noticed before how bright Eden's eyes are. They are a brilliant blue, so sharp and clear they look like a piece of sky.

My father shakes his head. He tries to regain his composure. "You're so young—" he starts, as if we don't understand a thing.

He shrugs again. The way he shrugged about stolen pears and a stolen princess and now our stolen lives. I close my eyes. I want to open them and see this room the way I used to: my father smiling special smiles at each of us and attendants happily flitting around, bringing out different foods and drinks, a sunset outside the window, all the answers to every question I've ever had answerable by my father, the Good and Gentle King.

It's hard to know what a Good and Gentle King is, if

you've never been outside the castle. It's impossible to know what a kingdom needs, what a kingdom *is*, if you've never stepped onto its soil.

I open my eyes. There's the Always Day sun and the long table piled with food and the attendants and my father, but I can't make it look the way it used to look. My father helps himself to another piece of chicken. Somewhere in Ever, people are fighting over half a turnip, some slices of stale bread, a crop of tiny potatoes.

Somewhere in the Home on the Hill, Reagan and her mother are trying to protect a kingdom that is falling apart.

Sometime long ago, this place belonged to other families, and now it's ours, and I don't know why or how or if we deserve it.

I never wondered before, about deserving it.

And here we are, watching my father eat chicken and shrug away our worries.

"What did you do?" I ask, my voice low first, then louder. "What did you do to the witches?" My feet are rooted to the floor. I stand up. It feels good, to stand. I'm so solid I'm not even hungry. I feel a little like Reagan, standing in the water, not wavering even as her skirts try to pull her down. I feel a little like a queen, the kind that is still and quiet even when they're not trapped in a box.

Mostly I feel like a person who has three days to try to survive, and I am talking to a man who is making it harder for me to get out alive. He keeps licking his goddamn fingers and adjusting his ridiculous robe and looking somewhere else, his eyes not quite on us, as if there are a hundred other things on his mind.

How often has he looked past me? Or someone else? How many times has he not cared about someone else's needs over his own?

And how often have I?

My heart beats out a terror that could make me weak but is making me strong instead.

"Tell us what you did to the witches," I say again. "Just tell us."

Maybe I sound like I'm accusing him, but all I want is to see something that tells me Reagan is a liar, Reagan misunderstood, Reagan's mother is crazy, the world is the way I want it to be.

Show me she's wrong, I say in my head. I beg him to be the man he's promised us that he is. The one they've written songs about, built statues of in the center of town. The one I've felt lucky to have. The one who would do anything for us.

He doesn't say anything. He half smiles, starts to roll his eyes like it's a big joke, except I can feel my heart slowing, my body begging to give up. I can feel three days left turning to two. I can feel something Slow turning True.

"You have to help us," I say. "You're the king. You're our father. You have to help us break the spell. The spell that you caused. You did this. You keep shrugging. Why are you shrugging at something this huge? How can you shrug at me when I'm going to die?"

"Jane. My god. You're hysterical," my father says. "Look at you. You're out of control. You need to calm down."

I almost believe him, that he did nothing wrong, that he's never done a single wrong thing. I really almost do. He's so confident, his voice at once sure and light, dismissive and patronizing.

Except I'm not hysterical. Inside, maybe, my body is rebelling, is working itself up into some kind of frenzy. But I have never stood more solidly on my feet. I have never been so sure of something I have to do. I don't yell or flail or throw a tantrum right here on the floor of the castle, even though it would feel good to let go like that.

I am not hysterical.

I am not making something out of nothing.

I am fighting the Spell of Without and asking for his help. And he is refusing.

He won't answer why. We don't know why they stole that princess eighty years ago, and he's saying we don't know why this spell was cast, but spells have reasons and princesses don't just disappear and I am not out of control. I do not need to calm down.

Not now. Not ever.

My father is lying.

My father, the king, is a liar.

And if he is a liar, it might mean that Reagan is telling the truth.

My fingers feel a shimmer. The palms of my hands hurt. My shoulders lift on their own, a jolt of strength.

I look at my sisters to see if they know it too. If they feel the same shimmer in their hands, the same sureness in their hearts.

They stretch their fingers. They squint at the man before us. They clear their throats, and Alice looks like she would cry if she had the energy.

The smell of chicken is still in the air. My father doesn't know what I would do for a bite of it. He doesn't know what my body is telling me to do. He is a man in a robe who doesn't seem to know anything about desperation.

He'll see. I'll show him what it means to fight for your life.

14.

REAGAN

We can't sleep; the smell of royal fear is too thick in the air. Willa climbs into bed with me, nuzzling her nose into my pillow, asking me to tell her stories until she falls asleep. "I can't sleep with all that smell," she says.

I nod. I can't either. None of us can.

When she finally drifts off, I wander downstairs to be near my grandmother. I've avoided her since coming home. I didn't want to know what she would say about the Spell of Always Day. I didn't want to see her disappointed face or get another lecture about all the ways my magic is failing her.

But she's the only person I want to talk to now. I want to ask her about what I felt with Jane, that little glimmer of something. The light on the moat. The shimmery thing that Abbott felt too.

She's where she always is, in her chair, smoothing the wrinkles in her hundreds of skirts. I take her in. Something in her face reminds me of Jane. It's in her mouth, hiding around her jaw. Even the way she sits—straight-backed, trying very hard though she is physically suffering—is just like the princess.

"You look a little like Princess Jane," I say, even though I'm not sure either of them would want to hear it.

Grandmother looks startled; then the look passes, and I guess I imagined it.

"Maybe this is how a person looks when they are waiting and hoping for a spell to be broken," she says pointedly.

"I haven't smelled it like this in a long time," Mom says instead of greeting me.

"Strong," Grandmother says.

"It was a bad day," I say. "We're all afraid."

"Yes," Grandmother says. "We are."

"You shouldn't cast spells out of fear, Reagan," Mom says. She gestures to the sky, to the Always Day.

"There was a good reason," I say, which is what they're really wanting to know. I want them to believe me, but I can see that they don't trust me anymore. My grandmother wants me to be a different kind of witch, a better kind. More like Willa or my mother.

Grandmother looks at me with raised eyebrows, and for the second or third or tenth time today, I miss my lonely existence in AndNot. She folds her hands in her lap. Her skirts rustle. "Bethly," she says, giving my mother the gentlest sort of look, "it's time."

Mom takes three deep breaths. Each one feels longer and sadder than the last. "It's been good to have you back," she says.

"It's good to be back," I reply, as if from a script someone else has written. We aren't usually formal like this, my mother and I. But things went wrong when we spoke in the morning, so we are more careful this evening.

"You've grown," Grandmother says.

"Yes," Mom says. "You've grown. And the older you get, the more potent your magic is."

"Powerful," Grandmother says.

"You are a powerful witch. You were before. And you are even more so now."

"Thank you," I say, even though it doesn't sound like a compliment the way she's saying it.

"Your grandmother is a powerful witch too. I'm not. Not like you. I consider that lucky."

"Your magic is—"

"My magic is simple. It's elegant. But it isn't big. Yours is big, Reagan. And big magic can be dangerous."

"*Is* dangerous," Grandmother corrects her. "And that attitude. Like your mother. Wanting things to change. Not knowing when to stop." She is looking at me hard, like I might be hiding something on my face that she's missed until now. A new freckle. A different shade of eye color. A wrinkle.

The things she's saying are true about me, I guess, but certainly not about my mother. Still, I don't correct her.

"When someone has dangerous magic, we have to be careful," Mom says. Her hands shake. "I'm so lucky I didn't have that."

"That's why you sent me to AndNot." I don't want to be dangerous, so I try to make myself sweet and easy and fun like Willa.

"We've spoken a lot, your grandmother and I, about how to proceed," Mom says. Her voice shakes faster than her hands. I'm starting to feel seasick from it.

"Proceed?"

"With your place. With your role in the family, in the Home."

"My role is your daughter, the disgraced witch. The fuckup." I mean to be humble, to listen and wait and do whatever she wants me to do. All I've ever wanted is to make her happy. The spell itself was to make her happy. But I fail, always. I fail at being quiet and sweet; I fail at protecting my mother; I fail at getting revenge; I fail at knowing what in the world she even wants from me. Five years in AndNot didn't help me figure it out. Maybe nothing will.

My grandmother shakes her head. She's disappointed in the way I've turned out too.

"We want you to stay," Mom goes on. "But what you did—you haven't been forgiven."

"By you?"

"By the family," Mom says. It pinches, because she doesn't rush to say of course she forgives me. "Those girls—you hurt them. And the queen. And you don't apologize, Reagan. Not really. All that time away, you were supposed to reconsider everything. You were supposed to regret what you did." She's shaking her head now too. The two of them in sync with their shame. "You were supposed to consider your family, and instead you're taking advice from a farmhand—"

Witches don't lie. I wish we did. "The king deserved to

174

be hurt," I say. "He deserved it for what he did to you. And you always said that parents are more hurt by their children's suffering than by their own. So I did what I thought would hurt him the most."

"It's my fault," Mom says. "I never should have told you about what he did to me. You were too young to understand, and too young to handle it. I knew that better than anyone."

Now it's me shaking my head.

"We all do the best we can," Grandmother says. "But that's not always enough. And, Reagan, your best isn't enough."

The room grows. I've heard people say that in terrible moments everything shrinks, but the room right now expands so much that I am tiny inside it. It grows so much that I am lost.

"*You* cast the Spell of Famine," I say. It's another thing we never speak of. That the Barren Fields are barren because of my grandmother. "It's caused pain. *You've* caused pain too."

My mother shoots me a look that tells me to shut up, but my grandmother's response is slow and measured. "Yes. I cast that spell. Do you know why?"

I shrug. We've come up with dozens of reasons, Willa and I, over the years. But we've never asked. You don't question my grandmother.

"For the things they let happen. To your mother. To others. I gave it one last try, Reagan. One last punishment to try to shake them into caring about the king and what he does. All the royals, what they all do. What so many people do." She shakes her head, at the royals, I guess, but at all of us really. The ways we are all, always, letting her down.

Mom rubs her forehead. She's heard this story over and over, but I'm only now understanding what little I've been told, how many stories there are underneath the stories I've spent my whole life learning.

"I cast the Spell of Famine, and I built that spell carefully, so it could be broken if the king stepped down. A True Spell that could be Undone under the right circumstances. All he had to do was step down." Grandmother looks at me. She's teaching me something I never bothered to learn before. She tried to tell me a hundred times, probably. A good spell takes time to build. A good spell is delicately balanced and does exactly what you want it to do. A bad spell is one cast from fear or anger or sadness. Or even love. A bad spell doesn't have the breaking built in. I nod. I want her to know I'm understanding now, finally. She goes on. "That's it. I even told him he could tell his kingdom he did it for them. He could walk away a hero, if he would just leave the throne, let the queen rule alone, or let a new royal family come in. He could live somewhere far away by himself or with his family. But he wouldn't. He said I was unwell. That he'd be a hero anyway. That he'd help them through the Famine. That it would make him look even better. And that was it. That was the last of it. Our final try to do something about it."

"It didn't work," I say. It's not a question, because I live in Ever and I can see that things are worse, not better. Still, I try to straighten my back and raise my chin so that we can be two witches who made mistakes and not a perfect grandmother and her disappointment of a granddaughter.

"Of course it didn't work," Grandmother says. "That's what we learned. That type of spell makes things worse. So we don't mess with things anymore. Even if the spell is ever broken, the damage it's done, the people who have already died, already fallen ill—well. The spell was True, not Slow, so there's no fixing what's been done. Even the best-built True Spells are dangerous. So now we try to help when we can. We keep the moat filled with fish. We watch the weather. We send spells of ease when someone is suffering. We try."

"So that's it. You cast one spell, saw it failed, and never tried to help again?" I think about the people of Ever lighting their candles, waiting for the princess to return. And now the witches, waiting for goodness to return, for a king to change, for a people to see something they don't want to see. All of us just waiting for something that might be impossible.

"Over the years we cast dozens of spells," Grandmother says. "You think I let that happen to my daughter and did nothing? But our spells weren't reckless. We thought them through. You have to think a spell through. A True one especially, but a Slow one too, Reagan. We tried our best. We're still trying! We're waiting for the king to break the Spell of Famine. His people are getting tired of him eating whatever he wants while they suffer. Things will shift. They'll see. And when they see, he'll leave the throne. And meanwhile they light the Enchanted Candles, and that means they aren't forgetting the past. Change is slow. We are patient."

"The Spell of Famine was powerful and hurt people too," I say, my voice quiet with the surprise of disagreeing with my grandmother.

"When I cast the Spell of Famine, I was eighty-three years old," Grandmother says. "I considered other spells. Other ways to fix things. And after a lot of thought, I decided on the Spell of Famine. I knew what I was doing, casting a very serious True Spell, and I accepted that responsibility. I have earned the right to use powerful magic. You are so young to have cast such an enormous spell. Too young. And you come back and still don't understand—" She breathes heavily, my grandmother. "You've cast *another* spell in just a few days here! Again without thinking about what it means, about what other harm it could cause. We cast spells for a good reason. Your fleeting feelings aren't a good reason, Reagan. A good reason is one that's thought through, one that is considered. Look outside! Another enormous burst of magic without consulting any of us! Without *thinking*. Always Day? That's a spell *I've* never even used—" Speaking is hard on her body; the breaths she takes are hidden underneath pounds of fabric, and she has to stop herself from going on, from getting any more upset.

"The spell needs to be Undone," Mom says. "And if it isn't, we have to let you go. Somewhere else. Another kingdom. Whatever kingdom you like. You can return to AndNot. You liked it there. With the ocean. But if the spell isn't broken, you can't stay here."

"I—" Nothing comes. "I—" Still nothing. No words.

"We had decided to stay away," my mother says. "We

were waiting for time and distance to do their magic. We weren't going to cast any more spells. We were maintaining the kingdom at rest. And then you—well. I think if the Spell of Without is Undone, we can find a way to make it all work again. But if not, and you stay here, keeping everyone on edge—we won't survive that." She pauses. She wants to be very clear. "I won't survive that. The spell—it made it worse, Reagan. It made me remember even more what he did. I used to think about it only at night, after a nightmare, when I saw him. The last five years—I think about it every single moment of every single day. What he did to me. And what you did to them. And how unfair it all is, to have things taken without permission."

I crumble. I've stayed strong over five years, bearing the weight of my mother's upset, lonely in my cottage in AndNot, missing Abbott and Willa and the rest of my family, trying to understand why things went the way they did. But I'm tired from all that strength. I'm tired from today, from the things that were taken from me, too, without my permission.

"They all think he's so gentle and kind and good. The Good King. I couldn't stand it. Witches tell the truth. And that wasn't the truth." I'm begging for my life, but Mom isn't looking at me. She's looking at Grandmother.

"I wanted to forget all about it," Mom says. "Ten years ago we tried the Spell of Famine, and when that didn't work—it was time to move on. We had taken enough from people who didn't deserve it. It was my right to pretend it didn't happen, to let go. To try to survive that way."

"You weren't surviving! You were— He might have done it to someone else! I bet he has. You're a witch! You're a fucking witch who was raped by a king, and you want to just sit back and let him do it again and again and again. You want to sit back and let him be the perfect Good King forever?"

Mom steps back. She steps back and back and back. She holds my grandmother's hand.

"There are a hundred ways to be strong," Mom says. "There are a hundred ways to move on. A hundred ways to survive. I get to choose the way I want to survive."

I know from the way she says the word "survive" that I won't be hearing another word from her. We stand in that certain silence. They have told me what has to be done.

Undone. They have told me what has to be Undone.

"This is my home," I say. "I'm your daughter. Your granddaughter."

My grandmother nods her head. She looks sad but sure. "There used to be more magic, you know," she says. "Much more. But they—people with power—they didn't want anyone else to—they were scared. So now we are here."

"I don't know what you're saying," I say. I'm not supposed to speak that way to my grandmother, but she barely finished a sentence. Her words are a soup of half thoughts.

"We are the witches of Ever. We are what's left of magic. And it's my job to protect us." Grandmother's voice is steadier now, the words still nonsensical and the ideas still flimsy and not mine to understand. But her voice, at least, is strong. "Ever is my home. It's my job to protect Ever, too. Sometimes those things are in conflict. But we do our best. I protect the king-dom and the magic and it doesn't always work, but it keeps things at rest."

She keeps looking at the Enchanted Candle, like it mat-ters more than I do.

"I thought you were meant to protect *me*," I say. I am thinking of nights spent in Grandmother's lap, counting out layers of skirts, cotton and denim and silk and tulle, each tell-ing a tiny bit of a story I was dying to hear. She imprinted the stories onto me and made me promise to remember. She would fill cauldrons full of healing potions when I was sick or hurt, and she cast a strong Security Spell to keep out intruders after an incident with a brick being thrown at my bedroom window when I was seven.

"We have to be at peace with them," Grandmother says, not really responding to what I've said. "Your mother under-stands that. Even after what happened. She understands that all the world's magic is at stake. We don't go to battle. We watch the Enchanted Candle. We let it flicker gold. We hope they come around. We do our best. We stay up here. Away from them. To keep what magic we have left."

"So I'll stay away," I say.

"Too late for that," Grandmother says. "Five years too late for it. Fix it, Reagan. Or we'll send you back to AndNot. There's nothing more to say."

And like that, my grandmother isn't my grandmother. She has my grandmother's long fingers and blue eyes and waterfalls of white hair. She has the smell of her—woody and warm. But she is another being entirely, one who can banish me, without another thought about it.

A long time ago she whispered in my ear that I was special. That I was her favorite. She told me not to tell, and I didn't. I didn't tell a soul. But I kept it locked inside, and it woke me up every morning and sent me to bed every night. The best kind of secret, that lit me up and calmed me down. The only secret I've known about at the Home on the Hill.

But something in the way Grandmother speaks now—in riddles, then dismissing her favorite grandchild—tells me there are more secrets locked inside her.

Ever more.

15.

JANE

Our attendants change us from our brown dresses to our nightgowns. They are white and thick. The castle is cold, no matter what season it is.

"Tomorrow's another day," Olive says. "You will break your spell." The other attendants nod their heads. Sometimes I forget they're with us; then Olive will say something, and I'll remember. She was in the boat. She heard what Reagan said. She knows most things that I know.

I almost tell her what the royals in the woods did. But I don't. If I say it, it will be real. And I don't want that.

Nora's attendant brings out soap for our faces and fingernails; Eden's brings out brushes for our hair. Grace's attendant is busy with Grace, who is more forgetful as the day goes on, just as I am weaker and Alice is more tired. Tomorrow is always a new day; on that, Olive is right.

They wash our faces with damp cloths and brush our hair out. They make us cups of milk, steamed and sprinkled with cinnamon. Except for Olive, who sits by me as my sisters sip away. I remember the taste. Or at least I remember remembering it. It was sweet and thick. It was decadent and calm. It made me sleepy and satisfied.

Maybe it's meant to keep us calm.

I'm not drinking steamed milk with cinnamon, and I am not calm.

I am tired, though. My body is heavy with the wondering what's true, the almost knowing what happened, the worried weight of accepting what Reagan said. My body, my heart, keeps rejecting it.

I'll inhale—*maybe my father is that person*—and then I'll exhale much more loudly—*no, he can't be; he's my father.*

As they all sip steamed milk, my inhales get longer and deeper, my exhales shorter and harder.

Aside from my breathing, we are all quiet. My sisters don't speak. I imagine all of our minds racing through the same questions: *Can this be true? How will we know for sure? Could there be a mistake? Why does it feel so real? Does anyone else know? Do I know? Who is this man? Who are we? What is Ever?*

"There's so much more than the spell," I say to Olive. She bows her head. The other attendants do too.

"You need to focus on the spell first," Olive says. "Then, after—" The word settles in the room like too-bright light, like an ugly odor.

After.

My heart travels at lightning speed to my stomach, then farther down, to my toes, leaving the rest of me desperate and empty.

After.

I don't know if there's an after.

Yesterday I had a father who was a Good and Gentle King and a witch who was awful and a kingdom full of people who loved and respected me.

Today I'm wondering if we have any of that. I look for a sign—any sign—that my father is who he used to be and that Reagan is a liar and that Ever is the kingdom it was in the books I read.

But instead I can only replay the conversation in the moat and the one at the table and the long walk from Drum Drascall's house to the shore, and even though none of those things make sense to me, they all feel more real than the old truths, the old stories, the old life I thought we were all living.

My breathing quickens. "I don't know anything about after," I say. "I don't know anything about anything. I never did."

I start to cry. The tears making their trails down my face shimmer like my fingers did earlier. It's like a vibration, but it doesn't shake. It's a throbbing, but it doesn't beat.

"Jane," Olive says. "Your tears. They're—"

"They're pretty," Grace says. She walks across the room and wipes them from my face.

They glint and glimmer on her fingertips, the way light did on the moat earlier today. An impossible shimmer.

Magic, my brain says, but it can't be.

"It's because of him, so he's going to help us fix it," I say. I don't believe it to be true, but we have more time to break the spell, and Olive is right. First we break the spell. Then we fix the rest of it. "I'm going to talk to him. Without pretending.

Without all the lies. I'm going to tell him what I think is true and what he has to do."

"Jane." Olive tries a single syllable. She might know what I know, but she isn't going to die if the spell isn't broken. Everyone but Alice and me can be slow and methodical and careful and a hundred other things that I cannot be, because I cannot die and leave behind a king who does what this king might have done, a father who cannot possibly be the same father who taught me how to waltz and who read me stories about unicorns and let me play bare legged in the moat even when Mom said no.

"Now," I say, because there isn't time; there isn't any time, and the shimmer on Grace's fingers, the strange feeling on my face, on my arm embolden me. Make me feel less like a princess and more like . . . something else. "Now," I say again, louder.

"Okay," Olive says. "All right. Let me—I'll check on him first."

One of the other attendants—I think her name is Sara, but it could be almost anything—peers over Eden's head. "Are you sure?" she asks. It's a question I've heard a hundred times but never heard at all. Today it stops me.

The other attendants look up from their braiding and brushing and tidying too. Each of them with the same concerned face. One who I think is called Devon straightens themself up. "I can do it," they say.

"No," Olive says. "I'm fine. I'll go."

I hear the words in other moments when they washed over me. Strange half arguments about who would get the king his slippers, who would fetch him when a princess felt sick, who would accompany him to town when his attendant was on a visit home.

Are you sure?

I'll go.

You went last time; I can do it.

Are you okay?

Will you be okay?

It's fine, it's fine, it's fine.

I look at my sisters to see if they hear it: the attendants are scared of our father.

Still, I let Olive leave the room to tell my father I need to speak with him, ignoring the pound of my heart, the slip-slide of my sweating palms. A minute passes. Three. Eight. Twelve. Olive doesn't return to tell me he's ready for me. Alice's attendant prepares her stone-carving tools for her, and they head outside to begin tonight's sculpture. It must feel good, tonight, to bang on rocks, to break down something that seems powerful and unbreakable.

Alice has always known that even the biggest, hardest surfaces can be chipped away at, can change into something else entirely. I am learning, we are learning, that the world is changing in the way it only can when you leave your home and cross a moat and see the world for what it is.

What you should have known it could be.

Nora wanders off to bed, not saying good night. Eden and Grace stay in the dressing room, talking about nothing the way they've done since they were old enough for words.

My heart pounds, waiting for Olive, waiting for what's next.

My body strains to see everything the way it really is, to chip away at the hard surface of stone, to see the truth underneath.

Sixteen minutes pass. Nineteen. Twenty-two and I fly out of the room.

"Where are you going?" Grace asks. "Are you going to bed?"

Eden doesn't ask—she just follows me, and Grace follows her, so when I throw the door of my father's study open, they are at my shoulders. When I see, they are clinging to my hips, breathing into my ears.

Probably I have seen it before, without seeing it. I'm sure I've felt it in the way the attendants hang their heads and lower their voices and skitter this way and that when he approaches.

Probably it has always been this way. I have never had the life I thought I did.

And I have known without knowing.

They are in the far corner of the room. My father and Olive. She is biting her lip like that will make it pass faster. He has one hand on his desk, steadying himself.

But the other. The other is reaching up Olive's skirts.

It happens so fast it's hardly a decision I make, but rather a thing my body does because it thinks it has to, to survive.

I look away.

And by the time I look back, both his hands are on the desk and Olive is a few extra inches away from him, and the moment might never have happened.

Except, of course it fucking *did*.

I miss the doubts I had the second they are gone. I miss

the voice that said *not my father, not the Good King, just because something is starting to seem true doesn't mean it is.*

"My girls! It's past your bedtime. You need your rest," Dad says, like that flash of his hand under Olive's dress didn't happen.

"Ah, the princesses!" another voice says. "It's about time I formally met these enchanted, enchanting young women." I turn to the voice, and it belongs to the King of Soar, who I hadn't seen in the rush of terror when I first opened the door. I look away again and hate myself for it again. Was there a flash of naked skin where the King of Soar's pants stitch together? Did I see a look pass between the two men? Did Olive try to mouth something to me? I don't know. I look away and away and away.

"Excuse me," Olive says. "I need to turn down your bed, Jane." She lifts her head at last, and her face is arranged into a normal expression, but even so, I look away.

It's all I know how to do. It's all I've ever done. I've seen flashes of things. I've seen the edges of something awful my whole life, and I've looked away and locked it up. Over and over and over again. I am letting these things happen. The truth of it takes my breath away, makes me want to escape my own skin.

Olive sweeps by me, and I try to hear something in her footsteps or her breath that tells me what to do, but there's nothing. I feel a rush of wanting my mother. I need there to be someone else in charge, someone I can tell everything to.

I knew at dinner that what Reagan had said was true. Still,

seeing it is awful. Nightmarish. I pull at my skin, wanting to escape it.

I feel Eden's body tremble. Grace's is its usual sturdy self. She didn't see it. Or she's already forgotten it. "It's a pleasure to meet you, Your Majesty," she says, curtsying in the direction of the King of Soar. I don't want him to get one step closer to my sister, but he does, taking her hand and kissing it.

He kisses Eden's hand next, not registering or not caring about the scowl on her face, the way she has turned from tiny trembles to angry shakes. Then he reaches for mine.

No! my body calls to me.

But my hand lets itself be cradled and kissed. The insides of my mouth sour, and the emptiness of my stomach deepens. I don't speak but I don't leave, either, and they do not tell you in princess school what to do in this moment.

I don't even tell my sisters to leave. I don't even protect them. I am weak and scared and officially every bit as terrible as my father, the king.

"You have to help us," I say at last. My voice is louder than I intended. For years, all I've practiced is being heard without speaking. That's what my mother called it. *Queens don't speak to their subjects,* she used to say. *But that doesn't mean we can't be heard.*

My whole life I've worked on glances and smiles and shoulder hunches and nods. But I'm tired of positioning my body this way and that, as if there's nothing in my throat wanting to be said. I told Reagan I didn't believe her and I looked away from Olive and I can't find the words to tell my father that I saw him, I *saw* him, but I won't leave this room and slink away without asking for what we need.

Dad looks genuinely surprised at my voice; the goblet of wine he's holding is stuck between his chest and his mouth; his eyes dart around the room. Mine start to focus on the King of Soar. He's wearing a heavy leather robe, and he has a long beard. He's older than my father, more hunched, and he smells of something strong and metallic.

I could vomit. I yell instead. "We have to talk." Grace jerks back from Dad, and Eden holds me more tightly.

"Well, we certainly don't have to talk right now," Dad says. He gives a little shake of his head paired with a smile and an eye roll. As if I am just another daughter and not a girl on a quest to save herself and her sisters. I can't tell if he knows I saw him and is pretending I didn't, or if he truly thinks he got away with it.

Because maybe he will always get away with it. With anything. If the people didn't rebel during the Famine and during the Spell of Without and now during Always Day, maybe they wouldn't do anything this time either.

They've shown me what they think of anyone who isn't old and male and royal.

Maybe you didn't see anything, my brain says, hopefully, one last time. I want to believe it so badly, but my father's hand keeps moving through the air, haunting me.

And by the time his hand finds his side, makes its way into his pocket, hides itself, the hope is gone. His face looks exactly the same and completely different. If I looked in a mirror, maybe the same would be true for me.

I imagine Mom's crown on my head. I imagine a scepter in my hand, gold and thick and topped with an enormous diamond. My back straightens, and I don't move an inch.

"We *do* have to talk right now. We have no time. You will help us break the spell. You will tell our subjects to help us."

"Jane. I'm in a meeting."

"Dad. We will die." I match his tone. I hadn't noticed until now, but I'm nearly as tall as him. My whole life he towered over me, hoisted me onto his shoulders, held me above his head so I could see the world the way he did. But now I am eye to eye with him, and it happens. He stops being my father. It's only for a moment, a flash, but it shakes me up. He is the King of Ever and I am the princess and I will be heard.

"My girls have had a rough time of it," Dad explains to the King of Soar. "As you know. Things here are— Well, it's been difficult. I hope you'll excuse their behavior. We're under enormous stress."

"Of course," the King of Soar says. "We aren't accustomed to magic, but I imagine it puts stress on even the sweetest princesses and noblest kings."

"It's been hard for me," Dad says, "very very hard. We are all doing our best."

"And we're here to help," the King of Soar says. "We are in this with you."

I don't know if this is the way they've always talked to us and about us and around us, but it's suddenly awful. It's all turning ugly so fast—my father's hand, the King of Soar's smirk, the too-dark lighting of the study, the sound of attendants rushing around the hallways like frightened mice. And the words of these men who try to shut us up and dismiss us and tell us nothing is a big deal when time is moving so quickly away from us, and this hunger is about to turn True.

I try to imagine what will happen if I tell Ever who my father really is. I want to imagine an army, taking him from his throne, demanding a new leader, maybe throwing him in a dungeon somewhere.

But there is no dungeon in Ever. And there's no army. And there might not be anyone who is ready to go to battle against the king.

I take a step closer to the man I used to know. My sisters hover but don't advance. Grace plays with something on Dad's desk, and Eden's eyes shoot daggers at both kings. But I am the only one with a voice. I am the only one who can do anything at all.

"You will help us. You will tell them to help us. Because I know what you did. What you've been doing. You are the reason for the spell. You—you—there was a witch, and you—"

It's so hard to get the word out. I don't want to say it. It's such a final word, such an ugly one. I'll never have my father, the king, back if I say it out loud.

But I can. So I do. "You raped a witch. And just now, with Olive, you—"

Dad tries to stand taller. He tries his best, but still we are the same. He can't rise up any farther without standing on his tiptoes. And he does not want to be a tiptoeing king.

"I see you. I'm not looking away." I linger in the moment

193

and do what I should have been doing this whole time. I look at him. I look at them both. I do not look away. I don't know what Ever would do if they found out, and he doesn't know either, but I decide to believe they would care. That at least a few of them, enough of them, would care.

"I see you, too, Jane," Dad says. "You're hysterical."

My arms shimmer. My fingers pulse. My face feels like it's glowing. I look at Grace's hands, and still my tears are glinting there, too.

But it's my heart that's truly strange. It stops and starts in a panic of a thousand feelings.

"I don't know what you've heard, what crazy person you've been listening to in your weakened state. You haven't eaten in five years, we can't expect you to be yourself, but this is—this isn't acceptable. You're out of control."

"You keep calling me hysterical," I say. "You said it at dinner. And it wasn't true. And it isn't now."

"I'm worried about you," he says, but his voice sounds like a snake's, and the King of Soar has a funny smirk on his face, like he's been caught but knows he'll never pay for it.

None of them think they will pay.

But they are wrong.

"I'll tell them all who you are. Their Good and Gentle King. I will tell them what you did to make the witch cast that spell. What you are doing to their children that they send to work here in the castle." Images flash through my mind. My father's hand lingering on the shoulder of a tutor, his body squeezing too closely to an attendant's, the way women and girls sometimes shrink away from his hand, the sheer number of young people in our castle, and how many of them seem shaky and strange and then, suddenly, leave, replaced by newer, younger people.

The people of Ever might not care what happens to me, or to Reagan's mother or even to Olive. But they will have to care when it's their child, their parent, their loved one.

But my father doesn't seem scared of anything. "And I'll tell them all how crazy you are," he says. "How much this spell has ruined our would-be queen. How you are unstable and how the breaking of this spell isn't good for you. For any of you." He brings his hands together. I see now how ugly they are. How awful and large and roaming. "We won't be trying to break the spell anymore. It's not good for my girls. Look what it's done to you. What a state you're in. No. You'll be staying right here, right where you've always been. Safe and sound. All of you."

I have more to say, but Dad doesn't want to hear it. He's turned into the king—the one they don't know about. Decisive and cruel. Uncaring and too sure.

He lunges at Eden and Grace. They don't think to run. I wouldn't either. We've never run from our father. He's strong enough to get one of them in each arm and hold them there. Or maybe we're weak enough, hopeless enough to not know how to fight back. They hang like rags, like nothing, from his elbows.

"Get the other two," he calls out to no one that I see but someone, I suppose, whose job it is to sit and wait for the king to need something.

And when a king needs something, they have no trouble

getting it. So my sisters appear, as if by magic, as if there's a witch helping him and not us. Alice is draped in one horseman's arms. Nora is squirming against another.

Neither horseman will look directly at me.

A third horseman, the skinniest one, comes for me. It won't be a problem for him, of course. I can't fight. I can barely stand on my own. My mind is racing and my heart is thumping, but my body is useless. It practically sags into him.

"Please let go," I say. "Please just let us all go. We have so much to do."

"The tower," Dad says. "You're not safe out there. You'll be staying here. In the tower. Until you've all calmed down."

I try to imagine a world in which I am calm, ever again, and I can't. I try to fight against the horseman's grip. I cannot go to a tower. If I get locked in a tower, I will die.

It has never felt more real.

"What are you doing?" I ask, my voice finding strength and volume in the midst of my panic. "We can't go to a tower! We have to break the spell! We have to do it right now! Let go!"

"I don't know about all that," Dad says, as if we haven't all been studying magic for our whole lives. "I just know what's best for my girls."

I didn't know my mouth knew how to scream anymore, but it does. And the remembering is loud.

They carry us to the tower, past my bedroom, where Olive is turning down my bed. She follows, calling my name, but I'm worried answering will only make things worse or draw his attention back to her. So I only scream louder, until I can't anymore, the burst of energy so fleeting it's as if it never happened at all. Within a few minutes we are in the tower, which is small and circular and the highest point in Ever aside from the Home on the Hill.

The horsemen put us down, there's nowhere to go, and my father, the king, crosses his arms over his chest and takes a wide stance with his legs. "You'll be safe now," he says.

"We will die here," I say, and I don't apologize for the spit flying out with the words or the way my body leans toward him, like I might scratch or punch or hit, if I could only eat a sandwich first.

Dad pretends not to have heard me, and Olive takes my hand, maybe to calm me down or to remind me of something or just to be in this moment with me. My sisters start to cry, all of them except for Nora, who is wrestling a horseman, and Olive squeezes my hand and I think again of the Home on the Hill being the only place higher up than we are right now, and I squeeze Olive's hand back and there's that shimmer again, that glint on the water, that splash of sparkly tears, that thing between us, and between me and the witch, too, and before I can take a breath to tell him to release us or to call down to the subjects of Ever or to tell my sisters it will be okay, I raise my hands and Olive's into the air, and I am gone.

I am gone from that tower, from that castle, from that life.

And I am all of a sudden at the one place in all of Ever that I've never been but I'd recognize anywhere.

The doorway of the Home on the Hill.

16.

REAGAN

Their arrival is loud.

We hear them before we see them, a crash and a screech and a frantic knocking. Willa and I rush to the door. We had been sleeping, but the sound woke us in the same moment, propelled our feet, every bit of our skin knowing something was happening.

The ocean smell, the royal fear, so potent it chokes us both.

It is Jane and her attendant, Olive, and they are both ghost faced and shaking.

"Hi," I say, because when a grand greeting is needed, I can only come up with something shallow.

"Hi," Jane says. "I don't know why we're here."

"I don't know *how* we're here," Olive says. They cling to each other, and the places where they touch seem to glow. It could be moonlight sneaking in between them, or it could be drops of sweat or my own tired eyes. But it looks like something else.

It looks a little like magic.

Willa is still half in a dream, but she opens the door wide for the princess and her attendant. "Come on in," she says.

"You walked all the way here?" I ask Jane. She was struggling on the walk from Drum's house to the moat. I can't imagine her getting herself up the hill.

"No," she says. Her voice is a whisper of what it was earlier today.

"No?"

"No."

"We arrived," Olive says.

"We were in the tower. He was locking us up. And then we were here. I don't—I can't be here. Not without my sisters. Are my sisters here?" Jane is talking so quietly and so quickly it's hard to parse what she's actually saying.

"What tower? Who was locking you up?" I ask. I touch her shoulder to try to calm her, but instead there's a spark of something—electricity maybe?—and we both jump from it.

"Are my sisters here?" she asks again, louder, faster.

"No," I say. "Not as far as I know."

"We have to go back," she says. She closes her eyes. "GO BACK," she calls, like if she yells something, it will happen. She is skinnier right now than she was a few hours ago, and this feels like *it*, like the end, like the things that happen before the spell turns True. I want her to get a hold of herself, to start making sense again, but she's gone.

"Jane," I say. "Breathe."

She looks at me like she was lost and now she's found. "I'm scared," she says. "I've never been without them."

I nod. I try to take in what that means, but it's hard, since I missed my family for five years, and she is falling apart at missing them for five minutes. At first I think, *I'm so much stronger than her*, and roll my eyes a little. But louder than my own voice is my mother's, reminding me *there are a hundred ways to be strong*.

I give Jane a good long look, trying to see where her strength is hiding right now. It's hard to see anything but her darting eyes, her shaky hands, the shimmer of light clinging to her elbows, her fingertips, her hair.

"Let's go up on the roof," I say. "We can see the castle from there."

Olive breathes a sigh of relief and Jane nods and we climb the ladder to the roof.

"There it is," Jane says when we peer out at the castle. "The tower they're in. It's got a light on. I think I can see their shadows. Do you think they're okay?"

She looks at Olive first, who doesn't answer. When Jane looks at me, I get caught between the truth and a lie. We're all three of us thinking of the things men do to girls when no one is watching. "The only thing we can do to make them safe is break the spell," I say, which is a half truth and a half hope and a half distraction.

Jane nods. There's a glimmer of strength, a trying to take in something terrifying. "There's my mom," she says, pointing to the woman in glass. "I'm glad we can see her from here. She always knew what to do."

"Do you miss her?" I ask.

"It's so much bigger than missing," Jane says. My mother is just downstairs, but not all of her, not always. She's right.

It's bigger than missing, when you want someone to be who they used to be, or who they are meant to be, or who you want them to be.

"I miss my mother sometimes too," I say.

"When you were in AndNot?" she asks.

"Then, yes. I missed everyone then. But my mother—even when she's here, she can be not here." I know I'm saying something Jane can't understand, but it feels impossible to explain what it's like to love someone who isn't all the way here. Jane waits. I love her for waiting. And in that waiting, I feel a breeze of something that isn't air. *A princess wouldn't understand how things are with my mother,* I think, but in Jane's waiting, she feels less like a princess. I'm tired of thinking of Jane as just a princess and me as just a witch and the two of us as just girls in this kingdom. Olive paces the length of the roof, and I'm tired of thinking of her as just an attendant, too.

The queen is not the only one in an impossible box.

"She vanishes sometimes," I say when the breeze of not-air passes through us all, gives us all a shiver. "My mother."

"I don't know what that means," Jane says. It's direct but gentle.

"Witches are weird," Willa says. It is the Willa-est way to say something.

Jane laughs. I've never heard her laugh. It's louder than I thought it would be. Uglier. There's a snort in the middle of it. The idea of a snorting princess makes me laugh. And the two of us laughing make Olive and Willa laugh. Soon the four of us are lost in that laughter. Every second is precious, the spell turning True with every breath, but the laughter feels good, necessary.

Something happens to the sky. The color of it shifts, the way it does when a shadow moves or the sunset starts, but it is Always Day, so the light in the sky isn't shifting. It isn't turning darker. It's warmer. The light feels less harsh. More like strong moonlight or a million candles.

We all notice it. We don't ask one another what it is.

Instead I go on. "When we're upset, when things are too much for us, bits of us vanish—an arm, a foot, whatever. We go hazy. My mother goes hazy sometimes. Me too."

Jane surveys me. "You're all here right now."

"I am."

"But earlier today—I thought something was wrong with your shoulder. And your hand. I couldn't see your hand at one point. I thought it was just me. My vision can be—"

"I'm sure."

"So you're all here now, but your mother?"

"She's always missing something essential," I say. Jane nods, and I know from the look on her face that we love our mothers in the same way—ferociously, sadly, with pain and wanting and wishing for a different past.

"She's sad a lot?"

"Once a year she vanishes. The whole of her. She's still there in the house with us, but her body is gone. It lasts a week, usually. I always wonder if maybe it will last forever, if she won't come back one year."

"But she always comes back," Jane says. She looks out at her mother again. Her fingers dance, wanting to pull her out of that box I'm sure.

"She comes back, but something's always missing," I say. "A way she says a word. A lilt in her laugh. A twinkle in her eyes. A tiny, essential part of her. Gone. Forever."

"Once a year," Jane says.

"Yes."

"Oh." Jane takes an enormous inhale and lets it out. She knows why. She doesn't have to tell me she started believing me. It's been all over her since she showed up.

Her father appears on the balcony outside the tower. He waves to his subjects. And maybe also to us.

"I hate him," I say.

"He's my father," Jane says.

"Father" is another word like "princess," like "witch," like "attendant" or "girl" or "man" or "duke" or "king." It sounds like it means something specific, but it could mean anything at all. It means what we want it to mean, and then it fails.

For years, I suppose, he has been her father, and that has been a sweet word that holds eighteen years of memories and a certain kind of perfect love. But soon, sooner than I want to think, so soon I swear I can see it on her body right now, he will be the father who let her die, the father who wouldn't save her, the king who locked away his daughters, the man who cared more about himself, who let things happen, who is the reason they happened to begin with.

And here's Jane, still wanting him to be the father who

saves her, who apologizes, who was wrongly accused, who is the Good and Gentle King.

"We didn't get the clock," Jane says. "So what should we try for next? The hair? The tears? The clock again? Obviously the crown will be—I don't know how we'll get that."

"The tears," I say. Some objects will be hard, but those, at least, will be easy.

"Turner Dodd," Olive says. Jane nods.

"Who's that?" I ask.

"The saddest person," Olive says. She knows the kingdom better than Jane, better than the king or me probably too. It's hers, more than either of ours. "A young boy. He cries all the time. Everyone knows about him. Been the saddest boy in Ever since the day he was born. They all actually think he's under a spell himself."

"That's not the saddest person in Ever," I say.

"I've heard of him," Jane says. "They say he cries one bucket of tears every day. I've heard he isn't allowed to go to school because it was too distracting for everyone. Can we go to his house now? Do you know the way, Olive?"

"Oh, everyone knows the way," Olive says. "People bring him and his mother food and flowers and little gifts. Everyone's always trying to make Turner Dodd less sad."

"It's not Turner Dodd's tears you need," I say, louder this time. They both look at me.

"You said the saddest person in Ever," Jane says.

"He's not the saddest person in Ever," I say.

"Well then, who?" Olive tilts her head to the side.

"My mother."

"But Turner Dodd—" Jane starts. Some stories are hard to shake. Some truths are hard to see. She has been taught one history of Ever, one way that her people are. She knows her subjects' names like she might be quizzed on them someday, and maybe that's how someone turns from princess to queen. I don't know.

What I know is that the story of Ever she's memorized isn't right. The boy who lives down the hill, by the moat, and bellows out his woes all day every day isn't the saddest person. The loudest person rarely is. The king isn't good and the princesses aren't quiet and the witches aren't evil and my mother is the saddest person in Ever. I put her tears on the list of things they had to gather so that they could see her pain. So that they could know what was taken from her.

And it's time.

I bring my mother up the stairs, up the ladder, to the place where Jane and Olive wait, watching the castle, wondering what is going on in the tallest tower. Willa and Aunt Idle and some of my cousins follow. Grandmother listens from her place downstairs. I clear my throat, and Jane turns to see my family.

My mother's face is a cloud of worry, and her right hand is gone. She is missing a part of her neck. Her hands are busy fretting at her sides. "This is my mother. She is the saddest person in Ever."

Mom recoils from my words. She holds herself, her arms

wrapped around her chest like she's making sure her heart stays right where it's meant to be. She doesn't speak, not even to deny it, but her body is doing enough of that.

Olive bows her head as if my mother is the queen. Jane does the same, mustering out a strange curtsy. We don't know what to do with one another—witches and royals. People.

"Oh, Reagan," my mother says. "What have you done?" Her head hangs, but she doesn't cry. I suppose I've never seen her cry, something I hadn't thought much about when I demanded a thimble of her tears to break the spell. I was thinking of myself, in AndNot, and the buckets of tears I let out. It seemed like an easy-enough thing, to get tears from a sad person.

But looking at her now, I realize my mother would never cry in front of a princess. Maybe she would never cry at all. There is more than one way to survive, she told me. There is more than one way to be strong. I forgot, of course, that there is more than one way to be sad.

Turner Dodd's sadness is the kind that comes with buckets of tears. My mother's is a dry sadness. An invisible sadness. A hidden sadness.

Jane takes a step forward, and my mother takes a step back, afraid of this princess, of anyone with a crown and a title and a room in the castle.

"I need your tears," Jane says. "I'm sorry."

"I'm sorry too," Mom says. "I don't have any. I don't cry. Not now. Not ever."

17.

JANE

"Please don't apologize to me," I say. I am torn between looking at her and looking away from her. I don't know what's easier for her. Or for me. I don't know what I expected, but when
she's in front of me, she's just a person. A mother and a witch
whose fingers fidget and whose voice is soft. Her hair is parted
a little crookedly. There's a blemish on her chin. She shifts her
weight from one hip to the other.

She wants to help us, the daughters of the man who hurt
her. She's kind and good, but also human. I want to sit down,
lie down, have the time and space to understand the way our
lives have collided, have met up here and now, so long after my
father started all this pain. I want to hold her hand, to have her
be my own mother for a moment, for her to tell me it's okay,
that *she's* okay.

Then I hate myself for wanting anything from her.

And still, I have to want something from her. Something
she says she can't give me. Her tears. "We can't break the spell,"
I say, mostly to myself. "The spell won't be broken. But it's not
your fault."

I once asked Mom if queens always tell the truth, like witches do. She said no, they do not. And I always thought that was a strange answer, so for my last week in Ever, I will be the kind of almost queen that I imagined being when I was small and not bound by an impossible spell. I will be a queen who tells the truth.

The roof felt expansive when we first arrived. But it feels small now. Everything feels small, my whole body cramped, trying to fit into a life that is pushing me out.

"I'm sorry," Reagan says, and she sounds sorry, but it doesn't matter. Time is passing, and we don't have a single object from our list. We need time from a dying man and tears from a woman who never cries. And a crown from a man who would do anything—*anything*—to keep it.

Even if Abbott Shine were to give us his hair, we would have only one object out of four, and that won't break the spell.

"Why?" I say, because I'm exhausted and I can't ask a full question or even know what question I need answered. I want to know why we're here and why she cast the spell on us and why she made breaking it impossible and why I care about her when she hurt me and why she cares about me when my father hurt her mother and why we are on a roof and my sisters are in a tower and why Ever seems to just go on as if everything's fine.

I want to know why we are all hurting, in this world run by my father.

I want to know why he and the other kings aren't hurting.

I want to know why we didn't see it, and why we didn't want to see it.

"I thought—" Reagan starts. "I thought—" She tries again. "I tried—" She can't seem to finish a sentence. Five long, impossible years ago she seemed young but strong, small but sure. She was evil, she was ruthless, she didn't care, she was powerful and cruel, and I knew I'd hate her forever. She was a witch in a cape with raised hands and layers of skirts and a look in her eyes that I thought was evil but was rage, which is a different thing entirely.

I know a little about rage, which is running through me now. I try to direct it at the careless young witch who cast an awful spell and made it impossible to break. But the anger keeps folding back on itself and back to my father. Then it folds back further still.

To me.

And to the times I saw my father's hand touch Olive's wrist or a low part of her back that should never have been touched.

I take it like a punch, which it is. The fault is Reagan's and it is my father's, but also it is mine, for the times I chose not to see and the things I decided weren't important and the things I believed to be real even though everywhere around me were signs they weren't real.

That is what being a princess is, I think with a rush of shame followed by my mind trying, again, like always, to unsee what is right there.

I sit down on the roof, and maybe it is time for the spell to turn True; maybe it is right for it to turn True; maybe it is what I deserve.

All this time I've wondered why she had to place the spell on us, on me, but I know now. I know, seeing her mother and the invisible parts of her, standing here next to Olive, who I must have known was hurting, who I must have seen suffering, who never told me because I was too silly and selfish and scared to care.

"I did this," I say, words that are more a gasp than a sentence.

I don't know who hears me or if anyone does. We are each in our own universe of shame and hurt and worry, and the roof is barely big enough for all of us.

"You have to break the spell," Reagan's mother says, and her voice can't break a spell, but it breaks through the trance I'm in enough for me to listen. "Willa. Show them."

The young witch who was at the party with Reagan lifts something up that I hadn't noticed before. A candle. "It's our Enchanted Candle," she explains.

"We know about Enchanted Candles," I say. "To bring back the missing princess. To keep us safe."

"This is our candle," the young witch says. "It tells us how the kingdom is doing. It's supposed to be gold, always. Shades of gold. But now the kingdom isn't at rest." The flame of the candle is an alarming red, and even I know that can't be good. Reagan's shoulders jump, and I look out at Ever again. Of course it's not at rest. I don't need a Spellbound candle to tell me that.

"Reagan. Willa. There's a lot at stake if the kingdom isn't at rest," Reagan's mother says to Reagan and her young friend.

Her voice shakes, and for a minute my heart lifts, thinking she could cry. But she only straightens her back and leans forward. "If the kingdom isn't at rest—all of the magic will go."

Reagan squints and I shrug. A magic-less Ever sounds good to me.

"You mean all of my magic?" Reagan asks.

"No," her mother says. "All the magic. All that's left. All that we've been protecting. It can all vanish."

A voice comes up from the air. It's the voice of an old woman. I can tell from the places it breaks, the crackle of it. "It's happened before."

I search my brain for everything I know about the history of witches. They live in Ever because we were kind and let them in after they had angered all the kingdoms during the War by getting involved in the battles. We were a safe harbor, and they are meant to spend their lives making it up to us. They perform spells for us, and in exchange we protect them from other kingdoms. Their magic is weak, and they are unreasonable. No one else wants them. We are the good ones; we are the kind ones; they never appreciate us enough.

The history of the witches of Ever never mentioned vanishing magic or a past where there was more magic, more witches. The history I learned also didn't mention anything about a cruel king and a desperate search for power and a quiet-voiced witch who lived with a painful history while her abuser reigned over a broken kingdom.

There's a lot history didn't tell me, a lot my father left out and lied about and got me turned around on. I might not really know anything at all about Ever and witches and princesses and magic.

Reagan looks as confused as I feel.

"I'll work on Bethly," the voice says. "You go back out into Ever and fix this. Look at your cousins, Reagan. All my grandchildren. Missing wrists and ears. Even my own lips—it's urgent. I'm not strong enough to—without our magic—we are necessary."

I thought Reagan was meant to be saving my sisters and me, but her grandmother's voice insists she has to save her family too. Save us all.

"Go to that Abbott boy. Get the princess away from us. Get her away from you, too. Break the spell, then never go back into Ever again. Hopefully a new burlap skirt will wrap itself around you and will keep you where you're meant to be. Here. With us."

Reagan looks like she has a hundred questions trying to inch out of her mouth, but the voice stops speaking.

Reagan's mother fills the quiet space with a quiet voice. "I'll try," she says. "But I promised I'd never cry over it."

I know she's speaking about my father and the things he did to her, but I can't find words to say I'm sorry or I believe her or I wish it hadn't happened. I want to tell her about every nice thing he ever did, like that will somehow make it better, but it won't, of course. It won't make me any better either. I keep scrolling through our family memories, like there is some pathway that will make this all make sense. And maybe there is that small dusty road, but it hurts to travel on.

Every happy memory of him will have to turn sour, every bit of history I had will be rewritten. And if everything around me has to be reconsidered, so do I. Olive bites her lips so hard I'm worried they will bleed. The way I hate myself grows, takes on a new shape.

"I shouldn't be here," I say. "I shouldn't be anywhere." The words don't make sense exactly, but they're close enough to what I'm feeling, seeing these witches, the way they are hurting, the things it feels like I could have stopped but didn't. I'm searching for the right way to be with this woman whose pain was big enough to make Reagan cast a spell on me. I grab on to Reagan, to steady myself. I'm wavy and weak.

"Hey," Reagan says, gentler than she needs to be, kinder than I deserve. "He did this. Not you. Maybe not even me. He did it. *He did it.*"

I hold on to her more tightly, and she holds on to me back.

The touch does what our touches seem to do.

There's a shimmer. A glow. A shock of a feeling in my body.

"Is this magic?" I whisper at last, asking the question I've been trying to hide from.

Olive takes a step toward Reagan's mother. Then another. Another. The steps are small and timid. They take forever. They aren't sure of what they are doing. But then she's next to Reagan's mother, and her hand hovers above Reagan's mother's arm, not wanting to touch until she gets a nod of *yes, you can touch me there like this.*

"There are so many of us," Olive says. "You aren't alone."

She doesn't blink. I can see the words work their way into Reagan's mother's hurting heart. We can all see her take them in, wrestle with them, worry they aren't true, see that they are. She lets go. Not all the way, not forever, but a little bit. Enough.

Enough.

Her shoulders unworry; her face unpinches; her heart ungrips just enough. And with that release, she starts to cry. I could fill a thousand thimbles with the tears that rush out. But I only need the one.

Olive rubs her arms, looks at the sky. We all feel it. The shimmer. The glow. The flicker of the candle from red to redder and redder and redder.

Willa shivers. There's a hint of a smile on her face, and she reminds me of Eden, before she was Spellbound. Not because they look alike—they don't. But because she is filled with the same hope Eden had. She hands me a thimble that appears in her hands from nowhere.

Bethly's tears don't stop.

"That's magic," the voice from nowhere says.

But I didn't need to be told. I knew.

18.
REAGAN

We have the tears. It is time to get the rest. Somehow. So we walk down the hill, toward the end of the spell, toward the things we hope we can change. It should maybe just be Jane and me, but Olive and Willa join us as if it is meant to be that way, as if the four of us are in something together.

"The handsomest boy," I say, like we are still just checking people off the list I invented instead of trying to understand what is happening between us and trying to save Jane and her sisters and maybe my entire family and the kingdom of Ever. And all the magic in the world.

"Abbott Shine," Jane says. I swear I can see her smiling. Or maybe it's me that's smiling at the sound of his name.

"Oh sure, locked in a castle your whole life, but you know all the beautiful boys," I say. It's the way I would talk to Willa, not a princess, but Jane isn't a princess anymore. Not like that. For an awful second I think I've said the worst thing in a serious moment, but then she laughs.

That great sound again. The snort. The heartiness.

"I'll miss that," Jane says when her laughter has faded and

the rhythm of our walking has taken over. "Laughing. I mean. If I can miss things when I'm gone."

"Don't," I say. "Don't give up."

"We have the tears," Olive says. "We can do this." I'd been thinking Olive was here to help Jane, and that's true maybe, but I see, I've been seeing, that she's here for the same reasons I'm here too. To punish the king. To fight back. Maybe when the spell is broken, more of him will be exposed, more things will change. The princesses know who he is. And if they are saved, they can tell their subjects. They can reveal their father. They can save their attendants. Maybe. Hopefully.

I put a hand on Olive, who has put an arm around Jane.

Willa nuzzles against me. "We can do this," she echoes Olive, and she sounds so sure I can almost believe her. Then the four of us are caught in this moment together, and there it is again, stronger now. The shimmer. The thing that feels like magic but can't be magic but so clearly *is* magic.

"Oh!" Olive says.

"What is that?" Willa says. She wiggles her toes, shakes out her arms.

"You feel it?" Jane asks. Olive looks frightened. Willa looks excited.

"What is that?" Willa asks again.

"It's something," Jane says. She rubs her arm, her heart, the back of her neck.

Olive considers her hands. She looks at the sky, which is day, but more golden than day usually is. Less bright and more warm. A new sky for Ever.

"Abbott Shine," Olive says. "That one will be easy."

I nod. "He's my best friend," I say. "Or he was. Is. I don't know. He'll help, though."

Olive smiles. Then grins. "He'll help," she says. "That's my brother. Half brother. But, you know, brother."

Jane looks even more confused. "Your brother?" she asks, like she's forgotten that attendants have families.

"Abbott Shine?" I say, like maybe she doesn't know his whole name, as if her brother is some other Abbott and not the one I've spent long mornings with on this side of the moat, the one who hates royals and sometimes witches, too. That cannot be her brother.

"I'm sorry," Olive says. "I was waiting for the right moment, I guess. . . ."

I try to see the ways they might be related. They don't exactly look like brother and sister. Or act related. Olive is a white girl with a small voice and a polite, timid way about her. Abbott is a half-black boy who says what he means and wasn't even scared of a home filled with witches.

But they have the same pointed chin and relaxed gait and their own ways of being brave. Of being strong.

"He must have hated you being in the castle," I say, remembering that of course he'd said he had a sister there. He said a hundred things to me that I heard but didn't listen to, didn't think about enough.

"He saw once," Olive says. She turns to Jane. "He saw your father. His hands." She speaks in code like my grandmother, but we all speak the same language now. It's the language of the secrets we've been holding and the wrongs that have been done.

"Oh," Jane says. She takes a shallow breath. Lets it out with another "Oh. Gosh. What are the chances?"

"It's a small town, Jane," Olive says.

"Five hundred thirty-seven residents," Jane says, and I smile, even now, at the way princesses are taught to see their kingdom. Numbers and facts and silence and distance.

A little like witches, I guess.

The rest of Ever doesn't get the benefit of distance. They are in it. They are struggling through it. It is what we made, but they have to navigate it.

"Abbott Shine," Jane goes on. "The one thing he wanted me to know was that he missed his mother and had the best little sisters in the world."

"And he'd do anything to protect them," Olive finishes.

"We have a lot in common," Jane says, and I think she means she and Abbott do, both of them desperate to save their sisters, and having a hard time figuring out how to do it.

But maybe she means more than that. I look at her to try to decipher it. When witches are struggling, we go hazy, but Jane's face is the opposite. It is coming into focus. She is sharpening, clarifying.

"Peach!" she says, so random I think I've misheard her. Or that her hunger is making her hallucinate.

Willa giggles at the strange exclamation, and I hush her. But Jane smiles at it. She has little sisters. She gets it.

"You okay?" I ask Jane. "Do you need a break?"

"I taste peach," she says. "I taste it. In my mouth." She grins. Licks her lips. She brightens. "It's there," she says. "It's in my mouth. *Peach*."

Her voice sounds a little out of control, like it might break loose and do its own thing. She's trying, I can see, to stay calm, to be a queen about it, but it's hard because her mouth is tasting again, after five years.

When spells break, they do so slowly, a little at a time. I wonder if Jane knows that. That spells don't shatter at once; they crumble and dissolve and shift. The taste of peach after years of nothing. A pocket of hope. A crack in a glass box. The sky turning from all bright to mostly bright.

Like it is right now.

"I love peaches," Willa says.

"I've never had a peach," Olive says.

"When this is all over," Jane says, "we'll eat peaches. All of us."

She might mean just the four of us. But she might mean all of Ever.

I don't know what it's all about, the buzzing and glowing, Jane tasting peach, the sky shifting, the breeze blowing, but it doesn't matter. We are walking again, without having discussed it, without even noticing the moving of our feet. I wonder if Olive's and Willa's and Jane's toes are scrunching and unscrunching too, experimenting with this thing between us.

It is a powerful thing that was supposed to be trapped up on a hill. A thing that isn't supposed to be pulsing between us all, changing the shade of the sky, bringing a princess from a castle to the top of a hill.

Magic.

And by the time we reach Abbott's house, it is singing in our limbs and sweetening our breath and making our hearts beat beat beat with something that feels a little like hope.

19.

JANE

He is waiting for us. Or maybe he is simply planting potatoes in the garden as he might do any other morning.

He is as handsome as they've all said he is, but it's obscured by how sad he looks. How worried. He keeps looking at the castle. He is so *real*. This is Ever. It is filled with worried people and heartbroken people and handsome people and terrible people. In my books, the subjects of Ever are one thing, one crowd that raises their chins to the castle and listens to the king and works hard and lights their candles and thinks of nothing but their royal family.

But Abbott Shine isn't looking to the castle in the hope of seeing a man in a crown or a bunch of princesses in silly gowns. He is looking for his sister. I wanted to know one thing about him, but there are a hundred things to know about him, a thousand.

"Abbott," Olive says. The way she says his name is so sweet it breaks my heart. She loves him like I love my sisters, in the way that makes you soft and striving. She can't even finish the second syllable before he is running toward her, stomping out the beginnings of plants, the tiny bit of vegetation the ground allows him to grow.

"My Olive," he says, and he's crying. He turns to Reagan next, and they embrace too, like old friends, which maybe they are. Half of my heart is with my sisters, locked in a tower, and the other half is right here, wondering at the impossibility of this beautiful boy and me loving the same people.

Hating the same people too. I realize it in a gasp, the feeling blooming in my heart before I've even had a chance to wonder about it. I hate my father. Maybe not the same way Reagan and Olive and Abbott do. But I hate him in a smaller, pointier, dizzier way.

I don't know how to greet this Abbott Shine. I am still a stranger in my kingdom, and the things I was taught don't work here. I half curtsy and half wave and almost offer my hand to be kissed but settle at last on bowing my head and whimpering out a thin "hello."

"Princess Jane," he says. It's not that he's not beautiful up close—he is. But now he isn't the idea of a person. He isn't who Alice carved into stone. He looks tired and hungry and sad and hopeless. I know, because I know the way that looks on people. "Welcome to Ever," he says. "What do you think?"

I look out at the kingdom, his view of it. All I can see are sad homes and sadder gardens and the tower that my sisters are locked in rising above leafless, fruitless trees.

And a bit of magic in the sky.

And a little bit more right here, on my fingertips.

"It's awful," I say.

"That's not very queenly," he says. Olive clings to him but smiles at me. I've failed her in the biggest, worst, ugliest ways, but here she is. A person I don't deserve. I almost ask again for the spell to turn True, so I don't have to keep feeling the way it feels to have been wrong, to have been selfish, to have been small and cowardly and silly.

But Reagan shakes her head at me, like she can see the shame on my face and doesn't want it to settle there.

I look for something beneath the shame and beneath the hunger and beneath all the ways I've ever learned to be a princess and a someday queen. I don't know the word for what I find there.

Or I do know the word, but it can't possibly be true.

Magic.

"I guess I'm not that kind of queen," I say.

"Not a queen at all yet," Abbott says. He tilts his head. He knows why I'm here. In Ever, everyone has a box they live inside, a category we have placed them in. I have always thought these things were true, something more than stories we tell one another at night.

We were wrong about who was saddest. But we are not wrong about who is handsomest. We know that, and this boy in front of us does too.

Abbott Shine gets a pair of scissors. I open my hands to use them myself, but he shakes his head. "No," he says. "I'll do it. My hair's been touched enough." He snips a curl from his head and hands it to me with a sigh. "I said I'd never help a princess."

"When the spell is broken, I promise we'll—" I start. But he doesn't let me finish.

"I've been promised a lot of things by people like you before," Abbott says. He looks at Reagan. She isn't like me, but I guess to Abbott she sort of is. "I don't need any more promises."

It's hard to stay silent, to not fill up the awkwardness with apologies and assurances. But I do my best to be quiet. It's a skill I should be good at. And with my silence in check, Abbott invites us inside. Olive doesn't need the invitation, of course. She rushes through the front door and hugs her father and a small child who must be her and Abbott's younger sister. She's told me about her little sister before. "She reminds me of you," she's said. I immediately look for what we have in common, but it's right there; it's crystal clear; it's not some hidden trait or inner strength or quality of character.

Her sister is skin and bones. She is starving.

She plays with the hem of my dress, gravitating toward me like she knows me and asking over and over if I am the princess.

"I am," I say, but it doesn't feel so true anymore. "I'm Jane."

"I'm Bess," the little girl says. She looks like Abbott—her face just as lovely, her eyes as big, her skin the same light brown shade, her chin as sharp. She could be four or twelve; the shape of her body is so small and wrong and hungry that it's impossible to know. She is not the size and shape she is meant to be, and her hunger hurts me almost as much as my own.

"She's why," Olive says.

"Why what?" I ask.

Abbott makes a noise like I should already know, and

Reagan looks to the sky like she wishes she could fly up there instead of being down here talking to us.

"Why I stay in the castle," Olive says. "We need to be in his good graces for her sake. Even though he—"

"Oh," I say, still not wanting to hear the words. I bring my hands to Bess's ears, to cover them so they can't hear what we're talking about. Whatever age she is, she's too young, and I know that because I am too young and Olive is too young and we are all too young for this.

"She knows," Olive says. I shrink. Even this small child knows the thing I decided not to know. The thing I saw but didn't see.

"Everyone knows," Abbott says.

Reagan tilts her head even more toward the sky, the hurt of it so big that she can't bear to look at us. She would do anything for her mother, which I understand, because I would do anything for mine.

"The whole kingdom can't know about— They love him," I say.

"Some of them do," Abbott says. "But the rest—we're scared of him," Abbott says. "You know the difference, don't you?"

I think of my father in his tower, giving speeches, and the way the whole town gathers, claps, nods their approval, calls his name. And the way they're waiting for his permission to help us. I think of the attendants whispering to one another, trying to give one another breaks, trying to make it tolerable, living in our home.

The way Drum Drascall's wife looked at us with sad eyes.

The way the royals in the Woods That Were didn't seem worried that someone would find out about what they were doing. The way they call him Good and Gentle, but maybe only because he likes to be called Good and Gentle.

The bells ring out from the castle. It's a sound I know well. A beautiful chiming that signals a speech from the king. We all tilt our heads up, like Reagan, who is lost in the clouds. And we watch the tower until he appears. Which he does. With four princesses by his side. If I squint, I am sure I can see that they are dressed in silk. I am sure, even though they are too far to see clearly, that they are wearing heavy crowns and smiles that hurt.

"It is time," my father begins. As with every speech, there is an enchanted crystal vase below his chin, and the sound spreads across the kingdom. "It is time to remember the past." I look at my sisters for signs of something. Life? Pain? Okay-ness? I don't know, but I'm too far away to see anything except their tied-back hair, their jutting chins, the heaviness of their gowns.

"Some of us know what our kingdom survived when our princess was kidnapped. How hard our kingdom fought to find her. How much Ever battled with other kingdoms who we thought might have taken her. The chaos that ensued. The pain and brutality and effort of the War We Won. The answers never came. The princess was never returned. So many lives lost, so many kingdoms blaming one another, and still we don't know what happened to our sweet princess. It was a long time ago. I wasn't there. You weren't there. But we know. We were in crisis. And now we are back in that same place."

I realize how very little I ever knew about that war. That princess. Inside the castle questions didn't arise. We memorized words and dates and names and recited them back. I was the fastest, the most accurate. And I felt smart, knowing all those facts.

But I knew nothing.

"How can we trust the other kingdoms," I asked once, "if we don't know for sure who took the princess?"

"It's for the best," my mother said. But that wasn't an answer, of course, and we both heard the nothingness of it. "Maybe we don't really trust anyone," she said moments later. "But peace is better than war."

It was a very queenly thing to say. But when I try to think about it now, it doesn't mean much. It doesn't promise anything. It doesn't help me know Ever and our history and myself.

"Why would someone take her?" I asked back then.

"She was rumored to be very beautiful." My mother paused. She looked at me, and I couldn't decide if I wanted to be beautiful enough to take or plain enough to stay safe.

I know now.

"Why candles?" I asked. I could see my mother's interest in talking about the War We Won and the princess we lost was waning.

"The witches," she said.

"And we trust them?" I asked. "I thought we didn't trust anyone."

My mother kissed me on the forehead. She was done

answering questions. Maybe because she didn't know the answers.

Or maybe because she didn't like them.

Those candles made Ever look beautiful, from the castle. Dots of light all over the countryside. Little golden orbs that reminded us that we were the only magical kingdom in all the kingdoms of the world.

"Let's not forget that we won the War We Won," Dad booms now from his perch. "We won, and we chose to protect the witches." Abbott makes a sound that's like a laugh, if a laugh could be exhausted and heartbroken. "We don't negotiate with those witches. We did them a favor. Now they want us to sacrifice to break a spell, and that is not what we do in Ever. We protect our kingdom, above all else. I love my girls. But I love all of you more. I have to. I am King of Ever." He says it again, "I am king," and it booms out over all of us, so loud I want to cover my ears now.

"Princess Jane the Spellbound, Princess Jane Without, has left. She has run away from her palace. She has abandoned her people. And her family. Her young sisters. We stand here, in unity, as your royal family, and ask you not to help her."

My heart stops. It's only for a moment, and no one would know except me. But it stops. My breath, too. The blinking of my eyes. The clicking of my mind as it processes words. It all stops. And then, because I still have a day to break the spell, it all starts again, foggier, clunkier, worse than before.

But my mouth tastes berries. And cream. All is not lost. Most, but not all.

My sisters bow their heads, but from a certain angle, it could look like a nod of agreement.

My sisters, trapped in that tower, without me—Without so many things—can't do a thing.

There is applause. The people of Ever applaud my father and his plea to let me die.

The sound is deafening. There is cheering. *"Ever forever! Ever first! Ever above! Ever Without!"*

And in the echo of that awful noise, my hands rise, on their own. They stretch up to the sky, to the Always Day, to the never night. There is a crash. The sound of glass.

I close my eyes. I try to look away, as I've done for years, as I did to Olive, as I promised I would try not to do again, but still I don't want to see what I've done; I don't want to see what might be wrong.

"Jane. Oh, Jane. No," Reagan whispers.

"Oh!" Willa's shock is quiet but powerful.

I hear Abbott's cry. It strangles itself. Olive's cry is behind it, a weep that turns wild. The gasp of their father and the sound of a body hitting the ground.

I do not hear a little girl shout. I don't hear Bess.

"Open your eyes," Reagan says. "You have to look."

"I can't."

"You cast a spell," Reagan says. "You cast a spell."

I open my eyes. Right in front of me, frozen, trapped inside a glass box, is Bess.

229

20.
REAGAN

Jane's arms come back to her sides as her eyes open and she looks at what she's done. For a moment, I think it's only Bess in a box, and the cruelty of it, the senselessness, astonishes me.

Then I see the home next door, a box in the backyard with Abbott's neighbors trapped inside. And when my heart slows down enough to let me listen, I hear the shouts of all the people of Ever. There are more people in boxes. Women and girls. I look up at the tower, and they are trapped in boxes too, all four of Jane's sisters caught in their hung-head, clasped-arms poses, all of them on display, just like their mother.

The boxes cover the empty gardens as we look this way and that. Glinting across town. Startled into stillness by the moat.

Women in boxes. Girls trapped behind glass.

"What did you do?" Olive asks. She looks at herself, decidedly moving and unboxed. She looks up, as if a glass box might be dropping from the sky to get her at any moment too.

But there is no glass box for Olive. Or for me. Or, of course, for Jane.

"I—" Jane starts. "I—" She keeps shaking her head, back and forth and back and forth. She rubs her arms.

"How?" Olive asks. She goes to her half sister in the box. She presses her hands against the glass, bangs on it, but it doesn't move an inch.

"The way all magic happens," I say. "A moment of necessity, a moment of clarity. When something feels essential. But this isn't essential. Shouldn't be essential." What I don't say, but what we're all thinking, is that this looks more like the kind of spell I might cast than the kind of spell a starving princess could conjure up. I check my waist to make sure there's nothing new affixed there, that I haven't accidentally let my magic get the best of me again. I'm covered with my dozens of layers, but there's nothing new on top of the thick flannel from the Spell of Always Day. "Jane? Why would you do this? When we're finally collecting some of the things we need?"

Jane is frozen. Not like the people in their boxes. Her hands can move, and her eyes can blink. But she is stuck in one place, trying to understand what her raised arms and rage have done.

"I wanted them to know how I feel," she says at last. "To have the people you love trapped. I wanted them to understand. I didn't mean—I thought about what it would be like if they had *their* wives and mothers and daughters in boxes. But I didn't—I'm not a witch. It was just a thought. I'm not magical." Even saying it, I think she knows it's not true. I think she's known for a while. There is magic among us. And it isn't just mine, and it isn't just Willa's. Jane's spell isn't strong enough

231

to reach a powerful witch like me or Willa. We are free from glass, and so is Olive. My heart pounds.

I take Jane in. There is one thing that makes a witch a witch. It won't be hard to see. It will be right there, wrapped around her waist, forever.

Witches can't hide the things we do. We can't pretend away our mistakes. They never leave. We are nothing like royals, who can pretend it's someone else's fault, who can blame other kingdoms or their subjects or witches on top of a hill. We live with our decisions.

Even the ones that didn't feel like decisions at all.

"Jane," I say. She sees it. Olive sees it. Willa sees it. Abbott sees it. Anyone could see it.

Around her tiny waist there is a skirt. It falls all the way to the ground. It is blue. It is wool. It looks itchy and uncomfortable.

It will be on her forever.

The weight of a spell, wrapped around her waist.

"Jane," I say again, to make sure she's really paying attention, something I know is hard for her lately. "You're a witch."

21.

JANE

It is an impossible thing.

I have only ever worn my dresses, hand-stitched by Olive, loosening every day, promises of all the ways in which I am dying. I have only ever worn one dress at a time, one color, one layer of skirt, one long line from my head to my toes. It's what princesses do; it's what princesses wear; it is how it has always been and how it will always be.

Except. There is now another skirt wrapped around me, bluer than my blue dress, heavier than I would ever wear in May, a material not right for royalty. "Take it off!" I say, because when something strange is tight around your waist, you want it gone.

"It won't—" Reagan starts. "I'll try." And she does. But there's no button or zipper. The fabric doesn't pull or slide. It doesn't tear. It's not going anywhere. "The skirts are permanent. They're forever," Reagan says. "That's why we're supposed to be careful with our spells. Even Slow ones. The spells can break, but the skirts are forever. That's why my grandmother is stuck in one place. Her magic is too heavy. She's done too much, over the years."

"I didn't do anything," I say. My voice shakes, and I hold back tears. The skirt makes me more aware of my waist and therefore more aware of my body, which I have been desperate to avoid thinking about for five years.

"But you did," Reagan says.

"You did," Olive says, her voice still a screech and a shatter as she watches Bess's frozen figure.

"How?" I ask, but part of me—the part that felt my arms rise up high—knows. We sit in the uncertainty of what's happened. We listen to all the families of Ever cry and yell and curse the witches, not knowing it's their own princess who cast the spell.

"It's a strong one," Reagan says. "Strong and strange. You have strong, strange, big magic." The glass boxes from my spell aren't like the one Reagan's magic made that my mother is stuck inside. That one was a perfect rectangle. These new boxes, from what I can see, are odd shapes. Some are cramping their prisoners; others are big enough to fit ten women when there's only one. Some have smooth edges or points or cloudy glass. Some, like Bess's, are lifted up from the ground, floating a few feet above it, untethered.

I try to take it all in, but it's too much, so I keep closing my eyes, like that will give me an escape from what I've done. "I'm a princess," I say. "I'm meant to be queen."

"You're a witch." The voice that says it is hard. Durable. There's no question mark. It comes from behind us and is accompanied by a smattering of fast-falling footsteps, a blur of a woman who is now here, as fast as any magic could make her appear. She is old and familiar. Last I saw her, she was trying to feed me lemon cake and was eyeing a beautiful clock. She is someone's wife, so she should be in a box. That's the spell I accidentally cast. All wives and mothers and daughters in boxes, except for witches.

But here she is anyway: Lady Lill.

"You're a witch. I'm a witch," she says simply. I look at her curiously, worried she's ill, ranting, suffering some sort of brain injury. But she looks clear. "We're all witches." She isn't breathing hard, even though she came here in a hurry. She isn't sweating. She doesn't look like she's walked, much less run, the mile between her home and Abbott's.

"You're a friend of witches," Reagan says, trying to correct her. But Lady Lill shakes her head.

"No," she says. "I'm a witch."

Her hands go to the buttons of her dress. It's the same dress she was wearing when we went to visit her. Long. Black. Odd. For a reflexive moment, this seems strange. But only for a moment. I remind myself that a person might have one dress, and nothing else. Days ago, it never would have occurred to me. The thought of a closet with one dress inside would have made me laugh. Or at least wrinkle my forehead in confusion.

I do not miss that girl, that princess I am saying goodbye to. I do not miss that small life, that dreamy ignorance, the way Ever looked from my side of the moat.

My arms start to lift again, wanting to cast a spell to bring new dresses to the subjects of Ever, but most of the people who like to wear dresses are in boxes, and the rest need so much more than silk and tulle and a pleated skirt.

Lady Lill unbuttons the dress from her neck to her toes. When she's done, she slips the whole thing off. I look away; a princess is meant to stay modest.

I have always been good at looking away when it's important.

But I do not want to be that kind of princess anymore. I take a breath and look right at her. She's not naked. On top she has a velvet blouse that used to be nice. On the bottom she has skirts. A dozen of them at least, maybe more. Some of them shimmer. Some of them look heavy. Some of them are lacy.

I touch my new skirt, wishing it was shimmering, wishing it was made of lace or silk or chiffon—something more fit for a princess. Then I quiet those thoughts. I am not owed a sparkly skirt, a castle, an attendant, the life I was living. The skirt I have is right for the magic I performed. It is mine. It is what I deserve.

"Why are you here? How are you here?" Reagan asks. Willa touches the layers of fabric like they are her friends, like she's been searching for them. I look for Olive, who has been quiet for all of this. Olive, who has done nothing but everything I've wanted for years piled on years and now is standing next to her boxed-up sister, broken.

It is a familiar scene. Olive knows how to stand by someone who is Spellbound. My thirteenth year stretched on and on in a rage of loneliness, and Olive would sit with me while I let out my tears, ripped at my skin, stuffed sheets into my mouth to stop it from wanting.

236

It's my turn to go to Olive now. She may not want me. She may blame me for the things my arms did in anger; she may hate the way she's spent her life locked to my side. But if she hates me for anything, she must hate me the most for looking away.

I looked away.

"I'm not going to look away," I say at her shoulder, and she lets me stay by her.

"My sister," she says, desperate and raw.

"I know," I say, because I do, because my sisters are there, in the tower, Without. I touch her arm, and there's that shimmer again, that magic, and she gasps at it.

"I don't want that," she says. I slip my hand from her arm and wonder if it's still there for her. The afterglow.

It's all over me.

"I came to tell you your past," Lady Lill says. "But also to give you my future." She reaches into a pocket of her discarded dress. She's been hiding something in its folds.

Not something. *The* thing.

The clock.

The clock from the oldest person in Ever.

It is ticking time away. And the second she hands it over, it stops. "He wanted me in a box," she says. "He was disappointed when I wasn't in there. They all want us—" She stops herself, emotion taking over. "You need this."

The clock is in my hands.

All that's left is the crown.

22.

REAGAN

"Tell us," I say. I know Lady Lill is meant to be respected, if she is in fact an elder witch. But right now there's no time for polite talking-around. The magical clock has stopped ticking. Ever is frozen. And the spell turns True so soon that I can feel the skirt around my waist tightening. A Slow Spell is a loose skirt. It lets you breathe. A True Spell doesn't leave any room between its band and your skin. A True Spell has a skirt that hurts. Only a pinch. But a pinch forever adds up to a lot.

"It should be your grandmother," Lady Lill says. "She'd be angry if I told you everything. She doesn't know—I shouldn't have my magic anymore. But I hid it. I pretended that it was gone. Your grandmother and I are the only ones old enough to remember what used to be."

"You know my grandmother?"

Lady Lill bows her head.

"I pretended my magic was gone, like everyone else's. I pretended to not be a witch. I didn't want to go to the Hill. I wanted to stay here. I was in love, and I thought it was worth

238

pretending, worth acting as if my magic was gone too." I can't piece her words together, can't quite seem to make them mean anything. "It's never worth it, hiding your magic. Not even for love." She shakes her head. If the clock she's brought us isn't ticking, it must mean Drum Drascall is dead. And maybe she's mourning him. But the bigger grief is all the time she spent being someone else, tucking away her skirts, denying being one of us.

"I thought witches had to live in the Home on the Hill," I say.

"I thought witches didn't fall in love," Willa says. My body blushes without my permission. I don't want Abbott to see, but he's right there, seeing me. Someday I'll tell Willa that Grandmother doesn't like it, but witches *can* fall in love. Someday I may even tell Abbott. But not today.

"Maybe you're not really a witch," I say, focusing back on Lady Lill. I'm almost hopeful. I want there to be rules, and I want them to be simple. Maybe I'll stop messing up if someone can tell me what exactly it is to be a witch and how to do it right.

Lady Lill thinks it over. "Witches have magic. That's it. That's the metric. If you have magic, you are a witch. You were still a witch when you lived in AndNot, Reagan. You'll still be a witch if they make you leave again. I'm still a witch, being out here, hiding everything. It can look however you want it to look. It can be whatever you want it to be. Don't let anyone tell you what a witch is."

I have so many more questions, but Lady Lill walks away

without another word; she doesn't want to be the one to answer them. And before we have a chance to call out to tell her to slow down, she is gone.

I look at Jane and Olive and Abbott. And all four of us look at what has become of Ever. It's not a place I ever loved. But maybe Jane loved it once.

And Grandmother loved it. That's why we stayed. And it kept us safe.

Mostly.

Now there's not much left to love. Just the sound of people crying, preparing for a battle against an invisible magic. My grandmother told me about the ridiculous ways people try to fight against magic. With swords and cannons and rifles. With fists ready to bang on things, ready to punch out a perpetrator, but you can't punch or shoot or cut the air. You can't fight with magic. It just is.

And even if you hide it in a home at the top of a hill, it's still there.

"Are we going?" I ask the people in front of me, who I guess are my friends or maybe something else that doesn't have a name yet.

"Yes," Jane says. She gives a last look to the castle. Her sisters in their boxes can still be seen in the tower. Her father is gone. She waves an arm, but I'm sure they can't see this far, or if they can, they're not looking in this direction. Maybe they're not allowed to. But she does it anyway, because she is theirs and they are hers and the fight continues. I love her for the bit of bravery.

"I don't—" Olive starts, looking at Bess and her mother and the hundreds of glass boxes ahead of us that we will have to weave our way through.

"Go," Abbott says.

"You should go," she says. "I'll stay here. You go."

"Olive," Abbott says. "You all don't need me. I don't belong in the Home on the Hill."

"Well, neither do I," Olive says. But Abbott only smiles. He knows something. I know it too. Jane is knowing it. But Olive doesn't know it. Not quite. Not yet.

"You can both come," I say, because I want to walk next to Abbott all the way there. "Please come," I say, because in spite of the way these days don't end and in spite of the way it feels to be a witch in Ever who everyone hates, I still have room to want him close by, to smell the ends of a fire on his clothes, to know he's there, breathing in time with me, seeing the same things I'm seeing.

That's what I missed most, in AndNot. The simple feeling of seeing the same ocean as someone else. Watching the same seagull poke the waves. I want to see whatever we're going to see next to him. I want to see it at the same time.

But Abbott is only taking steps back, away from us.

"You don't need me for this," he says. "Look at you all."

I want him nearby, but I know he's right. I see what he sees. Olive stands tall and doesn't look at Jane for permission to be anymore. She leans against the glass case with her sister inside and closes her eyes like she's conjuring something.

And maybe she is.

She raises her hands, dragging them against glass all the way into the air.

There's a crack in the glass. Maybe it was there before. Or maybe it happened just now. I don't know where one spell ends and another begins.

Jane misses it. She is already bounding after Lady Lill, letting weeds and thorns try to trap her ankles, deliciously unafraid of the men who are shooting at the sky, rushing at the moat, waving their fists at the Home on the Hill. There isn't room for fear. Not anymore. I suppose Abbott sees that. But he sees me, too.

"You're surviving," he says.

"Barely," I say. "I'm a mess. I'm—I keep getting involved and running all over and I haven't thought anything through and I didn't listen to you and then when I did listen to you, it still wasn't right and I like the princesses and I miss my mother and I don't want to be sent away but I can't stay here and, Abbott, I'm not sure this spell will break. And the things they say about me might be true. And maybe when those royals touched us in the woods they didn't mean to—and it wasn't as bad as what happened to my mother—and I didn't handle it with her quietness and her grace." It topples out of me, things I haven't wanted to say to Jane or my mother or Willa or myself but that rush out at Abbott and his beautiful face and his strong hands and kind heart.

"There's more than one way to survive," Abbott says. They are my mother's words, and they sounded wise and wonderful when she said them. But I hadn't thought they could be about me. I'd given them to Jane and Abbott and the other princesses and all the people of Ever with their many flaws.

The words are a kind of forgiveness I thought wasn't meant for a witch like me.

Willa runs after Jane, leaving me alone with Abbott.

Olive kisses the glass her sister is stuck behind and runs after Willa. There, around her waist, a light yellow silk skirt appears. It doesn't stop her. Not even for a second. I imagine the silk is light and soft and feels good, hitting her legs. She catches up to Jane and Lady Lill quickly. Olive has eaten and slept and loved and remembered and hoped for years. She can't wear a crown and she can't say no to the king, but she can run so goddamn fast I'm worried I'll never catch up, even with all my magic.

"Go," Abbott says.

And I do.

But I kiss him first. Because if I'm going to survive my own way, it can look however I want it to look. It can be messy, it can be brave, it can be scared, and it can be a kiss on the mouth with a boy I might love, no matter what Grandmother says.

"There is more than one way to be a witch." A whisper before my legs take over, and even my heaviest skirt can't hold me back.

23.

JANE

We run past hundreds of people in boxes. Everyone's mothers and daughters and wives. I don't know why I cast the spell that way, so that only women would be hurt. Everyone who is not a mother or daughter or wife stands by the boxes. Some of them cry. Some of them pound the glass. Some of them are running toward the castle, like the king might fix it for them.

But when has the king fixed anything, really?

And maybe the people who aren't women aren't in glass boxes, but they sort of are, too. The boxes my magic made are glass and misshapen. But there have been boxes always, at least while my family has ruled, while my father has ruled. The king and the people who think like him love boxes.

We have all been in boxes this whole time. Witch. Royal. Farmhand. Attendant. Spellbound. Good. Bad. And it's done nothing for us. It's been wrong. Even when it worked for me, it was wrong.

By the time we get to the Home on the Hill, I'm worn out from trying to rebuild everything I've thought I've known.

And my mouth tastes a little like dill. Like dill on top of cucumber, but that cannot be, because my mouth isn't allowed to taste and the spell is almost True and we don't have the crown with which to break it.

Still. Dill. Unmistakable.

"My hands are hot," I say when we get there. "Is this the spell turning True?" Every small shift in my body feels like it could be the end. Time is hard to track in Always Day; if it isn't too late, it is getting close.

"Mine too," Olive says.

Willa tucks her hands into ours and grins. "Witches' hands get warm when they're close to home," she says. Her heart is beating in her hands. Mine beats right back at her.

"This isn't my home," Olive and I say at the same time.

"If you're a witch, then it is," Reagan says.

A dozen witches are gathered in the living room of the Home on the Hill, sitting around a woman with a voice I recognize. She must be Reagan's grandmother. The voice I heard when I was on the roof. The voice that came from nowhere, came from here.

Her face looks nothing like Reagan's. It looks, actually, a little like mine. Not the way I look now, wasting away, but the way I look underneath the spell. She has my straight back and upturned nose and long hair and tired eyes. Being near her feels good, the way being near Reagan feels good. Better than good. Right.

My hands are warm. She feels like home.

Her legs are covered in skirts. It's beautiful at first glance.

Every kind of fabric, a hundred patterns, a thousand shades. But a closer look shows she is stuck beneath them: they are heavy; they are a punishment for a lifetime of magic.

"Princess Jane," she says when she sees me. "Your Spellbound."

"And the Spellbinding," I say. I hold out my skirt, wishing again and again that it were more like Olive's, something light and romantic and pretty. But it is mine. It is my magic.

"Ah," Reagan's grandmother says. "Well. Yes." She looks to her left, and I see Lady Lill is there. She fits right in, nestled between Reagan's grandmother and a tall woman Reagan introduces as her aunt Idle. It looks like Lill was always one of them and never lived among us.

Some of the younger witches react as I'd expected, oohing and aahing at a princess with a witch's skirt. And Reagan's mother shuts her eyes like she's not ready to see it. But Reagan's grandmother only nods and nods. "Willa," she says. "The candle."

Willa runs out of the room, then comes right back with a large candle that they all make space for, stepping away from it like its light needs room to breathe. It's the candle she showed us on the roof, except it's changed.

A tutor once told me I'd know magic when I saw it, and I see it now, coming from that candle. It glows a glittering rosy gold. Shinier than anything in our castle. It's hard to look at it, and the flame only seems to grow and grow. If I weren't in a room full of witches, I'd be afraid it would lose control of itself and start a fire, but the witches don't wince away from it or worry at it.

"The kingdom at rest again?" Reagan asks. She looks confused at the color.

"At rest is lighter," Willa says.

"But unrest is red," Reagan says. "That's not unrest."

Olive and I look at each other while everyone looks at the candle. Olive's been out in the world, at least. She knows more about Ever than I do, a fact I know now to be true that a few days ago I would have fought hard against.

But Olive looks confused too. She leans close to me, whispering into my ear. "I don't know much about witches," she says. "But when we are small, we're taught to stay far away from here."

"Why?" I ask. I know why we've stayed away, but I don't know enough about Olive's life, the lives of anyone in Ever, to guess at what they're afraid of, what they worry about, who they avoid, who seems like a threat. I don't know what she does on the few days off a year we give her, and I've never asked her what rules she and the rest of the subjects of Ever follow.

"Well. Because they're just as bad as the royals," Olive says. For years, I considered Olive an almost friend, but also an almost accessory. She was there; she was kind; I liked her; she required nothing of me.

Her words stop me. I look at her. Truly. The way I never have before. She's angry. She has always been angry.

"You hate us," I say. I've apologized. I've tried to do the right thing. I've promised myself I would protect her from my father from now on. But it's so small, compared to the rest of it. Of course her magic is good and helpful and mine is itchy and heavy and wrong. I shouldn't be confused by it. It's who we are.

"It seems sort of like you hate *us*," Olive says.

"We were Spellbound—" I say, and Olive shakes her head at the excuse.

"We've been hungry too," she says slowly. Witches who were watching the flame turn to us and listen. "We've been tired. We've been loveless and desperate to forget it all. We've been hopeless. For years we've been hopeless."

It's quiet, in the Home on the Hill. I'm quiet. There's a rage in me that wants to get out. *You're not hungry like me—you can still eat; even if you are tired, you have slept; you could try harder to hope, to love. You don't understand our pain. You don't understand the way it hurts.*

It's there, a tornado of defenses spinning and spinning and wanting to scream. Because my stomach is so empty, there could be a hole all the way through me and I wouldn't know. Because my sisters are locked in a tower, being forced to smile.

But Olive has been locked up. And others are locked up now. And all I've cared about is breaking my spell, eating a piece of chocolate or cheese or—god, I can almost taste it— plum.

Because of me.

Because of us.

Because of us.

I've been thinking about the crown. How I need it to break the spell. But my mind keeps stopping there. I'll get the crown. I'll eat a sandwich. I'll eat twenty sandwiches, I won't die, and this will all be over.

But that's not right, of course. There are other spells to be broken. Ones I can see, ones I did, like the girls in the boxes, but others, too, deeper down. All of Ever is under some kind of spell, and getting the crown from the king is more than a way to break the Spell of Without. It is more. It has to be more.

"We'll get the crown," I say to Olive. I look her right in the eye. I say the words carefully and hope she knows what I mean by them.

We don't have time to talk about it. Reagan's grandmother has cleared her throat, and the room has quieted immediately, like even that sound of hers is filled with magic. "Once upon a time," she says, "there were many witches."

I take a deep breath. I feel the world starting to shift around me. I was living one life, and this is the last second of that life. I breathe it in, enjoy it, even. For one more second I am Princess Jane of Ever, I am Spellbound, I am Without, but I will someday be queen. For one more second, all that matters is becoming queen, being quiet, staying in the castle, making sure my parents are proud of me for following all the rules.

And by the time I exhale, it's over. That life is gone.

"All women were witches. People all across the gender spectrum were witches. But most men weren't witches. And those men who weren't witches didn't like the witches having power. They thought men like them should have it all."

It sounds impossible, a world flooded with magic. "All

over Ever?" I say. "All those people were witches?"

"All of everywhere," Reagan's grandmother says. "In every kingdom." Her voice shakes a little. Maybe she never planned on telling this story. Maybe there is another reality, where I am just a princess and I become a queen and the people of Ever eat potatoes and wait forever for a kidnapped princess to return.

If it weren't for Reagan and her spell, maybe there would be that life for us all.

"We witches were rulers of every kingdom. Queens were witches. Princesses. Townspeople. Attendants. Some horsemen and dukes. The King of Nethering. All of us, witches."

I try to imagine it. A world where magic flowed from so many in the population, a world flooded with spells. A world where being a witch could mean anything, could mean being a king or a farmer or a princess, but always meant being a witch. A world where those without magic craved power. And got it. Men like my father, the king.

"My mother was a witch?" I ask. I want it to be true. But a witch wouldn't let herself be stuck in a glass box for five years while her daughters wasted away. She wouldn't. Would she?

"She has it in her blood," Reagan's grandmother says. "Like you. Like Olive. But she was born after."

"After what?" Olive asks. Her fingers play with the air.

I look at Reagan to see if she knows what's coming. She looks as confused as I feel. But her mother has a different look on her face. Something more knowing. She bows her head. Aunt Idle does too. Reagan's other aunts put arms around their children, holding them close. It is a story that was never meant to be told. I want my mother to shield me from the story too. Olive has a lost-girl look on her face. And because our mothers can't be here, we move closer to each other.

It isn't enough. It isn't the same. I wish and wish and wish for my mother to be out of her glass box. I wish with every bit of me for the spell to be broken. I am coursing with magic. I am surrounded by witches. But still, I am Spellbound.

24.
REAGAN

My mother puts her hand on the top of my head.

"You knew," I say. Her hand on my head is steady. It is here. It isn't vanishing.

She nods. There is more to her story. More to Grandmother's story. She wants me to hear it.

"You all know the story," Grandmother goes on. "A girl was stolen. A princess. What you didn't know was that she was a witch. The Princess of Ever. She was stolen from the castle and taken away by someone in some kingdom. And the queen—also a witch of course—fell to pieces. And you know what happens when a witch falls apart. She starts to vanish. Parts of her were vanishing and reappearing all day, every day. More than our Bethly has ever experienced. More than any of us has seen before. And that much vanishing and reappearing of hands and shins and lips and hips requires too much magic. All her magic. The magic started seeping from her. And soon, much sooner than any of us could have imagined, it was gone. She was just a woman. Just a sad queen. All the kingdoms got involved, searching for the young princess, accusing one another of taking her, then accusing one another of other wrongs, other ruinations. Wars broke out all over the kingdoms, magic bouncing around everywhere, making things worse, and the world was in a state of unrest. Ever was in a state of unrest. And in that unrest, more magic seeped out, more magic was used, and soon, almost all of the magic was gone."

I strain to picture any of it. We've learned the history of Ever, but it wasn't this history. I was told about the War; Jane and Olive were taught history too, but it wasn't quite like this. It didn't involve a world of witches losing their magic, a queen who was a witch wasting away. It was an entirely different tale.

Jane sits on the floor. Olive sinks to join her, then changes her mind. She doesn't have to do what Jane does anymore. She doesn't have to submit. She is a witch. We were all witches, once.

There's a shuffle in the room as we struggle to piece together what Grandmother is telling us. The air is tight and hot, and I'm certain we are all dizzy.

"The princess was finally found—" Grandmother says.

"No she wasn't," Jane interrupts. "We light candles for her to return. All of Ever is still waiting, hoping that someday—"

"She was found," Grandmother says again. "She was found even though you never ask why she was taken."

"Her beauty," Jane says, like that's the only possible reason anyone could want a young girl.

"No," Grandmother says with a laugh. "It wasn't her beauty. It was her magic. It was all of their magic. Young witches were getting kidnapped from all over Ever. The ones with the

253

strongest magic. But no one cared until it was a princess. Or, rather, people cared, but not the *right* people." Grandmother sighs, trying to rid herself of that reality, trying to remember what she was going to tell us. "That princess of Ever was one of those with special magic, and the kingdom of Soar was jealous of it. They wanted some of it for themselves. So they took her, setting off the War. They didn't know it would drain all the kingdoms, all the witches, of magic."

I squint, trying to see it. It's hard, to unsee the world the way it was, and to try to reimagine it through my grandmother's story. It's hard for me, but it looks nearly impossible for Jane, who keeps shaking her head and looking out toward the castle.

"They didn't plan for it, but they liked it." It's my mother's voice, not my grandmother's, that says the thing my heart knew. "They liked that we lost power; they liked that all of us witches, those who they found weaker and lesser in every way but our magic, didn't have something strange and special over them anymore. Those men, those men who never had to tell anyone who they were, wanted what they thought was rightfully theirs: all the power. And they got it. They liked the world without witches."

"But everyone loves magic," Jane says, but she doesn't even sound like she believes herself.

"Everyone loves magic under their control," Grandmother says. Mom quiets again, but it's no secret now, what part of the story keeps her up at night, what truth she wishes she didn't know. "And Ever got that. The witches were scared, all those kingdoms against us, magic draining from all the unrest—we needed help. And Ever helped. We would protect them. They would protect us. We were supposed to be grateful."

I've always thought Grandmother *was* grateful. For our Home on the Hill, for the safety of her family, for our small lives, our magic, our way of life. But the way she says the word now, it sounds like a joke.

"It was the kidnapped witch's idea, the whole thing. It took one year of mayhem, the loss of gallons and gallons and gallons of magic. The unmagicking of nearly all the witches in the world. The War continued, and the young witch knew the remaining magic wouldn't last. If something wasn't done, they would all turn mortal, there would be no magic left, it would be gone forever."

"And that's why Ever stepped in?" Jane asked. "To help the kidnapped witch? To save the magic?"

I put a hand on Jane's arm. Her sisters aren't here to do it, and she needs someone to ground her. I've only known her a few days, but I see as clear as anything that she needs her history to have something good in it. She needs the royals to have done something worthy and kind. She is the daughter of an evil king; she doesn't want to also be the heir to an evil history.

Grandmother sees it too. Jane's wanting. Jane's letting go. Jane's fight for something good in all that is terrible.

I don't know how to tell her it's not there. There is no good trapped inside all this bad. I don't know how to tell her that this is her history, no matter how she feels about it. The terrible things that have happened belong to the king, of course. And those things have hurt us all. Jane's hurt is right on the surface of her skin, just like my mother's, like Olive's. But she and her sisters protected their father. Benefitted from these horrors, and that piece belongs to them.

Still, none of us have escaped the king. We are all harmed by the world he's made. It's all terrible. And it's all ours.

"Most of the men in all the kingdoms preferred this new world," Grandmother says. "A world embroiled in battles, one without magical women, magical people. They were prepared to fight until every last inch of magic was gone. But that young princess, the young witch with the special magic, she used that magic to get herself back to her castle. And she threatened a spell. A big one. One that would stop the War and probably ruin all the kingdoms. The magic was draining either way, and she had nothing left to lose. She told the men that the only way to stop her from casting a terrifying spell was to stop the War. They were mad. They wanted all magic gone, and some still remained. They were at an impasse when the young witch said she would take the leftover witches to a home on a hill in Ever."

"She promised we'd stay away," I say.

Grandmother nods. "We promised to stay away if they promised to keep the other kingdoms from coming for us. We got to keep the last bit of magic, and Ever got to use it when they saw fit."

I look at Jane again. My hand is still on her arm, and her gaze is still on the castle. I can feel her heartbeat even though my hand is nowhere near her heart. It is that strong, that scared, that big. For a half second she looks away from her boxed-up mother and sisters.

"Nothing's real," she says.

"You're real," I say. "We're real."

I don't know what either of us means, except that somehow everything we know isn't what we thought it was, but here we still are. Our history is being rewritten, and we will both have to find new ways to understand it. But right now, Jane is shaking. I move my hand from her arm all the way around to her shoulder and pull her close to me.

Magic bubbles up between us. It is sweet and sparkly. It feels good, in the midst of all this. I think it does for her, too. I hope.

Grandmother takes a deep breath to go on. "That young witch didn't trust anyone. Not her own kingdom. Not the men who were once her royal subjects and friends and family. She was so scared she enchanted a candle to make sure she could watch over the kingdom of Ever," she says. "Then a candle for every person in Ever, so she would know what was happening down below the hill. Because a kingdom in unrest releases magic. She would make it her duty to keep Ever at rest. To keep things as they were, to maintain the magic in the world, even if it meant watching Ever turn cruel and unfair and broken."

We know, before she says it, what else is coming.

We know because of the way she looks ashamed at the choices she's made, and we know because of how scared she's been our whole lives. We know because she is draped in so many layers of fabric it seems nearly impossible one witch could perform so much magic. We know because she doesn't mind being anchored to her chair, stuck in a living room, never able to leave, never able to be taken.

Still, she says it. We need her to say it.

"I was that girl."

"You were a princess of Ever?" Jane says, squinting like she needs to see the resemblance. It's there. I saw it just the other day. I see it now.

"I was," Grandmother says.

"And your mother was the queen?" Jane is slow, and maybe it's from the lack of eating or maybe it's from the flood of information, or maybe Jane is simply careful in a way that I'm not.

"Yes. And later, when the Wars were over and the magic was gone, she had your grandmother. The first non-magical queen of Ever." Grandmother swallows. It looks like it hurts.

It is hurting.

Jane takes a few steps toward Grandmother. "We're related," she says.

Grandmother nods, once. She isn't one for sentiment, and even now, she's not rushing to hug Jane or calm her or let it be more than a fact, a moment, a truth that was hidden and is now out in the open.

"You were that young witch," I say.

"You were the kidnapped princess," Jane says.

"I had to protect the magic," Grandmother says. "I am still protecting the magic. This is still my kingdom. My flawed kingdom. My Ever. I want to protect it. And I want to protect us. And sometimes it's nearly impossible, to protect both. But witches make sacrifices, just like royals."

"But now?" Jane asks. She's scared. She knows, we all know, that by tomorrow, she could be the one who vanishes.

"We were meant to stay separate. That was the agreement. The witches on the hill. The royals in their castle. And the rest of Ever in between." Grandmother sighs. "It was working."

Olive shakes her head. It never worked for her. Or Abbott. Or Ever.

"Until I cast the spell," I say.

Grandmother shakes her head. "Until the breaking of the spell."

"Because the kingdom is in unrest?" I ask. There's so much I don't know about magic and even more I don't know about my family. Even Grandmother, who I thought I knew, who I thought I understood, who I thought was predictable just because she stayed in one place, is a mystery.

"Because the kingdom is coming back together," Grandmother says. Her eyes, ever blue, ever clear, ever dry, fill with tears. And finally, I see it. None of us knows. None of us understands. Not even Grandmother, who is really only the young princess who was stolen for being too magical, too powerful, and now just wants everyone to stay safe. "My magic is heavy," she says. "But my magic is scared. I cast a spell to keep us separate, but your magic is big and beautiful and stubborn, Reagan," she says. "Mine was only ever scared. Not built to last. Not built to battle against brave, bighearted magic."

Mom's hand finds my shoulder. Jane's eyes find my face.

"Bighearted," I say, like it's a question, a thing I can't possibly be. I am the reckless witch who cast the Spell of Without on all the wrong people. I am the one who ruined everything.

Grandmother nods. "Like your mother," she says.

I look at my mother, who has never seemed very brave to me. Of course, there is more than one way to be brave.

"Your mother is why we stopped telling witches what happened all those years ago," Grandmother says. "Or who I am. Who we all were, how many witches there were, how much magic." She says it gently, so it's not an accusation so much as a wistful recollection. Something that hurts but also fills her with pride.

"Because she couldn't handle it," Aunt Idle says. She rolls her eyes, as if she is tired of my mother, a thing that feels impossible.

"No," Grandmother says, shooting Aunt Idle a look that doesn't need any extra language.

"Your grandmother told us our history, and I couldn't stand being banished from our castle," Mom says. She shakes her head like she was foolish, back then, but I can tell she was brave. Is brave. "So I went there. To see the king. To demand he give us back our castle. I told him the agreement was over and that we could rule together. I told him forty-five years was a long time, and we were ready to return Ever to my mother, to the witches."

"Peas in a pod, you two," Grandmother says, as she's said before, but for the first time I believe her. My mother was not

260

always this cautious, quiet witch. She was bold. She was brave. She still is, I know, but it looks different now. A different kind of brave, like she's always told me.

She closes her eyes. I close mine, too. It's what we do when things hurt too much. It's what we do when we need to know something we don't want to know, when we have to understand something it will hurt to understand. It is what we do when we face the memories of the things that have hurt her. Hurt me. Hurt us all.

Then we open them again.

Sometimes, the opening hurts too.

"He didn't take it well," my mother says. She bows her head. "He said he was king. He said we should be grateful. And when he was done, he said I knew what I was getting into, when I came to the castle." I can't see her face, but I can tell from the sound of her voice, the choppy rhythm of it, that her cheeks are flooded with tears.

I take her hand, and it helps but also probably doesn't, really.

Olive takes her other hand.

She was brave and determined. She thought she could make things better; she wanted the royals to be kinder; she wanted to soften them. Like me, she came to the castle sure she could fix something.

Like me, she was wrong.

"I didn't know what I was getting into," my mother says, like it's the first time she's said it, like she's never before imagined that it wasn't her fault, not at all, not even a little. "I never could have imagined."

Grandmother looks out the window, to the castle, to the place where she used to live.

"For witches," she says, "we don't know much at all."

"For royals," Jane says, "we don't either."

The Enchanted Candle flickers pink and blue and red, from the things we are trying to understand.

Down below, hundreds of other candles flicker hundreds of other colors.

No golden flames anywhere.

25.

JANE

I join Reagan's grandmother by the window. Olive does too. Willa beside her.

"There's still the rest of the kingdom," Olive says at last, a little shy and a little angry at once. Because again we are witches and royals who have forgotten to care about everyone else.

"Yes, of course," I say, as if I hadn't forgotten Olive's sister in her box, as if I weren't so enamored with the bubbling up of magic inside me that I'd forgotten what I'd done.

"The spell will have to be broken," Reagan says. "You know about breaking spells."

"I don't know anything about breaking a spell I cast. I'm still trying to understand the breaking of a spell *you* cast." After five years of hating Reagan for her impetuous spell-casting, for not thinking through all the repercussions, I can't believe I'm just like her. Every bit as reckless and thoughtless and self-ish. Casting a spell, forgetting I'd have to Undo it. Not being sure how it all works.

"You have to break it before it turns True. You're not eighteen yet?" Willa asks.

"Not yet. Another month."

"Well. Then you have a month before it's True." I can tell that Willa loves studying magic the way I've loved studying the kingdom.

"A True Spell can't be broken?" I ask.

"Once it's True, the effects are permanent. So even if a True Spell was broken, the Spellbound would never fully recover," Willa says. "Some spells have the breaking built in. A rule made when the spell is cast that tells the enchanted how to fix it. But a spell like yours, like Reagan's, that doesn't have the Undoing baked into it—a spell like that has to be broken before it's True. Right, Reagan?" Willa looks proud of herself, but my head is spinning. We were told that magic had a logic, had good reasons, but I didn't understand what that meant, how intricate their rules were, how delicate the whole thing was.

"You've studied a lot more than I have, Willa," Reagan says, and the way she looks at her cousin, I can see the love right there on the surface, all soft and easy and sweet. It's the same love I have for my sisters.

"I don't know everything," Willa says. "But I know we need to break these spells soon. Now. For the people of Ever to survive."

"And my sisters."

"And your mother," Reagan's mother says.

"My mother, the queen."

"One of many queens," Reagan's mother says. Because if her mother was once princess, then maybe she is meant to be queen. Maybe Reagan is. Willa could be queen, or one of the

264

other witches. It's possible I am not the heir to the throne, that being queen is not my destiny. It seemed like a straight line. The oldest daughter of the Queen of Ever.

Except that was never the true story.

We all look at Reagan's mother. Bethly is a serious woman with curly hair and a strong jaw and a stronger silence. She looks spent from telling her part of the story. Reagan's grandmother does too, all of us exhausted by history.

"It's time," Bethly says.

"No," Reagan's grandmother says.

"We can't be afraid forever," Bethly says. It sounds like it is hard to say. That choosing not to be afraid is, somehow, terrifying. Being afraid is safe. It keeps you locked up in the Home on the Hill, casting small spells and watching a flame to make sure everything is okay. She's spent practically a whole lifetime pretending there is no magic tucked into the very fabric of the kingdom, pretending every person she watches from her Home on the Hill might not be a witch, and pretending that every witch wandering the halls of her home couldn't someday be a queen.

Being afraid means not seeing the way your father, the king, looks at attendants and tutors, chefs and visiting royals. That fear is comfortable, like a castle you never have to leave, like a story told so often you never wonder if it's true or not.

"It's not safe," Reagan's grandmother says.

"I know," Bethly says. "But nothing's safe."

She walks over to Willa. She watches the flame as it threatens to lick the ceiling. The whole Home could burn down. Ever could crumble into flames. Women could end up in boxes forever. Men could trap them in the woods. The night may never return. That spell too will turn True in another day, on Reagan's birthday. And then, if Willa's right, it will be nearly impossible to break. So many rules at work that we didn't know about, so many witches we'd never heard of, so many secrets buried all over the kingdom we thought we knew, even though we'd never seen an inch of it.

"The kingdom was never really at rest, anyway," Reagan's mother says. She leans forward, closes her eyes, and blows out the flame. Like it's a birthday candle. Like it's nothing.

26.

REAGAN

When our candle is blown out, the second it unflickers, the candles below are extinguished too. One minute they are flicking their dangerous colors, and the next, Ever is just in Always Day, not a candle to be seen. Not a speck of extra light on the horizon.

We can hear them gasp.

We can hear the men of Ever whisper and wonder at what is happening to their little kingdom.

Grandmother closes her eyes. She's told a story today that's been weighing on her for years, heavier than decades' worth of spells wrapped around her waist. "Stay here," she says to Mom and Willa and me. "Let these girls go. Let them go and work out their magic themselves. Let them fix it. Let them unwind it. If you go with them—we can't put that back together. We won't ever have this again. We won't be safe."

I've wondered, from time to time, what my grandmother might have looked like when she was a girl, when she was seven or twelve or almost eighteen like me. But I think I can see it now. She is that little girl, thirteen years old, stolen away from her home, which just so happened to be a castle, and her mother, who happened to be the queen. Her eyelashes flutter with nervousness, and she keeps looking around like she wants to remember every detail of the life we are living this moment, before it might change.

I wonder if that's what she did, when they took her.

"What did they do to you?" I ask.

Grandmother looks surprised that there could be more questions. She's told the story that's gone untold for years. And it turns out she's bad at predicting how we feel about it.

"Kings and princes have been doing the same things to princesses and witches for ages," she says.

"And to attendants," Olive says.

Grandmother's surprise grows. "Yes," she says. "I suppose that's true. Even when there was magic. Always. It was a king's kingdom, and we all suffer for it."

"In very different ways. With different consequences." Olive's voice is clear, and I see how similar they are, Grandmother and Olive. They have both been waiting their whole lives to speak, thinking maybe it would never happen. They are both finding voices that were buried, and they are both finding their balance right now, right here.

But Grandmother has had power her whole life, and Olive is just starting to wonder if some is meant for her, too. Suffering for my grandmother is living in the Home on the Hill, which is secluded but beautiful, filled with food and love and flickering candlelight. Suffering for Olive, for Abbott and Bess and so many others in Ever, is more base, more immediate, bigger.

"Stay here, Reagan," Grandmother says again, not quite looking at Jane or even Olive. "You've tried. You've helped these witches find their magic. They've made their own messes. You belong here. With me. It's better this way."

She can't leave, of course, but I see that she'll never want to either. Maybe she cast hundreds of spells, and the layers upon layers of skirts weighing her down are the price she pays. Or maybe, maybe, she cast hundreds of heavy spells so that she'd never have to leave, never be taken away again. Maybe the spells are bits of bravery, or maybe they are signs of fear. I don't think I'll ever know.

I don't think she knows.

But I will not cast a hundred spells. I will not sit in a chair and give orders. I will not let my magic turn True and wait to see how it ends up changing the world.

"We have to keep Ever at rest," Grandmother says, her words on a loop. So much is changing here and now, but she's trying to hold on to the way things have been.

"We can do better than a kingdom at rest," I say. I see now that the golden flame, all the golden flames, were meant to keep things predictable and calm and contained. But there's more than the golden glow of a calm kingdom. There's more to life than waiting on top of a hill and hoarding your magic.

Grandmother wants nothing to change, but of course everything already has. It's too late for the things she wants. It was too late when I cast my spell and too late when Mom tried to talk to the king and too late, probably, the second they declared it the War We Won.

269

We can't be at rest when the king still has his crown. I started something, or continued something that had started long before I showed up. And now it's time to finish it.

And besides, there is no flame that tells us how Ever is anymore, but we know. We can hear the bellows and see the hundreds of glass boxes catching the sun's flare, reflecting it out.

That candle had glowed for years, and with one breath of air it was gone.

Magic doesn't have to be forever.

Even the strongest flames are extinguished.

Spells are meant to be broken.

"We have to go," I say. "We have spells to break."

"We have magic to do," Olive says. Her fingers dance, like they are itching to experiment with her new abilities.

"We have spells to Undo," Jane says.

She has never sounded more like a queen.

27.

JANE

We run through Ever. Running is doubly hard, from the spell placed on me and the spell I cast. But we run, because time is running out. We have to get the crown. We don't have a plan for how or when, but we run—me, Reagan, Olive, Bethly, and Willa, who is the youngest and the surest and the most ready to fight.

"Oh, Jane," Bethly says over and over and over again until it stops sounding like my name and becomes an admonishment of what kind of princess I am. Or what kind of witch, I guess. Or maybe just what kind of person.

"I don't know how to break the spell," I whisper to Reagan. "I can't believe—I'm so thoughtless. I don't know how—"

"Yes you do," Reagan says. "You know how spells work. Remember what Willa said. Breathe. Think. They give you something. And then you perform an Undoing. Just like my spell. It's the same."

"It hurts," Bethly says. "The Undoing." She puts a hand on my arm, and it's a mother's touch. God, I've missed it. I move away from it, because how good it feels makes the rest of me ache. It makes me hungrier for all of it. Food and my sisters and my mother and a better world.

"That's fine," I say. "Everything hurts."

"You just have to choose what you want from them," Willa says. "They can bring you presents. Or you could banish them all to Farr or AndNot. Make them fight in a battle. Make them give up their land." Her eyes shine. She has a hundred ideas. Willa is always full of ideas.

But.

But.

Drum Drascall is already gone.

The royals in the woods were from other kingdoms. And they were royals, not subjects.

I try to remember what I'm punishing the people of Ever *for*. Everything is turned upside down and inside out, and after a day being away from the castle, I don't feel so much like a princess. Somewhere along the way, I lost my shoes, my tiara, my diamond earrings, my certainty.

I dig my feet into the Ever earth a little. It's so dusty and dry; who knows if it will grow anything again. The people of Ever, what's left of them, sit in their used-to-be gardens on their once-upon-a-time farmland, and they howl at the glass boxes with their loved ones inside. They don't have anything left to give me.

"I can't ask for anything," I say to the witches next to me. "What would they have to give me?"

"What do you need?" Reagan asks.

I look at the castle. It is still. My sisters in their boxes are as frozen as my mother on the lawn. All that's left of my family is me and the man who was once my father and was once the Good and Gentle King and is now someone else entirely.

If I could magic things back to the way they were before the spell, I wouldn't. That before wasn't real. It didn't exist. Not the way I thought it did.

There's only one thing I need, and the people of Ever can't give it to me.

The king steps out onto the balcony of the highest tower. My sisters in their boxes beside him look as lifeless as they did the last time he was on his balcony giving a speech.

"What did I do, what did I do, what did I do?" I say under my breath.

"Jane. Just do better this time," Reagan says, like it's that easy. I spent years learning what it meant to be a queen, but everything about it was wrong.

"I can't," I say. It feels true enough. I can barely think or stand or hope. For a moment, I don't even want to fix it. I don't want to break the spell I cast, and I don't want to break the spell Reagan cast. I want to stand right here until someone else fixes it. Maybe I even want to die. Slip away and never know what it is to live in another kind of kingdom.

Reagan must see it. She pinches my arm.

"Don't look away," she says. My heart squeezes at all the times I have done exactly that. I close my eyes for one second, then force them all the way open. Train them on my father. Look for edges of glass boxes with princesses inside, hidden behind him.

"People of Ever," the king says. From a certain angle, he still looks like my father. There are the same gray threads in his beard, the same oversize fur robe, the same enormous crown that I can't imagine him ever handing over. But mostly he looks like someone I don't know at all. "It is now that you need your king more than ever. I see that. I understand that. I am here for you. As I have always been here for you. Through the Famine. Through the Spell of Without. Through all of our suffering."

He says the word "suffering" like he knows what it means. But the Famine didn't hurt him. And the Spell of Without didn't hurt him either. He looks like a man who is hurt. He is excellent at playing the part. But I watch his hand as it straightens the crown atop his head, and the way his arms cross over his chest after.

There is a smattering of applause, but not the thunder he is used to.

"I am the only one who can get us through these terrible times," the king, my father, says. He sounds so sure about it. He sounds like the hero of a story that no one is telling. His voice is loud. And mine is soft. But he is up in a tower, and I am right here, right here on the bare, dusty ground of Ever, ready at last to fight.

"People of Ever," I say, surprised at the way the words feel in my mouth. "We can break the spell. We will break it together." I don't mean to sound like him, but I do a little. I sound a little like a someday maybe future queen and a little like a Spellbound princess and a little like a brand-new witch and a little like Jane, just Jane, a person in a blue dress and a wool skirt who would do almost anything for an apple.

The taste of it, I swear, sneaks onto my tongue. A tang. A sweetness. It's gone before I can enjoy it. But it was there. Apple.

I tell them what they have to do to break the spell.

28.

REAGAN

"To break a spell," Jane says, "there is a sacrifice and an Undoing. It is time to break the spell. The one on you. The one on me. The one on all of Ever."

The unboxed people of Ever look up. They are wary of this princess, with her soft, starving voice and her shaking hands. And they are wary of the king in his tower. And they are wary of the rest of us witches, walking around when so many other people are trapped in glass.

"To break the spell, you will go to the castle. You will cross the moat. We will get the crown."

There's a pause.

There is always a pause when you tell someone how to break a spell. There was a pause two days ago, at the Thirteenth Birthday. It felt like a hundred years, but it was probably barely three seconds. Still, it is a distinctly quiet thing.

"We can't," a white man leaning against his wife's glass box says.

"It's *water*," a person with an upturned nose cries.

"We don't cross the moat," a young kid in a thick sweater

says, as if we need Ever to be explained to us.

"Well, today you do," Jane says. Her back is straight. She pulls her hair up on top of her head in a messy knot. She hikes her wool skirt up.

Olive, my mother, Willa, and I follow suit, pinning up hair, tying up layers and layers of magical skirts, readying ourselves for the cool water.

Jane steps in. "It's just water," she says.

"They're Spellbound to be afraid of it," Willa says. Jane knows this, of course. We all know this. "They can't cross the moat."

"I think they can," Jane says. She takes another step in and another. She walks straight to the middle of the moat, where the water is nearly up to her neck.

"It's not safe," Turner Dodd says. The one who is not, in fact, the saddest person in Ever. He's sad, though. A lot of them are, it turns out. So much sadness packed into this one little kingdom, and we had to use magic to get a thimbleful of tears. I shiver from all the things I'm still trying to understand.

Jane laughs. Right there, in the middle of the moat, soaking and starving and Spellbound. She laughs so hard I start to laugh. Olive laughs a little too. Willa giggles. Even my mother gives a wry smile at worry over a moat when the world is falling apart.

"Ever isn't safe," Jane says. "What do you have left to be afraid of?"

The king in his tower booms out objections. "Subjects of Ever can't cross the moat," he says. "Think of what it will do to the kingdom. It's not how things are done. It's not safe. It's not right." But I keep laughing, and the unboxed, unbound people of Ever look at a sea of glass boxes and miles of Barren Fields and the everlasting day and the Woods That Were and their king in his tower holding his crown onto his head like it means something, like it matters, like it makes what he says matter more.

There is a splash. And a splatter. And a series of waves.

There is Abbott Shine up to his waist in water.

There are two young children atop their parents' shoulders.

There is Turner Dodd, crying as he takes the world's smallest steps into the moat.

There is a rush of two hundred sets of legs in every shade of skin feeling the cold of the moat for the very first time. They scream, a few of them, in alarm at the temperature of it or the wetness maybe. They shiver and worry and wonder what might happen. They gasp.

They're afraid. That hasn't gone anywhere. They are Spellbound to be afraid, so they are afraid.

But they are in it, wading in the shallow end at first, then joining Jane in the middle. And by the time Jane makes it to the castle, to where her mother is waiting for her in a glass box, the whole of unboxed Ever is in that moat, walking and floating and swimming and running and screaming and crying all the way to the other side.

I watch with my mother as Willa runs across the moat. She splashes and shrieks. She does it alone and doesn't seem to notice we aren't next to her. And we watch Olive lift her chin up high and walk through, catching up with her half brother waiting for her in the middle, holding her hand for the harder half. She won't be alone in that castle again.

Mom is shaking next to me. She doesn't want to go. "You don't have to," I say.

"I know," she says. She licks her lips. There's nothing there to lick, but she does it anyway. She stares up at the king in his tower. He is looking right at us.

"Look what you've done," he says, to her or to me or to his daughter, it's hard to say. "All I ever did was try to be a Good King."

What we want more than anything, what I know my mom wants, and what I want so badly I can barely breathe, is for him to apologize and say he was wrong. That is the ending we deserve.

He will never give us that.

It would be nice, to be given everything we deserve.

But it's not necessary. And if he won't give it, we'll just take it.

We're goddamn witches. Don't tell us we can't.

29.

JANE

I don't let anyone in until Reagan and her mother are all the way across the moat. I won't let them enter alone.

"We're ready," Reagan says when she reaches shore. I look at Bethly. She is soaking wet and gripping her daughter's arm. But she is as ready as the rest of us, pulling her shoulders back, lifting her head, taking big breaths, like she might blow the whole thing down.

There's a flurry of conversation among the subjects of Ever. They want their wives and daughters and mothers unboxed. Mostly. Mostly they do. But they also want to know if this is the only way.

"He's a Good King," a man who looks like my father says. Maybe he's dined in our castle before. Maybe he came to my Birthday. Maybe he himself is a good man or a kind man, but he is wrong about my father. "He's the Gentle King," the man goes on, shaking his head and speaking a little more loudly, a little more confidently, drumming up support. People nod.

"He sent wood to fix our roof," one says.

"He saved my child from the moat once," another says.

"Think of how the queen fell in love with him. Because he was so good to her. So unlike other princes and dukes from other kingdoms." My heart twists at this one, thinking of my father and mother but also of Grace, who pinned her every hope and dream on their love story. A story I am taking apart. A story we may never tell again.

"He sent us pineapples when my mother was dying," a person in a green coat sighs.

"He kept the witches away."

"He reached peace with the other kingdoms."

"He loved his children. Let them be themselves. Didn't try to force Alice into being a prince. Didn't stop Nora from playing in the mud, or Grace from her daydreaming. Never laughed at their dolls or ribbons or gowns. He let us all be ourselves. He is Good." There is finality to this last statement, and again my heart wrestles with itself. Images flash in my head: of my father letting me try on his crown, letting me sit on his throne, calling me Queen Jane. My father brushing my hair, learning how to French braid it. My father making us pancakes, and making tiny miniature ones for our favorite dolls. My father lighting his candle, hoping for the princess to return, bringing it to my mother in her glass box in the evenings and talking to her about his day. My father telling me I could love anyone and be anything.

My father, the king.

But also: there's the image of his hands on Olive, his shadow making attendants shiver, a long-ago time when I thought I heard him say something about what kind of girl would let a man hurt her, how silly a girl like that must be, how weak.

His straight back at Eden's Thirteenth Birthday.

The way he smiled at the King of Soar, the Prince of Droomland, the Princess of Thorner, nodding as they each appraised us. His scowl when he called me unstable. The quick, easy way he locked up my sisters.

And Bethly. And Olive. And the ways they each hold their body, leaning back a little when you get too close, looking worried at what might happen next.

If a queen is silent, I guess I won't be queen.

"He shouldn't be king," I say. My voice is weak. It is weaker every second. The spell is so close to True that I can feel it in my bones, rattling around, readying me for something awful. I try again. "My father isn't the Good King. Or the Gentle King. Or the king that cares about any of you." I look out at the people of Ever, what's left of them. They keep whispering among themselves, looking from the castle's tower to the moat they conquered, to their loved ones in boxes, to me. Over and over and over, they land on me.

But I don't know what else to say.

My father knows what to say. Of course he does. He opens his mouth, and like that, my chance to say the truth, to change the world, to break the spell, slips further away. His voice is booming where mine is weak. His is steady where mine shakes. He is tall where I'm small and thick where I am broken. He is in his robe and his crown, and he is the highest point in Ever; he is the king; he is their King.

"My poor daughter," he says. "She is so confused. She's brought you over here in some fit of hallucination. It isn't her fault. We all know whose fault it is. She's never been the same, not since the spell hit. Our prized princess, our someday queen. That girl is gone. Look at the girl in front of you. We should be thanking the heads of every kingdom for considering taking her in, having their children marry her. She barely knows her own name. She hasn't eaten in five years. Don't forget that. She's not capable. Not now. Not like this." He shakes his head and lets his voice falter, lets it sound as if he is going to cry from the pain of it, but the tears don't come. "You know me," he says, and I know they feel like they do. "You know what kind of king I am."

30.

REAGAN

"I know what kind of king you are," a voice from the crowd calls out. I make sure it isn't me who said it. I have been trying to find my voice, wondering if my mom will find hers. I listen for her breathing and mine. We take big breaths, like we are about to speak, and then we don't.

I look for the origin of the first voice to speak. And when I find it, I put my hand over my heart. The voice belongs to Abbott Shine. He is not a princess or a witch or Spellbound. He is handsome and tall; he has a voice that is lower than I ever thought his voice would reach. He is just like them, except he knows a different king than they do.

"Give us the crown," he says. He could chant it or yell it, he could say what was done, but it's not his story to tell. He lets the words ring out on their own, and he waits. We all wait. The people of Ever shuffle. A princess they can deny. A witch they can hate. They try to decide how to ignore Abbott Shine, too, but it seems harder.

"I know what kind of king you are," another voice says. "Give us the crown."

This time the voice is a sweeter one, but surprisingly strong. The voice of my mother.

"I know what kind of king you are," Olive says next. "Give us the crown."

There is the sound of glass cracking. A spell isn't broken all at once; it comes tumbling down in bits and pieces. Jane's spell is breaking down. Her magic is entirely her own: big and strange and reckless but also ready to break apart, open-hearted, changeable.

"I know what kind of king you are," Willa says. "Give us the crown."

"I know what kind of king you are," someone says, their voice caught up in a sob, the sound of someone who has kept a secret for a long time. "Give us the crown."

More glass cracks and shatters, and a few of the now-witches of Ever break out of their boxes. They shake out their hands when they do, the feeling of magic unfamiliar in the tips of their fingers. I can hear glass breaking inside the castle too, the sounds of attendants and maybe princesses escaping their curse.

"I know what kind of king you are. Give us the crown," some of the people emerging from their boxes call. Not all of them. Not even many of them. But a few. Enough.

The temperature of the kingdom lifts, the warmth of a hundred witches finding one another, the feeling of magic coming back, rushing back in. We were always witches; we just didn't know. Whatever happened between Jane and me has unleashed all of that magic back to its rightful owners, all these decades later. I watch the king's hand travel to his fore-head, wiping sweat away. It snakes around to the back of his neck, where he lifts up his robe, airing himself out.

"The kingdom is meant to be at rest," the king says. His voice is less steady. He clears his throat and tries again. It isn't much better, though. "The kingdom can't be at rest with all this chaos. Without a king in a castle. Without the witches out of the way. This isn't safe. I'm telling you, this will be like the long-ago War We Won. Do you want to be at war again? Do you want another Famine? Do you want things to get worse?"

"I know what kind of king you are," I say. "Give us the crown."

A dozen more glass boxes break. A dozen more witches step out into Ever, wondering why the air feels hot and charged, why their arms are begging to be raised, why they suddenly smell something too sweet and a little like coffee—the royal fear. The king's terror.

"You can't trust a witch and a princess over a king. Your king," the king cries.

"What about a dozen witches?" I say.

"What about a hundred?" Jane says. She looks out at Ever. A young girl, newly emerged from her box, raises her arms. An enormous cake appears in front of her. Another new witch raises their hands, and a silk gown appears on their body. Turner Dodd's mother raises her hands and stops her son's crying. Lady Lill raises her hands, and the king is no longer in his tower but right here, among us, on the ground, on the shore of the moat.

He is smaller than I thought he was. Grayer than he looks in his tower. His crown is askew.

"Is this what you want?" he asks the people of Ever, all of them in different states of surprise and fear and excitement and pride. "Is this really what you want?"

There's the sound of more cracking glass. It's the loudest shatter yet, because it's right here, practically on top of us. We move out of the way of the falling glass, some of us screeching in surprise. There is more to be afraid of than just a king in a tower or a witch on a hill.

But when the shock is over, when the glass is all on the ground and my mother can magic it away, the fear is worth it. Because she is here with us again. The Queen of Ever. Out of her box. Moving her limbs. And turning to the king with a sureness reserved for royalty, reserved for queens. A certainty that comes from sitting in a box, watching the world go by, worried she'll never be able to make it better.

"You are not a king," the Queen of Ever says, her first words in five years, but still they sound sure and easy, a little like music. "Give us the crown."

31.

JANE

I don't recognize her voice. I thought I'd remembered it all these years, replaying her advice in my head, going over and over and over the things she'd told me about what it would take to become a queen. But she sounds completely different from the memory of my mother.

A still comes over Ever. They've waited a long time to see their queen move and speak. I wonder if she's what they want her to be, if she fits their memories better than my own.

"Is the spell broken?" I ask Reagan, who looks every bit as surprised as me that the queen is out of her box. The king's crown is still on his head, so it shouldn't be possible, but boxes are breaking everywhere, and I have a sudden desire to eat. I look for my sisters. I'll be able to see in their eyes if they are still Spellbound.

"It can't be," Reagan says. "He didn't give us the crown. I didn't perform the Undoing. You haven't performed yours. Spells break little by little, but there's always a moment where they're totally done. The Undoing."

I imagine Reagan, like me, poring over books upon books to understand how magic works, how Ever works, what it means to be royal or magical or none of those things. We have both studied hard. We were both brought up to carry on a tradition that we didn't entirely understand. We both thought we were living one story, when really we were living another.

There was nothing in our textbooks about a king who shouldn't be king or witches who don't know they are witches.

I look up at the tower, and there they are. My sisters, out of their boxes. Nora grins. Alice lowers herself to the ground and maybe, maybe, finally sleeps. Grace looks alight with knowledge.

And Eden. Eden is filled with hope.

She rushes down from the tower, joining us on the lawn. She's brought something with her. "Here," she says. "I think you'll like it."

It's an apple, so red and shiny it could be fake, but the feel of it in my hand is so real that my mouth starts to water. "I can't," I say, because that feels true, because my father is standing there with his arms crossed and his head raised, daring us to take the crown from his head.

"I think you can," Eden says.

So I try. Because if Eden can hope, maybe I can eat. My lips meet the apple's skin, and for a moment I think it's just like always. I can't bite in. My mouth won't let me.

But it only lasts a second. My teeth break through. And I take a bite.

It tastes nothing like what I remember. Sharper than I thought it would be. Sweeter. Messier, too.

Like Ever.

It's gone in an instant. I am ravenous, desperate for more

and more and more to eat. Alice will probably sleep for a month. I will eat for the rest of the day. For the rest of the week, barely taking a rest. But the look of confusion doesn't leave Reagan's face. And she doesn't have a new skirt from the magic of breaking a spell.

"This isn't possible," she says to me and to her mother and to Willa and to whoever in Ever can hear her.

Reagan's mother puts an arm around her daughter. She looks at the king. Maybe it's the first time she's looked directly at my father and not immediately needed to look somewhere else, to make herself disappear.

"I'm not giving up my crown," my father says, pretending to be sure but faltering, since the Spell of Without isn't turning True but in fact is breaking down.

"That's just fine," Reagan's mother says. "There's more than one way to break a spell."

My mother smiles at Reagan's mother. They don't look anything alike, except for the ways they look at us. A hundred textbooks we read, Reagan and I. A hundred rules we memorized. I was taught that nothing was more powerful than the royal family. And Reagan probably learned that nothing was more powerful than a witch's magic. But all this time, there was the truth, there was the kingdom, there was bravery, and that was stronger than anything we learned about.

"And more than one way to rule a kingdom," my mother says. She raises her arms. It must feel good, to stretch like that after five years frozen. To feel magic rush through her after a lifetime without.

"This isn't right," my father, the king, says. "This isn't how it's supposed to be."

"We needed a crown from the King of Ever," Reagan says, looking to her mother for an explanation. "He didn't give his crown. Why are the spells breaking?"

Again, Reagan's mother looks at mine. Their stories have crissed and crossed for all these years, silently winding around each other, more complicated than they had to be. Made complicated by silence and shame and ignorance and fear.

They look out over the kingdom, the masses of people demanding the king give up his crown.

"A king has to have a kingdom," Reagan's mother says. "A king is only king because his people say that he is."

She smiles. It's a beautiful thing, rare and precious and about-to-laugh.

"There is no King of Ever," my mother says. She straightens her own crown, then reconsiders and takes it from her head. "We are a kingdom without a king."

"We are a kingdom with a queen!" an eager woman across the moat cries. There's a smattering of applause for my mother, the queen, and some grumbles, too. My mother shakes her head at the excitement, though. She gives in to Bethly's beaming smile, and one finds its way onto her face as well. She looks happy to have her smile back. Her voice, too. She looks happy, in a way she never did before.

She isn't still. She isn't quiet. She isn't ruling from a distance. She isn't the sun obediently shining on a garden.

"Are you still queen?" I ask my mother. "What does it

mean to be queen?" It is a question I asked when I was young, but I knew so little then. The question is different now.

My mother thinks for a great long while.

"There's more than one way to be queen," she says, the words of my mother and Reagan's mother echoing off each other again and again.

"You have to be royal," I say. But my mother shakes her head. We don't know what royal means, anyway. It has changed, over the years.

"You have to be quiet," Reagan says. She knows what lessons I learned and how hard it is to unlearn them. My mother shakes her head again. That one was wrong too.

"A woman," Willa says.

"No." My mother is sure on that point. We grew up thinking queens were quiet women and kings were gentle, good men, but all of that was wrong.

"A queen is a person with a crown," my mother says. Her arms raise and crowns appear on the heads of people all over the kingdom.

Willa touches the one on her own head. It looks small and delicate. Other crowns are large and opulent. Others are basic and sweet. "It's not that simple," Willa says. A crown doesn't fix the way things have been. A crown doesn't mean we are all the same. A crown doesn't change the years that have gone by, the way things have been, how much work it will be to change Ever, to change the world.

"It was never so simple, I suppose," my mother, the queen, says.

32.

REAGAN

Outside the walls of the castle, standing before the Waterless Moat, looking out at a world of witches, there is a man in a box. He is hunched and cross armed. He is gray haired and smirking. He still has a crown upon his head. He is not sorry. He is Jane's father, the once-upon-a-time king.

It is a perfect spell, because we cast it together. All of us, every witch in Ever. There are more of us than I thought there would be. Every woman in every kind of body, and others, who identify only as witch. And some men, too, who found the magic as if it were a sock they'd lost in the laundry, a key that had slipped through their fingers into the moat. Maybe there are people who are witches but want to keep that hidden. I don't know. What I know is that though some men *are* witches, it is only men who are *not* witches.

We cast the spell together, so that none of us would have to bear the weight of it alone. Each known witch in Ever was wrapped in a featherlight silver skirt, so thin you could forget it was there. Except that there is a king trapped in glass who refuses to be sorry.

If he is ever sorry, the spell will be broken and he will be banished to AndNot, to a small cottage I once lived in. He will be allowed to listen to the ocean and think about what he did. He will be free to walk the shore, but not free to hurt anyone else.

But for now, he is not sorry. Before the spell hit, he said he had done nothing wrong. He looked them all in the eye—my mother, Olive, a dozen other now-witches whom he'd hurt—and said he hadn't done it, they had misunderstood, they had wanted it, they had asked for it, he was king, and if a king does something, it can't be wrong.

It isn't true, but it also doesn't matter. In Ever, now, there are no kings.

There is an empty castle and an expanse of avocado trees and raspberry bushes and fields of greens and wheat. Jane works in what were once the Barren Fields, always stealing bits of food for herself. A cherry tomato. A bite of pear. A mushroom growing from the ground, earthy and delicate at once. Her mother works alongside her, loving the sun on her arms, the breeze in her hair, the way her limbs move when she wants, still when she wants.

Jane wears her crown in the fields. It is a sight to see. A queen of Ever in thick pants and a heavy sweater, digging holes in dirt, picking fruit from trees, looking around before popping it in her mouth, always closing her eyes at the taste.

She doesn't want to miss a single bite.

Willa wears her crown by the moat, where she spends most of her time. She teaches spells to new witches and is always forgetting an ingredient, a word from a chant, a detail. She thinks she is a teacher, but she is a light. A tiny light by the moat, a person who is both strong and sweet, both brave and silly, unlikely, perfect combinations that are befitting a queen of Ever.

Olive wears her crown as she walks the kingdom of Ever, checking on magic, making sure no one has cast a spell so large it will weigh them down, so unruly it could unmagic a kingdom full of witches. She makes sure no one has lit a candle. Sometimes a non-witch tries. Sometimes a non-witch says we are dangerous, that our magic is evil, that we have made Ever a terrible place to live. Sometimes a non-witch says it is our duty to forgive the king. Olive assures them it is not.

Olive speaks to the subjects of Ever in her gentle voice, and they believe she is soft when in fact she is unwavering. There is so much they don't see of her, so much they miss.

So much they miss about us all.

"He is not the king," Olive says when they ask and ask and ask. "There is no king."

I'm not sure if there are queens, either. There are people with crowns. There are witches with skirts. There are people who don't want either, who want both, who want the past, who think the future is already here.

Jane's mother said a queen is a person with a crown, but she also said it was never so simple as all that. We could hand out a hundred crowns, a crown for every witch, but it wouldn't make us all the same.

Maybe I am not a queen, or maybe I am, but I wear my

crown in the Home on the Hill, where I sit on the roof and watch over Ever. Sometimes I miss the smell of the ocean. Sometimes I miss the sound of frying berries. Sometimes I wish I could live in a home as one of only a few witches in the world, not knowing that there is magic everywhere.

And on those days, at those times, I go down to the moat with Willa and wait for Abbott Shine to join us. He always does.

"Look what you did," he says, and he points at the gardens of vegetables and flowers, the women with skirts tied tight around their waists, the bursts of magic that explode in the sky a dozen times a day, the never-night sky that keeps us safe, the Woods That Were so that no one can hide what they're doing.

Sometimes we miss the way things were. The sky turning from light to dark. The woods with their tall trees and worn paths and hidden nooks. A fairy-tale kingdom with parties and jewels and enchanted princesses. A Good King. A beautiful queen. A clear role for everyone. Five hundred people in boxes fit just for them.

But the way things were was never the way things were. Night was never just a starlit sky. Woods were never just trees. Not really.

I keep looking at what Ever has become, the beautiful and the ugly parts in a strange sort of harmony. If we lit the candle, it wouldn't be gold. We are not at rest. We are changing. We are trying. We are failing. We are trying again, harder.

It is an imperfect and unbalanced Ever. It always was. Maybe it always will be. Even magic and crowns can only do so much.

Abbott and I talk about Ever, like we used to. Some days he is angry and some days he is hopeful and some days he is too tired to talk about any of it. Willa tells us about Jane, who magics up more crowns, then fewer. She tries spells and then promises to never cast another one again. She doesn't know quite who to be. Neither do I. Neither does Abbott.

Neither does Ever.

"We need to write a new story of Ever," Willa says. "A true one." She opens up a notebook that looks like the one Grace used to use; maybe it *is* the one Grace used. She doesn't need it anymore. And Willa begins to write the truth of Ever, the way she sees it.

She leaves room for more histories. More fairy stories. More once-upon-a-times and a-long-time-agos. Behind the castle, Alice chips away at stone, carving and recarving the people of Ever, trying to tell our story in marble, never getting it quite right, never finishing.

Alice carves and Willa writes and Abbott worries and my gaze lands where it always does. On the king in his box, sure he has done nothing wrong, waiting for something other than his own heart to break the spell he's under.

We sit on the edge of the moat, dipping our feet into air that used to be water. And we think about the magic that used to be only mine.

We wait for a night to come, but it doesn't.

It won't.

I won't let it.

Not again. Not Ever again.

ACKNOWLEDGMENTS

This book has been a challenge, a gift, a thrill, a surprise. There are so many people to thank for helping this book move from the vaguest of ideas to a full-blown world.

As always, a gigantic thank-you to my agent and friend, Victoria Marini, who is my rock, who makes me feel capable, and who I am so grateful to have spent the last eight years working with.

I've been beyond lucky to work with my editor, Liesa Abrams, on this imagined fairy tale. This book and I both needed her buzzing brain, her big heart, her patience, her faith, and her brand of magic to push this idea to places I never knew it could go. Thank you, thank you, thank you for the long list of ways you showed up for me, for this process, and for this story. It is a gift to work with you. And a huge thank-you to Jessi Smith for her incredible editorial input and creative energy, which played a huge role in sculpting this story.

An enormous thank-you to everyone at Simon Pulse who has worked on this book from the million different angles bookmaking requires. Specifically, thank you to Heather Palisi and Katt Phatt for the incredible cover and thank you to Chelsea Morgan, Sara Berko, Brian Luster, Jen Strada,

ACKNOWLEDGMENTS

Rebecca Vitkus, and the wonderful sales and marketing teams for all your hard work on and support of *Ever Cursed*.

A very special thank-you to Sarah Gailey for their incredible, generous, valuable insight. And thank you to other readers who brought vital feedback to this project, helping me find the best path to tell the story I intended to tell.

This is the first novel-length book I've written since having a baby, and I have to thank everyone who helped me find a space to be a parent and a writer, and everyone who helped make that space beautiful and safe and valued. Thank you to Fia's grandparents for being available whenever we needed it, the incredible women at Fia's day care, a long list of beautiful friends, and an impressive roster of babysitters, including my valued friend Alisha Spielman. And a very special thank-you to the other moms who gave me support, gave me inspiration, and gave me comfort. The list is long but includes Jess, Caela, Aly, Dana, Lauren, Katie, Nita, Anna, Monica, Carolyn, Carla, and many more at all different stages on this journey.

And thank you to Frank, for always, always saying yes to my writing life.